This is a work of fiction. Names, cha
either are the product of imagination
resemblance to actual persons, living o
entirely coincidental.

RELAY PUBLISHING EDITION, NOVEMBER 2024
Copyright © 2024 Relay Publishing Ltd.

All rights reserved. Published in the United Kingdom by Relay Publishing. This book or any portion thereof may not be reproduced or used in any manner whatsoever without the express written permission of the publisher except for the use of brief quotations in a book review.

Jo Crow is a pen name created by Relay Publishing for co-authored Psychological Thriller projects. Relay Publishing works with incredible teams of writers and editors to collaboratively create the very best stories for our readers.

Cover Design by Blacksheep Designs.

www.relaypub.com

THE COMPANION
JO CROW

BLURB

'WANTED: Companion for sick wife.'

Landing a job caring for the **unresponsive wife** of celebrity podcaster Colin Harrington could be the best thing that's happened to me in a long time. I get a place to live, a paycheck and a way to salvage my comatose career.

It's my **last chance** to finally prove the doubters wrong. I have to make it work.

All I need to do is survive a few months in the eerie, high-tech halls of the Harrington's mansion. But caring for Colin's wife Kara is testing the limits of my sanity. Doors seem to open and close on their own, shadows shift in the corners of my vision, and I can't shake the feeling that **I'm being watched**.

I wouldn't mind if it was Colin watching. He's **been through hell**, and it *has* been years since his wife's accident. Maybe it's time he moved on—and maybe I'm the one who can help him.

Then I find a cassette tape that reveals **a shocking truth**…

Someone in the house has a dark secret—one they'll **do anything to protect**. But they're not the only ones with something to hide.

I have a secret of my own.

CONTENTS

Prologue	1
Chapter 1	3
Chapter 2	12
Chapter 3	25
Chapter 4	35
Chapter 5	45
Chapter 6	53
Chapter 7	59
Chapter 8	68
Chapter 9	74
Chapter 10	84
Chapter 11	91
Chapter 12	104
Chapter 13	109
Chapter 14	114
Chapter 15	116
Chapter 16	124
Chapter 17	132
Chapter 18	138
Chapter 19	141
Chapter 20	154
Chapter 21	161
Chapter 22	169
Chapter 23	173
Chapter 24	181
Chapter 25	188
Chapter 26	193
Chapter 27	195
Chapter 28	198
Chapter 29	202
Chapter 30	206
Chapter 31	207
Chapter 32	213
Chapter 33	217
Chapter 34	222

Chapter 35	226
Chapter 36	230
Chapter 37	238
Chapter 38	245
Chapter 39	249
Chapter 40	253
Chapter 41	257
Chapter 42	261
Chapter 43	267
Chapter 44	271
Chapter 45	273
Chapter 46	278
Chapter 47	284
Chapter 48	288
Chapter 49	296
Chapter 50	304
Chapter 51	312
Chapter 52	316
Chapter 53	319
Chapter 54	322
Chapter 55	327
Chapter 56	332
Chapter 57	339
Chapter 58	347
Chapter 59	352
Chapter 60	359
End of The Companion	363
About Jo	365
Mailing List	367
Also By Jo	369

PROLOGUE

*Y**ou would look at me and think—she has everything.*
But you wouldn't understand. Nobody would.

This is the only way it can end.
Because when she wants something...she gets it.
This is the story of how I die.

1

If any of the neighbors had seen me standing in front of the Harringtons' house looking the way I did, they may have called the police.

And I wouldn't have blamed them. I'd tried to tame my frizzy hair and dress in my nicest clothes, but despite my best efforts, it was clear I did not belong here, on this scorching driveway winding down to a multimillion-dollar house. From the outside, I could easily be mistaken for a crazed fan who had broken into this sanctuary of clean driveways and perfectly maintained gardens.

Or worse, paparazzi.

I swiped off some sweat with the back of my hand and looked down over the house. It was just as it had looked online: a modern house, white, all clean lines and sharp angles. Tall glass windows broke up the exterior, reflecting the surrounding landscape of trees, meticulously trimmed lawn, and a polished black marble statue at least ten feet high.

The house looked like a sculpture. Some architect had definitely won an award for it.

This was a home for the kind of people who never broke a sweat, with hair that always looked effortlessly glossy. Actresses, famous podcasters. That is to say: people like the Harringtons.

I started walking down the driveway toward the house. The hot asphalt stuck to the soles of my shoes, which came free with a terrible *smack*.

I tried not to think about how much hinged on this interview, but with every step, my intrusive thoughts grew louder.

My career. *Smack*. My dreams. *Smack*. Everything I'd worked for in LA, everything I'd sacrificed. *Smack, smack*.

I was so immersed in my thoughts that I didn't look up at first. But when I did, I was transfixed by movement in the small upstairs window. My steps faltered.

The reflection of the bright blue sky and shimmering sun obscured its features, but there it was—a black silhouette of a person, pulling the curtains to one side and staring down at me. I mean, I was *sure* it was looking at me, even if I couldn't distinguish a face. It froze me into place, as surely as a butterfly pinned onto a board.

And then, as soon as it had appeared, the curtains dropped, and the shadow was gone.

I took a deep breath. I was being stupid. If I was interviewing candidates for a live-in job, I'd want to sneak a peek at them too.

So I kept walking.

How much really hinged on this interview?

Everything.

As I approached the door, I reached out to ring a doorbell—only to discover there wasn't one. The entire door and the surrounding walls were made of a smooth, black slate that didn't have any features at all, much less a doorbell. I'd spent so long panicking about the interview during the drive over, and up outside the house, that I only now realized I was in danger of being late to an interview I couldn't afford being late to.

Right as I was contemplating hammering on the door, there was a sound like a vacuum seal being released, and the door swung open effortlessly.

The man standing in the doorway was undeniably attractive. His hair was glossy and black, and his shirt was bright white—almost blindingly so. Either it was new or he had access to an industrial-level bleach I had never heard of.

He had a question etched on his face.

Probably wondering if I am about to attack him.

I quickly lowered my raised fist. "Hi, I'm Anna. I'm here for the interview?"

"Anna Albright?" he asked with a smile. "Perfect! You're right on time."

My spirits lifted a little from the positivity; maybe I didn't look as out of place as I'd thought. I straightened my posture and tried to exude confidence.

"That's great! I'm really looking forward to meeting the Harringtons."

The man smiled widely and gestured for me to come inside. As he closed the door behind us, it glided shut and closed with another vacuum-like *woosh*.

"You've already met one!" he said cheerfully. "I'm Colin, Colin Harrington. Sorry, I should have introduced myself earlier. It's been a hectic morning, with all these interviews."

I cringed inwardly—less than a minute in, and I'd already made a mistake. I should have known it was too much to hope that the Harringtons kept a hot, eligible doorman. To hide my embarrassment, I gestured at the door.

"How do you…open it?" I asked.

"Oh, it's a smart door," Colin explained. "It recognizes us."

"Oh."

Obviously.

Colin laughed at my bewilderment. His laugh was bright and infectious, and for a moment we both chuckled at the door.

"I don't understand it either," Colin confessed. "The security team showed me how to use it, but all I remember is something about *heatprints* and *voiceprints*. Whatever that means. But you can open it with this handle from the inside…unless the triple lock is activated…"

Colin experimentally turned the knob on the door, but nothing happened. He shrugged and motioned for me to follow him.

The opulence of the Harringtons' house quickly made me forget all about the door. It was hard for me to believe anyone actually *lived* here. The room we were standing in looked like a lobby in a fancy hotel. And wait—was that a waterfall *inside* the house?

My thoughts were interrupted by a young woman with highlighted hair shrugging her strapped bag onto her shoulder. She seemed to be getting ready to leave. Dangling from her immaculately manicured fingers was a piece of paper. "I'll just leave this here, Colin," she said, motioning at a clear glass table the size of a bed, so clear it almost blended entirely with the room. A small stack of papers sat neatly on the edge of it, like a perfectly rectangular cloud floating in mid-air.

"Ah, perfect. Thank you for coming along, Emily," Colin replied.

"No, thank *you,* Colin," the woman said. She gave Colin a warm smile that instantly dropped as she turned away and passed me on her way to the door, giving me a quick once-over as if to say, "What do *you* think you're doing here?"

I clenched my hands into fists and followed Colin through the house. I *was* a good candidate for the job. I'd prove it.

Colin led me through a pale corridor into his office and motioned for me to sit down. I handed him my CV over the desk. As he read, my eyes wandered around the room.

It was sleek and modern with minimal decor. Art hung on one wall. One of the pieces looked like someone had crudely splattered fruit onto a canvas with a spray can. It reminded me of the stuff my hometown vandals graffitied onto the gas station wall. Who knows, maybe one of them had branched out to high-brow contemporary art now.

Colin noticed my gaze and asked, "What do you think?"

"It's...are you a big fan of apples?" I asked, gesturing toward the piece.

Colin burst into laughter. He shook his head, his dark curls falling softly over his eyes. "No, no. It was a gift from one of my podcast guests who happens to be an avid collector of up-and-coming contemporary art. I keep it there to please him. Your reaction is refreshing. One of the candidates called it *sublime*."

I relaxed ever so slightly in my chair. If Colin was down-to-earth like this, maybe I still had a chance.

"And that one?" I gestured toward another piece of art, a portrait of a woman in the nude, with her features exaggerated, colored in bold dabs of purple, red, and black paint. So much paint caked the canvas that it resembled crusted dirt or dried blood.

Colin pushed his hair back and glanced at the portrait. "Ah, that's my wife. Kara. Most people notice that one first. She commissioned one of her favorite artists to paint her portrait. She is a big fan of contemporary art."

I struggled to think of something diplomatic to say, but thankfully Colin thought it was time to get down to business.

"So, how did you hear about this opportunity with us?"

"Actually…my dad told me about it. He's mostly retired now, but he used to work in Hollywood. I guess an old acquaintance of his heard about the role and knew I was here and…open to work…" I cringed inwardly, wondering how I sounded. A grown woman with her dad still helping her get jobs.

"Well, connections are vital. Especially in this industry. I can tell you, I am a very well-connected man, and look how I'm doing." He smiled and extended his arms so I would take in his surroundings.

I looked around, nodding, hoping I looked adequately impressed. I'd been so distracted by the loud artwork before that I hadn't seen the framed certificate hanging on the adjacent wall. I tried to make out what it said: *Certificate of Self-*…was that "Mastery"? "Ministry"?

What kind of school would someone like Colin go to?

"It's nice to see a father guiding his child. Are you two close?"

Absolutely not.

"Fairly," I lied.

Colin tapped at a point on my CV where I'd listed a range of jobs: waitress, maid, and bartender.

"You mentioned a relative at a care home?"

"Just to show that I have experience caring for..." I trailed off. What *was* Kara's condition, exactly?

"That's good to know. Just so you are aware, we already have a nurse for Kara. What we really want is someone who can keep her company and talk to her. Make her days more lively and stimulating."

I nodded eagerly. I could definitely do that.

"I work from home here and there, but most days I'm downtown," Colin continued. "I wouldn't want her to be lonely when I'm gone." He handed my CV back to me. "Hold on to that for a moment. Did you have any questions before I introduce you to Kara?"

"This is a live-in position, am I right?" I asked, tucking a strand of blonde hair behind my ear. It was an old habit from childhood, when I'd needed to calm down. But it wasn't doing much for me at the moment: I could feel my cheap polyester shirt clinging to my underarms and my back, clammy from the sweat.

"Yes. At least for the summer. Most of Kara's friends have left town, and it gets pretty quiet up here. Whoever we hire gets free rein of the house. We want this to feel like home. Is that okay?"

Free rein of the house.

Surely that includes the sound studio? My father had mentioned that as a potential perk of this job.

But I bit down the question. Too soon.

I nodded.

"Great. Let me take you to my wife."

Colin led me out of the office and through the lobby-like space, up a set of polished stone steps that seemed to float off the wall and onto an upper landing, the walls adorned with more abstract paintings. My shoes squeaked against the giant, seamless slabs of white marble.

As Colin led me through the house, he asked if I had listened to his podcast. I admitted I hadn't. Of course, I'd heard *of* it—one of the top ten most listened to podcasts out there. From what I understood, Colin talked a lot about self-improvement. It's hard to care about something like self-improvement when you're constantly worrying about how you're going to make rent. Once I could get by day to day, maybe I'd "look inward."

"Well, that might be a good thing," he said, after my admission. "I have a bit of a tough-guy image on my podcast, which intimidates some people."

I found that hard to imagine—Colin had been nothing but friendly since I'd walked through his door.

"You seem different from a lot of people I've met in LA," I admitted.

"I get that a lot. Maybe it's because we keep to ourselves. We try to stay out of the public eye as much as possible—the media really put us through the wringer following Kara's accident."

Kara's accident. I tried to retain a neutral expression as I remembered what I'd heard. *Kara Harrington's drunken fall. Controversial Hollywood star's ascent cut short.*

The media had been relentless; it had chewed Kara to a pulp. There'd even been a big controversy about privacy when a paparazzi had snuck onto the grounds to get pictures via the house windows: an illegal practice, but the tabloid had still run with the pictures.

"Maybe that front door isn't such a bad idea," I offered.

"I'm glad you think so." Colin's voice held a hint of amusement. Then his smile faded away. "They wrote some pretty terrible things about Kara."

"Don't worry. I'm not one to dig around online looking for dirt," I reassured him. "They just write anything that sells, right?"

"Good. It's all garbage anyway," he said, leading me along.

I followed Colin down the hallway on the upper landing. The truth was, I had researched the Harringtons online. Aside from the flood of tabloid headlines, I'd read an interview where Colin expressed his deep hatred for the media, so I'd laid off the internet sleuthing after that. It seemed like I'd made the right call.

Truthfully, I didn't care about what I might find.

There was nothing I could discover that would scare me away from this job.

2

Colin pushed open a pair of pale double doors at the end of the hallway at the top of the stairs.

"So this is Kara's room," he said softly.

The room was dark, lit only by a dimmed, muted light that made the sharp edges of furniture blur into their surroundings. The decorative objects and fabrics were neutrally colored, unoffensive, and impersonal, reminding me of a therapist's office or an airport lounge. Over the bed hung a painting of a city skyline at sunrise. It was the only glimpse of sunlight in the otherwise gloomy space.

Kara sat in a wheelchair facing the curtained window, her back to us. I could only make out the head of tousled brown hair. She appeared to be motionless.

Colin brushed past me toward the window, gesturing for me to follow.

As I approached, I could see Mrs. Harrington in more detail. Unlike Colin, I'd seen countless images of Kara in ads, films, or tabloid magazines. It was odd to see someone in person you had seen in pictures for years. Elements about her face I'd never noticed were instantly apparent: the slight bump of her nose, the fine lines at the edges of her eyes, the beauty spots under her lip.

Of course, she looked sick now, her pale skin almost translucent in the odd light, her sculptural face turned gaunt.

"Kara, this is Anna," Colin introduced me. "She's come to meet you and see if you might get along."

There was no response from Kara.

"Hi, Kara, it's lovely to meet you," I spoke up. "I hope we can get to know one another and spend the summer together. I would like to help make sure you have everything you need." I glanced at Colin, who nodded in encouragement.

"Kara enjoys reading," Colin continued. "But she can't do it so much on her own now. Perhaps you could read her something?"

Read to Kara? Acting and using my voice to convey emotions was the one thing I excelled at. This could be my chance to stand out from the other candidates.

"Oh, sure," I replied. I walked over to the bedside table and picked up a book before returning to my spot by the window. Kara still hadn't opened her eyes, and I wondered how Colin knew she was even awake. With shaking fingers, I flipped to a dog-eared page, trying not to think about what would happen if I failed.

If I didn't land this job, it would be goodbye LA and hello sweet backwater hometown in Minnesota.

I'd worked so hard to make it in this city. I'd made a *lot* of sacrifices. But if this didn't pan out, none of it mattered.

No pressure, right?

I drew a deep breath. *Just another day in a recording booth,* I told myself.

Trying not to let my thoughts bother me, I opened the book and began to read aloud. It took me a moment to shake off the awkwardness of the situation—standing in a dark room, reading to an unresponsive woman—but once I started reading, my words flowed more smoothly, and my pacing became more even.

As I finished the chapter, I looked up to see Kara staring straight at me.

I almost dropped the book.

"Oh," I said. "Did you like—"

But I never finished my question, as after what I could only interpret as a contemptuous gaze, Kara turned her head toward the window and focused on the curtains. I glanced over at Colin for help.

"I think that is enough for today," he said gently. He leaned down to kiss Kara's forehead before guiding me out of the room and down the stairs. He explained that she hadn't regained her speaking abilities yet, so sometimes she communicated in unique ways, but I was only half listening through the ringing in my ears.

That was it. My one chance at staying in this city, and it had somehow come down to reading lines—and still, I'd blown it.

Colin had to repeat himself a few times before I realized he was asking me a question.

"I'm sorry?" I asked.

"You have such a lovely voice," he said. "You are obviously a professional. Have you acted in anything I'd know?" His face brightened. "You must have heard about my offer to use the sound studio! Are you working on something right now?"

His compliment would have warmed me if I wasn't on the verge of tears. I mustered all my acting capabilities to smile brightly at Colin.

"I have a role in an animated series. It's a really exciting opportunity."

A role that could restart my career. A role I will lose if I don't provide a sound studio for the project.

"Well, I wish you the best of luck in your project, Anna," Colin said sincerely. "I'm sure you'll do a fantastic job."

I would have, I thought darkly to myself. But I forced a smile and nodded at Colin.

He frowned as he checked his phone. "I need to take this call. Do you mind showing yourself out? Just leave your CV on the pile over there."

"Of course," I replied, the job slipping away from me like a distant light fading across the horizon.

"Thank you for coming, Anna. Truly." Colin shook my hand briefly, lifted the phone to his ear, and walked away. I heard his shoes against the marble and then the click of the office door closing. Disappointment lurched in my stomach.

As I leaned down to add my CV to the stack, I couldn't help but notice the one that had been placed before mine by the young, put-together woman who had preceded me. It was printed on thicker, textured paper, almost like cardstock. *Of course it was.* I skimmed the contents and couldn't believe what I saw. Was there really a course for *rehabilitating exclusive individuals*?

Screw that.

I swiped the pretentious CV and put mine in its place. That perfectly primped, over-qualified candidate wasn't desperate for this position like I was. I crumpled the page and shoved it into my pocket before storming out of the posh house and toward my beat-up car parked in the driveway.

The car came alive with a tired rattle. I quickly glanced back at the house one more time. My eyes found the upper story window, but there was no one there.

I turned my eyes back to the street and stomped on the gas.

It was an hour-long drive back to my apartment, but it felt like a completely different world from the pristine streets of the Pacific Palisades. The roads were dirty, littered with garbage, while the buildings were worn down and covered in graffiti and perpetual grime no one seemed responsible for cleaning.

As soon as I pulled up to my building, I could see that my landlady had followed through on her threat from a few days ago: my belongings were scattered all over the sidewalk, spilling out of haphazard boxes.

Pressure building in my eyes, I quickly dodged out of my car and started loading everything in. As I bent down to pick up a box, my pencil skirt—the only skirt I had—rode up uncomfortably high, but I didn't have time to fix it. I shuffled toward my car with the final box. Just as I was about to lift it in my trunk, the bottom gave way and scattered dog-eared books everywhere.

My landlady chose that moment to appear at her doorway. She stood there with a smug look on her face, wearing a faded floral cardigan despite the heat, which had plastered it against her leathery arms. Her frizzy hair was sticking to her forehead, and she crossed her arms as she smirked at me.

"Didn't think I'd actually do it, did you?" she taunted. "You young, entitled freeloaders always think you can get away with everything. Well, I'm no bleeding heart. You don't pay, you don't stay!"

I wiped away tears threatening to fall with the back of my hand, refusing to give her the satisfaction of seeing me cry. I slammed my trunk shut, circled to the front, and hopped in as she hobbled after me.

"And don't think I'm not expecting that overdue rent!" she yelled as I drove away.

And I kept going. I didn't know where I was heading. I had nowhere to be. Someone once told me sharks must continue to swim or else they will sink to the ocean floor. I don't know if it's true, but I couldn't stop driving.

I pulled up a hill and continued on for another ten minutes before my car finally reached the top. The chirping of crickets filled the air as I turned off the ignition, stepped out of my car, and sat on the hood. It had been years since I last visited this spot. It was where my ex first took me when we started dating, trying to impress me with a secret view of the glittering city below.

"Welcome to LA," he'd said with a smile. And in that moment, it had felt like this was where I was meant to be. But as time passed, it became clear I didn't have what it takes to make it in this city.

I couldn't claw my way from the bottom to the top like I'd thought I could. I had the drive; I knew I did. Every fiber of me wanted to make it, and I was willing to do anything. But I just couldn't catch a break.

There was another thing I'd have to do. The thought circled in my head like a wasp, and I didn't realize I was chewing on my nail until I tasted blood.

I needed to call my father and tell him the truth: I had failed and would have to come back home.

He'd never approved of my dream of becoming a voice actress. He'd told me, point-blank, that he didn't think I had enough talent. That I would never make it in Hollywood.

I'd taken that as a challenge. I'd been determined to prove him wrong.

I'd never asked him for money, not that he would have offered any. But he knew I wasn't exactly thriving out here. When he mentioned the job with the Harringtons and Colin being an "audio star" I could learn from, I saw it as some kind of concession. Maybe, just maybe, he'd finally accepted my dream.

But now I'd only proven him right.

My finger hovered uncertainly over the black, cracked screen of my phone. My reflection stared back at me in dozens of shattered fragments.

I had a sudden flash of a memory, of picking the phone up from a dark, wooden floor, of vaguely noticing the screen had cracked. Of flashing lights. The sound of an ambulance. Choking. Gurgling. A fleshy hand clawing at me, and then growing limp.

I tucked my phone in my pocket and forced the thoughts away, taking deep breaths. The lights of the city blinked absently below me.

I'd come here to follow my dream. But the definition of a dream is an imagined experience: something not real.

The aggressive electric chiming of my phone raised me from my clammy sleep.

I'd wrapped myself in the backseat of my car, but the interior was already heating up in the rising sun.

I grabbed my phone and wiped the rest of the sleep from my eyes.

Shit. Lunch. Micky.

Micky was an audio producer and director I'd met at an event for voice actors, and he had a role he thought I'd be *perfect* for. Not words I'd heard in a while. Micky was the only person who'd had the nerve to speak to me during the entire event.

He'd offered me a potentially great gig—maybe even enough to restart my career, if it all panned out. There was just one catch. It was an indie project he was funding himself, and he'd already found an actress who could provide a sound studio for free.

If I wanted the role, I needed to match that offer.

The Harringtons had a state-of-the-art sound studio that, as their live-in employee, I'd have access to.

Nailing my interview had been critical.

The Harringtons would never hire me for the job following my disastrous interaction with Kara. Now, I'd have to break the news that the sound studio was a no-go, and he'd have to drop me from the last project that would keep me in the city.

I wrote out a reply to Micky saying I'd be late and clambered out of the car and switched to the driver's seat. I dreaded having to tell Micky about my failure, but it was best to get it over with. There was just someone I had to see first.

Someone much more important than Micky.

It was a terrible day to drive a poorly air-conditioned car; as the sun climbed higher in the sky, the heat became almost unbearable. I pulled into the parking lot and stared at the building across from me, trying to cool off by waving the car door back and forth.

I sincerely regretted sleeping in my polyester shirt, which was practically glued to me by two days' worth of sweat. I wistfully thought back to the shower at my old apartment. I'd never thought I'd miss it: the creeping mold in the corners of the chipped tiles, the company of cockroaches that persistently skittered through the vent by the ceiling. What a difference a day makes, right?

I glanced darkly back at my car. One of the advantages of living out of a car, at least, is that your wardrobe follows you anywhere you go. I dug around my bags and procured a simple T-shirt and unassuming yoga pants. Not the most elegant outfit, but I was confident the person I'd be visiting wouldn't judge. After attempting to surreptitiously shuffle into my new clothes, I locked the car and headed over the lot.

The Green Village care home was both a posh and a misleadingly named establishment; it lacked any actual greenery and was located in a busy, corporate area. The building itself was a sandstone-colored multi-story structure that resembled a villa.

As I entered, the familiar nurse at the front desk gave me a wave, and I made my way down the pristine tiled floor toward room 107, my footsteps echoing softly in the empty hallway.

My routine was familiar: adjusting the bedcovers and replacing wilted flowers, checking the charts at the foot of the bed, and observing the comatose figure before me. The only sounds in the room were the soft, persistent hum of the air conditioner, the distant conversations that carried down the halls, and the slow but steady breathing of the unconscious patient. On a monitor, the rhythmic spike of a heart rate.

The minutes ticked by. Soon, I'd be late for lunch with Micky. Still, I found it difficult to tear myself away.

Leaning over, I placed my hand on his arm and whispered, but there was no reaction. No indicator that he knew I was there at all.

Micky had chosen a trendy plant-based burger joint for us to meet at. It had an ironic name, bright blue seats, and annoyingly named menu items. Micky sat across from me with his glasses slipping down his nose as he perused the menu.

A waitress carrying a pitcher of water shuffled over to take our order.

"I'll just have water, please." I gave her a small smile, hoping it wouldn't be a problem.

"Don't be like that, Anna," Micky groaned as the waitress filled my glass. "You'll make me look bad. This one's on me—get anything you want, okay?"

He turned to the waitress. "Double fries and the Double Smash Burg'r."

"I'll have the cheeseburger," I said.

"So a Cheezy Dream for you?" the waitress asked in a monotone, as if the words had been drilled into her.

"Sure," I replied, my heart going out for her. I'd worked my share of odd jobs trying to support my dream. She would probably much rather be out there pursuing hers than stuck here, forced to parrot dumb names.

The waitress left, and Micky turned to me. "So, Anna, any news?"

I took a sip of water to buy some time, feeling Micky's eyes watching me hopefully. But there was no point in sugarcoating it.

"I think the interview was a bust. Mrs. Harrington didn't like me."

Micky frowned. "I thought she was a vegetable."

I cringed at Micky's inappropriate choice of words but pressed on. "It's hard to explain. I just had this feeling."

Micky scrunched his lips childishly in dismay. "This blows. I want to work with you."

"Too bad the project can't afford to rent a studio," I sighed, not for the first time.

"It's an indie project," Micky said defensively. "We have to save money where we can. My other actress brings a studio to the deal—I just can't overlook that."

I hadn't wanted to plead with Micky for the job, but now I was desperate. "You could pay me later, once the crowdfunding gets going? That way we could afford a studio now. Like you said, there's a dedicated fan base, and once the pilot is out, crowdfunding should be a breeze—"

Micky stared at me skeptically. "I like you, Anna, but without a free studio thrown in, you'd still be losing the project money."

I dialed up the passion. "I'm worth it, Micky."

"I don't know, Anna…I just don't think it's going to work out."

"You won't regret picking me, I *promise*."

Micky frowned at me. "But what will you live on in the meantime?"

I gulped. I hadn't told Micky I'd been evicted, and I doubted revealing the fact would improve my argument.

"I'll pick up a part-time job. Find a more affordable place to stay." I tried not to dwell on the logistics of what I was suggesting: finding a job to afford working another job I wouldn't get paid for. I'd need a permanent address to land a job, but how would I find a place to stay with no money to put down and little guarantee I could pay rent? What would I tell a landlord—that I might star in a fan-favorite video game animated adaptation that may or may not be crowdfunded months down the line?

"You'd downgrade? No offense, but isn't the place you're leasing sort of cheap already?"

Before I had time to say anything, the waitress arrived with our food —two juicy burgers and a mountain of hot fries that made my mouth water just looking at them. As I took a bite and tasted the savory non-meat melting in my mouth, I instantly forgave the place for its headache-inducing furniture and odd naming conventions. It was divine. When had I last eaten?

A bit of food dribbled down my lips, and I wiped my chin. I caught Micky staring, and he moved his gaze, abashed. I tried to ignore it. Micky was a nice guy, but I couldn't imagine anything between us. Unfortunately, I wasn't sure if Micky saw it that way.

There was an awkward pause.

Just then, my phone rang.

Thank god.

I probably broke a record with how quickly I snatched it up and pressed it to my ear. "Anna Albright," I announced breathlessly.

Warmth filled my ears as Colin's voice came through the line.

"Anna, Kara loved you. Are you still interested in the job?"

I could hardly believe what I was hearing.

Kara had loved me, and now I had the opportunity to work as her personal companion.

I'd be spending the summer in the Harringtons' opulent house. Not only that, but I would also have access to Colin's sound studio, where

I could record my lines for Micky's project. A project that could save my floundering career.

"Anna?"

"Yes, yes! I'm here." I motioned excitedly to Micky across the table, who gave me a questioning look. "I would absolutely love the job!"

"That's great news. When can you start?"

I gave Micky a big thumbs-up. He smiled back at me, but there was a strange look in his eyes I couldn't quite place.

It didn't matter. I got the job at the Harringtons'. And everything was going to be okay.

3

When I arrived at the Harringtons' the following morning, I encountered another obstacle besides the high-tech door from my first visit. A sleek black gate blocked the driveway that led down to the Harringtons' house. Rails lead behind a cube-shaped bush where the gate must have been retracted the day before.

Like the door to the Harringtons' house, this gate didn't have a console, button, or handles. I wondered if this gate, too, picked up heat signatures.

As I stood there, stumped by the elitist gauntlet of gates and doors and beginning to break a sweat, a voice behind me startled me out of my thoughts.

"Can I help you?" a middle-aged man asked with a hint of suspicion in his tone. He was wearing activewear and sneakers I would usually associate with a teenager. His skin was remarkably smooth, and his shirt, like Colin's, was blindingly white. It must come with the territory, I decided.

"I'm here for work," I explained, wanting him to know I wasn't just some lurker he should call security on. After all, he might be seeing me often. "For the Harringtons. For Kara Harrington?"

"*Kara* Harrington?" He raised an eyebrow.

"Yes, I'm her new live-in companion. I'll be helping her out and keeping her company," I offered.

He glanced at the house as if it was included in the conversation. He shook his head with a snort, then narrowed his eyes at me.

"Well, good luck with *that*," he said and turned to walk away.

"Um, nice to meet you…I guess," I said uncertainly, not sure what to make of the interaction.

He was mumbling as he walked. From what I could make out, "crazy" and "bitch" seemed to be among his mumbled words.

Rude. But at least he knew I wasn't there to rob the place.

Not that I'd be much of a threat if I couldn't even pass this gate.

Just then, a disembodied, slightly distorted voice came out of the gate.

"Anna! Welcome. Just come on through," it said cheerily.

With a sense of relief, I watched as the gate slid noiselessly to one side, disappearing behind the bushes. I hopped back in my car and slowly inched down the driveway toward the garage. As I approached, the doors parted to reveal a smiling Colin Harrington. My heart grew lighter as he walked up to my window, which I quickly, manually, rolled down.

"So how does that gate work? Telepathy?"

Colin laughed at my dumb joke. "The security system pinged me that there was someone at the gate. But if you're coming and going, it can tell if you're carrying a key."

Of course.

I looked over my shoulder to see the gate soundlessly slide back over the driveway, barring the way back up onto the street.

Colin pointed out a spot in the back of the garage for me to park among the expansive collection of luxury vehicles.

I got out of my car, careful not to bump into anything that would surely cost more than my life, and made my way over to where Colin waited.

He led me inside, where the layout of the house was becoming familiar to me: On the first floor, there was a spacious kitchen and a sunken living room that overlooked a glittering pool visible through a glass wall. The corridor leading to Colin's office branched out to several other rooms, of which a disproportionate amount were lavish restrooms. Upstairs, marbled corridors curled around the house, and a glass-lined balcony offered views of the shared spaces below. Doors were tucked under outcroppings of white rock, softly lit from underneath by hidden lighting that gave off a subtle, warm glow.

I didn't want to think about how expensive this place was. I bet even one step on the staircase cost more than my car.

Colin caught me staring down as we climbed the stairs.

"The steps are from Italy. Repurposed from an old castle."

I nodded, as if suitably impressed. Colin laughed.

"I'm kidding. I have no idea. Probably some quarry in Colorado."

I relaxed. Rich, charming, *and* funny. "Thank you for having me. I'm so pleased to be here."

"*We* are so pleased you are here. And thankful you could start so soon."

He led me into Kara's bedroom, where she was reclining in a chair, attended to by an unfamiliar woman.

"Anna, let me introduce you to Flora, Kara's nurse."

Flora was a petite woman with soft features, her long hair pulled back in a braid. She wore a crisp white uniform that fit her perfectly.

"Nice to meet you, Flora," I said.

"A pleasure," Flora said. Her expression seemed to be in direct contradiction with the statement, but I smiled, resolved to make this working relationship the best possible.

Unsure of what more to say, I leaned toward Kara. "Good to see you, Kara. I hope you're doing well?"

Kara's lips formed words, but they came out as a barely audible whisper. I leaned in closer to hear her better. My? Mine?

"Please do not disturb Mrs. Harrington while she is trying to sleep," Flora said, patting my arm. I reluctantly withdrew. Had Kara tried to tell me something?

"Well, I'll leave you two to it," Colin said. "Flora can show you to your room. I'll be downstairs in my office."

"Yes, Mr. Harrington," Flora piped up.

Colin left and the door closed, leaving Flora and me hovering in awkward silence.

"Sorry...I thought she said something to me."

Flora considered me. "Sometimes Mrs. Harrington says odd things. It has to do with the accident. It's just babble."

I glanced at Kara to catch her reaction, but there didn't seem to be one. Kara continued to gaze listlessly ahead of her, at nothing in particular.

"How much does she…um, Kara, understand?"

"Mrs. Harrington sometimes expresses satisfaction or displeasure with non-verbal cues. Beyond that…well, she has not been cooperative in neurological exams. So, do not expect riveting conversation."

I winced. Even if Kara didn't understand what was happening around her, it was jarring to hear Flora talk that way about someone who was present.

No wonder Colin wanted someone else to keep Kara company.

"Her wristband has a button which she has learned to use to call for assistance," Flora continued, handing me a pager. I'd only ever seen one on TV.

"Old-school," I murmured, turning the thing around in my hands.

"I'll show you to your room," Flora sniffed. I couldn't help but think she was stiffer with me now that Colin had left us alone.

Flora led me out of the room and down a corridor with a glass railing overlooking the kitchen and living area below.

"Mrs. Harrington's wardrobe," she indicated curtly as we passed a door. Flora hurried me wordlessly past another door. I motioned over my shoulder.

"And that room?"

Flora ignored me.

"I'm excited to be here," I tried.

"I can see," Flora said dryly.

Safe to say, I've met my new best friend.

We passed a few more doors for which I received no explanation, and finally an elevator that went down to the ground floor. As we walked,

Flora explained her shifts: Flora cared for Kara in the early mornings and checked on her again in the evenings, while I was expected to keep her company during the day and check in at night if needed.

I was losing count. *How many rooms does this house have?*

I followed Flora down the stairs to a hallway lined with ceiling-high glass windows overlooking a pool and rolling hills. In my peripheral vision, I could see the sparkling ocean.

"Wow."

"We are advised not to use the pool," Flora said, noticing my reaction.

"Oh," I said, slightly deflated. Colin had told me to treat this place like home, but Flora seemed to be laying down a lot more rules. She probably had insights about working here that I didn't. I wasn't going to give up on using the sound studio, but maybe it was safer to stick to Flora's advice when it came to the rest of the house.

After glancing wistfully at the pool, I followed Flora down the corridor and through the kitchen and living space toward a set of stairs leading downward.

Underground, we entered into a cozy family room complete with bean bags, as well as a room I was pretty sure was a movie theater. I had to hurry behind Flora, but I kept glancing around, trying to drink everything in. Was that a backlit bar built of quartz? Would I be living here?

Flora led me to a small room. It was a cozy space with a comfortable bed, warm lighting, and wooden shelves lined with books.

"This is yours," she said.

"It's great," I said, and meant it.

"You'll probably have to go home to get some stuff."

"Oh no, all my stuff is in my car," I said absently.

"*All* your stuff?"

Shit. I didn't think Flora would be that impressed if she found out I was effectively homeless.

"All the stuff I need," I corrected quickly, tucking a strand of hair behind my ear.

Flora pursed her lips, studying me, but pried no further. I hoped she was satisfied with my answer.

I really didn't need her digging up dirt on me.

I didn't have many essentials to move into my new room—my car was mostly filled with odds and ends like books, pots, and pans—so I only grabbed the duffel bag stuffed with all the clothes I owned. Flora had given me a clicker for the garage doors, which I accidentally bumped while hoisting the duffel. The doors slid open surprisingly quietly, but not quiet enough to get past Flora. The door into the garage whipped open, and Flora looked at me quizzically.

"Leaving already?" she asked.

"Nope!" I faked a laugh and shifted the box to my other hip, reaching for the clicker in my pocket. "Just a little clumsy!"

Flora disappeared back inside, and I let out a sigh of relief.

I looked out at the clear sky as the garage doors slid closed; only scraps of clouds hung overhead, curled like question marks.

I wasn't sure what the expected dress code was, but when I saw how simply Flora was dressed, I figured I could manage with the little I had for now. Once I started earning some money, I'd be able to afford better clothes. And with this job and Micky's project, that hopefully wouldn't be too long.

As I walked back inside the house with my duffel bag, I noticed Colin saying his goodbyes, just finishing a call. I waited.

"Great. Thanks, man. Eyes forward." Colin pocketed the phone and turned to me.

"Anna. Settling in?"

"Sure! Flora gave me a tour of the house," I said. "But she didn't have time to show me the sound studio…"

"Of course!" Colin replied enthusiastically, catching my hint. "Come along."

He led me downstairs to an unassuming door and gestured for me to enter.

Inside was a massive, sleek console, double monitors, speakers, and a microphone, all clustered together behind some futuristic-looking desk chairs and leather couches. Everything was glossy and pristine, as if it had just been brought home from a store and unwrapped. The recording booth itself, behind a wide, spotless pane of glass, had extensive baffling, a table, seating, and several more microphones. Above the door to the booth was an unlit red light.

Colin watched me. "Do you think it will do?"

"It's perfect," I said reverently.

Colin mulled over the room, as if taking it all in once again.

"Kara and I both used it all the time, but now I mostly use it for sound editing and an episode here and there. Most of my guests prefer to record out in the city. But this place is special."

There was a bright electric chime, interrupting Colin from his recollections. He went for his phone and frowned.

"Sorry, I really need to take this. Feel free to look around."

I settled into the rotating chair in front of the giant console, taking it all in. I was used to making improvised booths in my closet, stringing up sheets and blankets to muffle sound, but here I was, in a professional sound studio. And I had free rein. This had to be good enough for Micky.

I ran my hands over the console. My finger grazed a curly edge of clear tape on the edge of the console, out of place in such a pristine environment. I stared at the tape for a moment, this small, irritating flaw in an otherwise perfect space. Now that I'd seen it, I couldn't help myself. I idly scratched off the corner and began to peel it away. Strangely, it curled off the edge of the console and underneath the desk.

I got down on my knees to pry off the tape, but then I noticed it was attached to something larger, secured with multiple strips of tape. Had I accidentally pulled something loose? Was this meant to be here? The Harringtons must have had the money to pay for proper repairs or fixes, and not have to resort to cheap hacks.

As I examined closer, I realized the tape wasn't just a quick fix or haphazard attempt at fixing the console—it had been carefully placed there. It was holding something in place. I pulled off the last of the sticky tape and along it, dangling, was a cassette tape.

I held the cassette in my fingers and turned it around. Written on it, in bold letters, was the name *Kara*.

I froze.

Why did I suddenly feel like I was doing something wrong?

A knock on the door made me jump, and I impulsively shoved the tape into my pocket.

Flora opened the door and peeked through.

"I looked for you in your room. It is time for you to help with Kara. Follow me."

I followed Flora up the stairs, not listening to half of the things she said. I could feel the outline of the tape through my jeans.

Who would go through the trouble of hiding a tape like that? And why?

4

On my first morning at the Harringtons', I woke up to a stranger in my room.

I jolted up from bed in alarm. I'd stayed up way too late and fallen asleep listening to Colin's podcast, curious to learn more about my employer, and my groggy mind took a moment to register the intruder as a wide-eyed, young maid.

"I'm sorry," she said in heavily accented English, looking down at her feet. "I didn't know someone was here." She quickly excused herself, not meeting my eye once.

I rubbed the sleep from my eyes with the back of my hand and got up. It was useless trying to fall back asleep now. I wondered who had forgotten to inform the maid I would be staying here.

The maid wasn't the only stranger in the house. When I headed upstairs to find something to eat, I found a delivery man stocking the fridge. Outside, beyond the floor-length glass windows, someone was tending the lawn. After a moment, a man dressed in a nondescript black suit walked down the hall from Colin's office carrying a pile of papers and exited through the front door.

They all ignored me. I hoped it was because someone had at least told them what I was doing here.

I'd asked Colin whether I'd have a shelf in the fridge to keep my food, and he told me to help myself to anything from it, as it was regularly stocked with premade meals and snacks made by a local catering company. I scanned the contents and noted that the meals were all exactly what I'd expected from the Harringtons: collagen-infused bone broth. Zucchini noodles with hemp pesto. Activated charcoal lemonade. Maybe I'd live longer or get that glowing Hollywood skin by virtue of super food summer, but my heart already ached for a good burger, and I hadn't even got through my first day.

Resigned, I helped myself to some chips and broccoli dip while I flipped through the script for Micky's show. But my thoughts kept returning to the cassette tape I'd found the night before. Why on earth had someone hidden it like that? Was it an old tape, or had someone intentionally chosen to record on such outdated technology? And if so, why?

What would I find if I listened to it? And how *could* I listen to it? Did they even make tape players anymore?

I kept checking my phone to see how much longer until it was time to go upstairs and meet Flora, who would walk me through caring for Kara. Like Colin had warned me during the interview, my job as Kara's companion also involved assisting her with some basic tasks.

Flora was waiting for me upstairs in Kara's bedroom. Without so much as a good morning, she began to administer instructions.

"There, go and fetch Mrs. Harrington's clothes," she said, nodding toward a door on the far side of the room. Inside, I found a walk-in closet with rows and rows of elegant loungewear in a wide range of beige. It was surreal. Here *I* was, picking out clothes for *the* Kara Harrington. Not for the first time, I wondered if there'd been some misunderstanding, if Colin had made some mistake in picking me for the job.

But that didn't matter now. I was going to prove that I had what it took, that I belonged here.

I picked two outfits and brought them out to show Kara. By this point, Flora had propped Kara up in bed and against her shoulder.

"What do you think?" I asked Kara. "We could go for a deep V-neck top, or this roll-neck cashmere sweater?"

"Don't bother," Flora said. "Just pick one."

I studied Kara. Hadn't Flora said yesterday that Kara was capable of expressing satisfaction and disappointment? And if that was the case, shouldn't we at least let her voice her opinion on the few things she could?

But Kara didn't react in any way to either of the outfits. So I handed the sweater to Flora, who began guiding Kara's long arms through the sleeves.

"Only natural materials for Mrs. Harrington. Helps regulate body odor." Flora glanced at me. "Sweat. Sometimes urine."

I glanced at Kara again, her head still hung over Flora's shoulder as Flora maneuvered her into her wheelchair by the bed. Flora was talking like Kara wasn't there. How did we know how much she understood? What if Kara understood everything we were saying?

Not long after I had considered this, Kara started tapping her fingers on the armrest of her wheelchair in rhythmic patterns, her delicate wrists making little jerky movements up and down. It reminded me of something I'd learned back in scouts in Minnesota.

"Is that morse?" I asked.

Flora stared at me as if I'd asked an inconceivably stupid question. I might as well have asked if Kara were casting a spell.

"Mrs. Harrington taps if she must use the restroom. Unfortunately, that is the extent of her communication." Flora glanced at her watch. "My shift ends soon, and we haven't covered everything. But this will have to do for now. I will go prepare the medicine downstairs. Take Mrs. Harrington to the restroom and get her resting in bed ready for her second injection."

Anyone would have thought *Flora* was my boss. But I supposed I had to give her credit for being particular about Kara's care, even if she wasn't very personable.

"Okay," I said chirpily, suddenly aware of what I was about to do. Though I'd gone on about my caretaking experience in my CV, the truth was I hadn't worked as a caretaker before. I'd certainly never helped anyone use the restroom.

Flora disappeared through the door without another word.

"So," I said, stupidly chirpy again. "Let's get you to the bathroom." I cringed—my words had come out in a sing-song tone, like something out of a kid's cartoon show.

But Kara didn't react. She sat slumped in her wheelchair, staring out into the distance. If she had heard me, she did not show it.

I wheeled Kara off into her restroom, where every surface seemed marbled. I couldn't help but think that it wasn't the safest environment for a recovering patient. What if Kara were to slip? A fall like that onto a hard surface could be ugly.

At least there were handles installed on either side of the toilet, but I wasn't sure how much strength Kara had. Flora had picked a great moment to throw me into the deep end.

"Okay, I'll just lower your pants now," I said, trying to keep my voice steady. "And then we can get you onto the toilet."

Silence.

I began to roll down Kara's expensive cashmere slacks. It felt…invasive. I glanced at her. She was still staring off, but I could swear her gaze was more pointed. Concentrated.

Since she was still sitting, I could only pull her clothes down so far. So, I scooped my own arms under hers and helped her lean against me as I pulled down her underwear. Moving Kara felt like handling a mannequin; she was rigid yet fragile at the same time. With my shorter frame, her head drooped over my shoulder. It was lucky she was so light. Was this how Flora did it? I was close enough to smell Kara's morning breath. Her breathing tickled my neck.

As I pulled her up, the wheelchair started to roll away behind her. I had forgotten to lock it.

"Shit," I said. Trying not to panic, I shuffled closer to the toilet and maneuvered Kara onto the seat as best as I could. Kara's hands gripped the railings, shaking. I had to hold onto her to prevent her from falling over or leaning too far to one side. Once she was somewhat stable, I adjusted her shirt to make sure it wasn't caught under her.

Flustered, I glanced up at her face, which seemed furrowed in concentration. Too late, I realized I was staring at her face as she defecated.

I averted my eyes and scanned the room for something else to do. We'd gotten this far—now what? Thankfully, I spotted a console on the toilet. After deciphering the buttons and testing a few different options, I was relieved to find a button that activated a little showerhead at the back of the toilet. At least that part was easy.

After drying her off with a towel and securing the runaway wheelchair, I carefully helped Kara back into it.

"How's that for an icebreaker?" I attempted to joke as I returned her to her bedroom and settled her onto the bed. At this point, I didn't expect a response from Kara and thankfully, she stayed silent. It seemed fair given the situation.

"Okay, all settled," I told her with a smile after I'd settled her onto the bed and drawn her cover. "I'll get better with practice. You'll see."

Kara's eyes flitted from me to the window. I followed the gaze to a framed photograph on the windowsill. It must have meant something to her because she kept looking back at it.

"Do you want it?" I asked, retrieving the photo and returning to the bed. In it, a slightly younger Colin and Kara had their arms looped around one another. Kara's face was half hidden by a sheer veil.

"It's a lovely picture. Is it your wedding day?"

Kara's eyes kept returning to the picture.

"Do you want to hold it?"

The tiniest, most imperceptible nod. I felt a rush of satisfaction. Maybe I had some sort of magic touch. Despite what Flora said about Kara, here we were, communicating. Connecting.

I placed the picture in Kara's opened palm. She moved her eyes down to the photo.

Then, suddenly, Kara's hand twitched, and the framed photograph tumbled from her grasp down onto the marble floor, shattering into pieces. Shards of glass skittered across the smooth floor.

"Kara! Oh no." I looked down at the wreckage. "Are you...okay?"

Kara simply closed her eyes.

I was on my knees picking up shards of glass when Flora returned.

"What happened?" She demanded.

"Kara dropped the frame," I explained.

"*Kara* dropped the frame? Don't blame your own clumsiness on someone who can't speak up for themselves." She pointed across the room then shook her head. "You must be more careful. And account for your own actions."

I gritted my teeth. The injustice was painful, but I didn't know how else I could defend myself. "Okay."

"Make sure to get every piece so no one gets hurt."

"Okay," I repeated.

Flora drew some kind of amber solution into a syringe and began injecting into Kara's arm. Flora's thumb pushed down on the plunger, willing more of the substance to slowly seep into Kara.

"Never touch any of Mrs. Harrington's medicine. It is strictly my responsibility," Flora said sharply.

I wondered if that was the end of my admonishments for the day.

"Is that clear?" she asked pointedly.

I forced a smile on my face. "Crystal clear."

The Harrington's residence had every gadget imaginable—except a cassette player. But I was determined to find a way to listen to the tape I'd found. My best bet was probably rummaging through the boxes of technology stashed in the back of the sound studio, but I hadn't had a chance to spend much time there since finding the tape. Ordering a device online would have been easy, but it felt presumptuous to start having packages delivered to the Harringtons'. And, unfortunately, I didn't have another address to ship it to.

My mind raced with possibilities of what I'd find on the tape. Kara's preparation for a role? A clandestine conversation between Kara and some hot-shot director? Evidence of a long-forgotten affair? It had to be juicy if someone had gone through the trouble of hiding it like that.

But unraveling this potential secret would have to wait. I had to focus on my assignment as Kara's companion—at least until I could cobble some money together and record my lines for Micky's project.

After a week spent as a companion, Kara's and my relationship wasn't improving. The understanding I thought we'd had when she'd nodded at the photograph hadn't happened again. Maybe I'd imagined the gesture. But it was hard not to feel irritated, especially since she'd gotten me into trouble and made me look bad in front of Flora.

I tried to convince myself to let it go and stop overthinking. It had been an accident. Flora may have blamed me, but I hadn't been fired over it. I just wouldn't hand Kara anything breakable again.

Attending to her daily needs, it was becoming easy to forget Kara was a movie star. However, pieces of her past life—scattered throughout the house—quickly reminded me. Dotted on the walls were posters from Kara's most iconic movies as well as her covers from every fashion magazine I could name and some I hadn't known existed.

Down in the basement bar, there was what I assumed was a paperweight, but turned out to be an obscure award for Kara's performance in a historical biopic. I remembered the film; it hadn't performed as well at the box office as expected. Bad PR about Kara had circulated prior to the film's release—something about Kara yelling at a young crewmember on set—but I couldn't remember the details.

Whether or not she lost the studio millions of dollars, Kara still lived in this lavish house. I was learning wealth placed you beyond the repercussions of certain mistakes.

Kara's formal wardrobe was another testament to her fame and fortune. I often confused the doors to one of the expansive restrooms and her wardrobe, and I couldn't help but linger in the latter when I found myself inside. Okay, maybe it was becoming a habit. It was filled with rows upon rows of dresses, shelves of shoes, and a center console overflowing with accessories and jewelry.

This wasn't as much of a wardrobe as it was a museum. Would Kara wear any of this ever again? Or was it just a reminder of exactly what she had had before her accident?

I reached out to touch a luxurious silk dress. If this was what silk felt like, I wasn't sure what that other fabric I thought was silk had been. I couldn't help but imagine what it would be like to live like Kara. A walk-in wardrobe filled with designer dresses and diamonds, perhaps requiring an insurance agent for important functions.

As I emerged from the wardrobe and turned to continue my way down the corridor, my eyes flew wide. Kara was sitting in her wheelchair down the hall, staring directly at me.

My heart hammered wildly in my chest.

"Kara!" I exclaimed, once I had gathered myself. "You're out!" For the whole week I'd spent with the Harringtons, I had never seen Kara out of her room. I hadn't known she was capable of moving around on her own. Had she been secretly watching me all week?

Just then, Flora appeared. She was holding a light scarf in her hand. She must have brought Kara here and gone back to fetch something from Kara's bedroom wardrobe, the one with her practical beige clothes. Of course Kara wasn't moving about the house; she couldn't even use the restroom by herself.

"Why shouldn't she be out?" Flora asked. "It's her house." She flicked off the brake of Kara's wheelchair with her heel and started rolling her down the hallway in my direction. Once she reached me, Flora slowed down for a moment, then glanced between me and the wardrobe door. Heat rushed to my face.

"I recommend not snooping around, however much you are curious about Mrs. Harrington's lifestyle. Just some friendly advice."

Somehow, it didn't feel so friendly.

5

A few days later, I was wheeling Kara out onto the balcony for some fresh air when my phone began to ring. I pulled it out and glanced idly at the number.

"Sorry, I have to take this," I said.

Kara didn't react.

Why did I even say that? She doesn't care. She might not even hear me.

I pressed the phone to my ear. "Hello?"

A familiar voice responded. It was one of the nurses from the care home. I ran past the usual prattle. It was customary for them to call me once in a while with minor updates, but it hadn't been that long since my last visit.

"I wanted to let you know personally. We've observed some reflexive eye movements."

My heart skipped a beat. "What?"

"We wanted to let you know first. But it's also important to note that this may or may not be indicative of change. You have to understand, recovery is highly individual and challenging after such a long period of unconsciousness. We will keep an eye on the situation and let you know if it advances. I would...try not to get my hopes up."

"Of course," I said. "Thank you."

I hung up and stared out over the railing.

The sound of sirens growing nearer. A desperate choking, gurgling. A hand reaching out—

Suddenly, there was a painful jolt against my legs as Kara's wheelchair bumped into me. Surprised, I stumbled against the low railing, which came up to my waist, and instinctively gripped it as tight as I could. I was *really* looking over the edge now. A rush of vertigo hit me; it was a *long* way down.

I pushed myself back upright and twisted away. Kara, in her wheelchair, rolled forward to fill the space I had cleared, bumping softly against the railing.

I could have sworn I'd checked the brakes. Ever since the bathroom incident, I'd been extra careful.

But here Kara was, her wheelchair clearly brake-free. I quickly reached down and secured them with shaking fingers, apologizing profusely.

"I'm so sorry," I muttered. "It won't happen again."

I glanced down at Kara. Her eyes flitted away from me and back onto the horizon. For just a moment, I thought I saw a look there. Evaluation? Weighing me? But I was probably imagining it.

As I wheeled her away, a thought nagged at me: What if *this* was the balcony Kara fell from? My mouth went dry at the thought. Could Kara have been upset about being brought here?

And with Kara, how could one tell?

Someone had been going through my stuff.

I stood in the guest room taking stock of what little I owned. It didn't take long—a duffel bag, a backpack, and what I thought was worth hauling in from the car, all of which fit neatly on the guest room bed. To be fair, the bed was massive, but you get my point.

I didn't have much stuff to keep track of, so it was obvious that things had been moved around. Whoever had gone digging hadn't been exactly subtle about it: The charger for my phone had been wrapped up and placed on my bedside table, my shirts had been folded upon being rearranged, and even the underwear I heaped into the bag had been stacked into a neat pile without any regard for my privacy.

At first, I was oddly relieved to find that the cassette tape from the sound studio was still among my stuff. But then an uncomfortable lump formed in my throat at the thought of the maid finding anything among my belongings labeled with *Kara*. Especially after Flora had already told me off for snooping around. Would she tell the Harringtons? Could this cost me my job?

The next time I saw the maid, I'd explain. I'd tell her I found it lying around the house. And that I'd meant to give it back but had forgotten all about it. I'd be extra convincing.

I couldn't afford to lose this job.

Why *hadn't* I given the tape to someone? To the maid, or even Colin? Maybe I didn't want to seem like I'd been snooping. Or maybe it was curiosity.

It made sense that there would be things labeled with Kara's name. This was, after all, her house. But why had it been hidden under the console? And who recorded on *cassette tapes* in this day and age?

I didn't know why, but I felt like the cassette tape would tell me something about Kara—help me understand this woman I had been hired to accompany. A woman I knew everything, yet nothing,

about.

So, from then on, I decided to keep the tape tucked safely in my pocket.

Making friends with someone who is only semi-responsive and extremely uninterested is challenging. Making friends with someone who creeps you out is borderline impossible.

But I had a job. I had a place to live. And, most importantly, access to a fully equipped sound studio, which was not only my ticket out of poverty but back into voice acting work. Things may have gone to hell before, but I'd charted a way out of this mess. All it would take would be to pretend to be best friends with Kara Harrington, who was currently staring blankly through me as I propped up the cushions behind her and pulled a cover over her long, slim legs.

Kara was dressed in a beautiful midnight-blue silky nightgown hemmed with lace. Throw on some heels and dangly earrings, and I'm pretty sure I could have pulled it off as a dress at a high-end cocktail party.

I couldn't help feeling it was all wasted on Kara.

I instantly felt guilty for the thought.

"You have the nicest clothes," I said quickly. "Jewel-tones always look great on you."

Kara continued to ignore me, focusing instead on a potted plant in the corner of the room. That plant would most likely have been a better conversationalist. But there was also an underlying tension. Like a coiled toy ready to bounce. Kara's sudden, jerky movements always had me on edge, certain she would knock something over and Flora would come rushing in, accusing me. They really needed to get her a nice silicon cup. Kara was a jump scare waiting to happen.

I wondered if her spasming was painful, or if she felt much at all.

"Would you like me to brush your hair?" I asked. "You have such gorgeous, thick hair."

Kara's eyes flicked. I might have imagined it, but I could almost swear I saw her begin to roll her eyes. Then she directed her gaze to her bedside table, where a pile of books resided.

"Did you want me to read?"

The tiniest, most imperceptible nod.

Pleased we were finally communicating in some way after almost two weeks of being ignored, I reached for one of the books. As I scanned the covers—historical biographies, contemporary fiction, and even a fantasy novel from a popular film franchise—it clicked. These were all projects Kara had worked on.

"These are all films you've been in!" I exclaimed. "Wait, is this the novel for that space movie you did? The one where you played an astronaut?"

Kara closed her eyes. I was starting to think that meant *yes*. Or maybe *shut up*.

Just then, there was a knock at the door.

"I hope I'm not bothering you," Colin said, poking his head in.

"Oh, not at all," I said, and I couldn't help but smile. I'd been listening to Colin's podcast at night before going to bed, and it was hard not to subscribe to his brand of infectious positivity.

Not to mention, he had a pleasant voice. Deep, soothing. I liked having him in my ear.

I shook myself out of my thoughts and nodded at the bedside table.

"We were just about to read," I explained. "But I got caught up in going through the titles."

"I heard," Colin said with a grin. "It's a great line-up, isn't it? Kara has some killer projects under her belt."

"I can't argue with that," I said. Then, realizing my excitement, I glanced at Kara and tried to compose myself. "I'm afraid I was rambling on…"

"Don't apologize," Colin reassured me as he walked over to the bed where Kara lay. "I'm happy she has someone who talks to her like a friend. Most people talk to her like…"

"…she's not even there?" I finished his sentence, thinking of Flora, who seemed convinced Kara was capable of communicating only basic needs. To be honest, I wasn't sure what I believed. Sometimes, I thought I saw a flicker of emotion on Kara's usually impassive face in response to something I said or did. But maybe I was imagining it. Maybe I was projecting my own emotions onto her.

"Exactly," Colin confirmed. "And her other friends, well…most of them didn't exactly stick around after the accident."

"I'm sorry to hear that," I said. My heart broke a little for Kara. I knew how it felt to be pushed to the side and forgotten, closed off from a community. With all your old friends turning against you.

"Thanks. Anyway, you should call it a day—I can take over from here." Colin's blue eyes scanned the book titles on the nightstand. "*Sentinels of the Stars*," he read aloud. "A classic."

"Aren't there like a million books in the series?" I asked.

"One released every year," Colin laughed. "But at least that means there's material for film adaptations. I hear they're getting ready for the sequel. Hopefully, Kara will be better by then."

My heart sank. Having worked in the entertainment industry as a voice actor, I knew how long it could take for projects to make it to casting. But imagining Kara jumping around a set in a stunt harness, wielding a prop blaster rifle in even a few years' time seemed impossible.

But I couldn't say that to Colin. Not with his hopeful expression.

"I'm sure she will be," I said, forcing a smile. "Thank you, Colin. Enjoy the book."

"Oh, we will," Colin said. "Thanks, Anna."

"See you later, Kara," I said before heading out of the room.

As I slipped out of the door into the hallway, I braved a peek inside. Colin had begun to read the beginning of the book, and his voice was confident and comforting, a low, pleasant timbre. Coupled with his pleasant personality, it was easy to see how he had become such a popular podcaster. But I couldn't help but believe his optimism was misplaced. I could picture him in a similar situation, giving his caretakers little thumbs-up signs, interacting with physical therapy toys, and surpassing all odds. But Kara? Kara with her thousand-yard stare, condescending glances, and shaking hands? Kara limp against me like a ragdoll? It just seemed like she had already given up.

And Colin hadn't realized yet. He really didn't deserve this.

I shook my head, trying to focus on something other than Colin's thick mop of curly black hair—when my eyes landed on Kara again.

Except this time, she wasn't staring off into space or looking past me with indifference.

She was staring straight at me.

I froze before quickly closing the door.

Was I imagining it…or was there something I recognized in her eyes?

Hostility? Malice? Even…hate?

6

Rifling through the many boxes of equipment in the sound studio, I came across a cassette tape adapter.

I knew I should have left it alone.

But I couldn't help myself.

I still had an hour before Micky arrived for our first recording.

I hadn't exactly cleared Micky coming into the house to record for the show with Colin. I had a feeling Colin would be fine with it, but it still felt awkward to ask whether I could bring a guy into the house so soon after starting my new job. I was nervous about Colin getting the wrong idea.

I kept putting off asking and before I knew it, it was too late. I'd been meaning to, all week, but Colin was a busy guy. He was often out of the house, and when he was in the house, he was either in the sound studio or spending time with Kara, and I didn't exactly feel like I could interrupt him in either of those moments. And whenever we ran into each other in the brief time in between, well, Micky was the furthest thing from my mind.

And now it was too late to ask Colin. Micky would turn up within the hour, and Colin was out in town. Luckily, the maids were out, and it was too late for deliveries or for one of Colin's many assistants or associates to wordlessly breeze in and out of the house. Flora would be upstairs with Kara, hopefully busy bathing and medicating her.

I'd told Micky to meet me at the gate, and I could walk him directly to the poolside door that led downstairs, right to the hallway with the studio. If this panned out the way I thought it would, Micky would be in and out and no one would be the wiser. Then, later, I could clear the whole thing with Colin and save myself a *lot* of stress down the line.

I turned on the computer in the sound studio, and it chimed awake, filling the space with a pleasant melody. I quickly searched for a port for the tape adapter and found one. A few clicks later, I had an audio file on screen, ready to play. I glanced nervously at the door.

No one was in, as far as I knew. It was fine. Even if someone were to come in, I could always say I just plugged in the wrong suspiciously labeled cassette.

I double-clicked the file.

An audio clip blew up on screen, a mountain range of neon green linework sketching the audio level as the voice boomed all around me, displaced by the surround-sound, coming from everywhere and nowhere at once.

The voice belonged to a woman with a raspy tone, as if she had a cough or had been crying.

I don't know what to say. Should I start at the beginning?

There was a small pause and an indistinct murmur, as if someone was responding to her.

Okay. I'll just talk about how I feel in the moment, then.

I don't really know who to trust, or who to believe. I don't think I can trust myself.

I'm getting scared.

I have a feeling something terrible is going to happen to me. It's rushing at me, inevitable, like a wave. But there's nothing I can do to stop it. No escape. And no face to this enemy.

I'm scared.

And I don't know what to do…

I jolted as the door swung open and slammed my hand on the keyboard, killing the audio.

"Anna?"

"Oh my god, Micky, you scared me." I said, covering my face with my hands. Then I quickly straightened up. "How did you get in here?"

"The gate was open, and you weren't answering your phone," Micky explained. "I circled around to the pool and saw the door heading downstairs, so I thought I'd just come find you."

"I told you to wait for me." I pulled out the cassette adapter and tossed it underneath the console, hoping Micky wouldn't notice.

"Why?" Micky asked, frowning.

"It doesn't matter," I said. I couldn't believe Micky had snuck in without waiting for me. And it wasn't like the Harringtons or their staff to leave the gate open.

Micky appraised the sound studio, nodding appreciatively.

"This is amazing. The more professional our demo sounds, the better chance we have at getting funding."

Micky glanced at me, almost hopefully.

"We can do anything down here, and no one will hear us."

He walked over to the console and played with some options. He clicked on the microphone next to it and said dramatically, "In space, no one can hear you scream." His words echoed around the room. I couldn't help but crack a small smile.

"Well, let's get to it!" Micky said, clapping his hands.

We started going through the lines, and Micky had me run through a few different versions at the mic. After every version, Micky fiddled with the settings until he was pleased with the sound profile he'd created and saved for me on the studio computer, ready for me whenever I had the chance to record some lines.

"Of course, the more direction you have, the better the final product," Micky kept reminding me.

"Sure. But we can work remotely. I don't want to inconvenience you," I explained, though really, I was more nervous about Flora catching me smuggling a man into the basement of the house. "You don't have to come over here all the time."

"I don't mind coming over," Micky said. "It's a good excuse to see you, too!"

I forced a smile.

Oblivious, Micky dug around his bags and produced a bottle of cheap liquor. "We gotta celebrate!"

"Maybe just one drink," I suggested. I was starting to get the bad feeling that Micky had aspirations of hanging out and catching up, and I didn't want Colin or Flora walking in on us and getting the wrong idea.

I fetched a pair of glasses, and Micky poured us drinks. The liquor was sour, but it wasn't as bad as I'd expected. I relaxed into my chair, and Micky and I began to go over the characters. When he stuck to talking about work, Micky was a fine enough conversationalist. And he was passionate about this project. That passion carried, and I could feel myself getting excited about the story, the characters, and the possibility of where the project could lead with proper funding.

"With an established fanbase and a whole pre-built universe ready for adapting, we could have years of work ahead of us," Micky said gleefully, not for the first time, refilling my glass. "Who knows where this could go?"

I nodded in agreement, the warmth of the liquor trickling through me, a pleasant purr in my throat.

"And you really are the perfect pick for the role of the Countess," Micky said. "You *are* the Countess."

He'd said that at least three times already too. How drunk was Micky?

"Thanks," I said politely, wondering if I should wrap up the visit. I was becoming increasingly aware of my upcoming shift and more and more alarmed at the concept of having drunk prior to it. I had intended to have one drink, if that, but I had lost track of how often Micky had refilled my glass, and I felt slightly woozy. *Not good.*

"You could take inspiration from your surroundings," Micky said, waving his arm indistinctly, indicating, I supposed, to the general house. Liquor sloshed over his arm and onto the carpet. I tensed.

"It was really nice of Colin to let us use the studio," I said, trying to change the subject.

Micky swirled his drink. "What do you think about him?" he asked.

"He's certainly a good reference for the Count," I said, unsure where he was going with this.

Micky's eyes narrowed. He tapped his fingers against his glass.

"You know," he said. "Everyone *loves* the Count."

"I guess," I said with an awkward laugh. Something had shifted in the atmosphere. "He's suave, and handsome, and—"

Micky went on. "Yes. He's handsome and charming, but he's also…" He shook his head. "But people don't want to see it. Not like the Jester. The Jester is solid all around…"

Micky drifted off. I waited for him to continue, praying this wasn't going where I feared it might be. How many actresses had to deal with unwanted advances from directors?

But he just downed his drink, placed the glass back on the table with a slight wobble, and stood up. He shook his head and shot me a glance.

"So, you'll have the first batch ready for me by the end of next week?" Micky asked.

"Yes, absolutely," I replied, taken aback by Micky's abrupt shift. We had already agreed upon this deadline, and we'd barely gotten started on this project, but I now felt like an unruly subordinate.

He nodded absentmindedly and walked out of the room.

"See you soon, Anna."

I was left alone in the room, dumbfounded, with my half-filled glass still in my hand.

This opportunity with Micky could be my ticket to success and stability, but maybe I was being too naive. What if he wanted something more from me? Something I wasn't prepared to give?

And the thought of what would happen when he realized that made my stomach turn.

7

After being employed by the Harringtons for two weeks, I finally had a chance to leave the house.

Well, that's not entirely fair. Technically, I *could* have left during the mornings or evenings while Flora watched over Kara, but the scorching summer heat made staying in the cool, air-conditioned basement with its stocked bar of cold drinks much more appealing.

Besides, my main goal was to read my script and record my lines in the studio, so I couldn't complain. Things were finally looking up for me, right?

Today was different though. As I made my way upstairs for my shift, I saw Colin talking to what looked like an assistant dressed in a sleek black suit. Colin firmly shook the man's hand, quickly finishing his conversation, and intercepted me.

"Anna," he said. "I was hoping to catch you." He rubbed his hair idly, and his damp curls fell onto his forehead, as if he had just showered. I was strangely pleased he'd interrupted his conversation to talk to me, as if it somehow proved I was important. If nothing else, it helped me feel a little less out of place.

The other man gazed at me as he passed on his way out. I smiled, but my attention was on Colin.

"It's your lucky day," I replied, spreading my hands. "How can I help?"

"I was actually hoping you could drive Kara to her physiotherapy appointment."

"Oh. Isn't that…Flora's job?" I didn't care whose job it was, but it didn't seem like Flora to give up her responsibilities, and Colin must have noticed my surprise.

"It is, but I thought you could take over for today. It will be good for you to be familiar with the routine too. Just in case Flora is ever…unavailable."

"Got it," I said. I was sure Flora would never be *unavailable*, not if she could help it. But it wasn't my place to question what Colin thought was necessary.

Plus, I had to admit it sounded like a good idea to take Kara outside. Spending hours upon hours in Kara's room, with my own voice being the only sound to break the thick silence, was starting to make me uneasy. It had been weeks, but I still couldn't shake off the strange feeling I got around Kara. She reminded me of one of those paintings whose eyes appeared to follow you wherever you were in the room, even if she seemed to be staring straight ahead.

Maybe being out in the real world would make her less intimidating, surrounded by bustling traffic and cheerful physiotherapists.

"Great! Thanks a lot, Anna." He gave my arm a gentle squeeze, then called out, "Flora?" A moment later, Flora appeared pushing Kara's wheelchair.

"You'll show Anna the ropes?"

"Of course, Mr. Harrington," Flora replied. Her tone was neutral, though cold. She pushed Kara's wheelchair into the elevator, and I stepped in beside them. Colin gave us a cheery wave, and the doors closed shut. Suddenly, the temperature dropped by at least thirty degrees.

We descended to the garage, which I'd only seen briefly while parking my car in its corner. I tried to ignore it as we walked past the Harringtons' gleaming collection of cars, although I saw Flora glance at it with badly concealed disdain.

She could glare at it all she wanted. As long as she didn't ask any intrusive questions.

The Harringtons had enough cars to supply a small squad rather than a two-person family. I briefly wondered if they'd hoped for a larger family before Kara's accident.

There were two SUVs, a gleaming silver Maserati convertible, and a few vintage cars I couldn't place at the back. Flora wheeled Kara to a car in the front, a large black Mercedes van.

"The key is inside," Flora stated as she opened the door and pressed a button to lower a platform for Kara's wheelchair. Meanwhile, I circled around to the driver's seat and climbed in. The seats were pristine white leather and butter-soft, a stark contrast to my beat-up car which I was trying and failing to forget. I sank into it. I swear, in that moment, Flora could have said anything, and I would have let it slide.

After she'd loaded Kara into the van, I started the car and scrolled through the navigator menu until I found the address of the physiotherapy clinic.

"Drive carefully," Flora said before slamming Kara's door shut. From anyone else, it would have sounded like genuine concern, but coming from Flora, it sounded like an order. I steered toward the doors, which rolled aside automatically, and drove onto the street while Flora disappeared somewhere into the darkness of the garage.

The ride was smooth, more like flying than driving. And easy—the car practically drove itself. The air ventilation system provided a constant current of cool air, making me untouchable to the heatwave outside.

As I drove, my thoughts kept going back to the voice on the tape I found under the console in the sound studio. Even though Micky had interrupted my listening, the haunting words had rooted themselves in my memory, and I could recall the words as if they were being whispered directly in my ear.

...something terrible is going to happen to me.

The desperate undercurrent in that voice. The hopelessness.

There's nothing I can do to stop it.

The slight distortion on the tape made it difficult to identify whose voice it was. It reminded me of old smoky offices and bulky Walkmans, something from my parents' generation.

No escape.

But it had been clearly labeled with Kara's name. Did she record it herself, or had it been addressed to her? I'd need to dig up more clips of Kara speaking to compare her voice with the one on the tape.

Then again, Kara had altered her voice for different roles before. Maybe she was preparing to play a character? What was that movie she'd dropped out of before the accident?

I'm scared.

And I'd believed every word the voice said. Whoever spoke on that tape, they either sounded genuinely terrified for their life or could deliver an Oscar-worthy performance. That sort of performance wasn't easy. I knew that better than anyone.

Was Kara a better actress than I thought? Or had the indomitable Kara Harrington truly been afraid? And if so, of what?

I caught a glimpse of Kara in the rearview mirror and nearly slammed my foot on the brakes, which would have been catastrophic.

It wasn't just that she was staring right at me.

It was that she didn't have a seatbelt on.

"Oh shit."

I frantically scanned the road for a place to pull over. Finding none, I waited until we were stopped at a red light and then quickly jumped out of the van. Horns blared as the light turned green, just as I was tugging at Kara's seatbelts. Out of breath but relieved Kara was safely buckled in, I flung myself into the driver's seat.

The rest of the drive to the physiotherapy clinic was uneventful, but I couldn't shake the anger boiling inside of me, even as I maneuvered Kara onto the car's lifting platform and then wheeled her toward the clinic. I remembered Flora's words: *Drive carefully.*

Had she set me up to fail? Had this been some kind of sick test?

I had a feeling Flora wasn't too fond of me, but risking Kara's safety to prove my incompetence seemed extreme, even for her.

It occurred to me that Flora's hours must have been cut once I was hired, and I seemed to be acquiring more of her responsibilities. Since I'd emphasized caring for a sick relative on my CV, I'd been assigned duties typically done by a nurse. Helping Kara onto the toilet. Bathing her. Dressing her.

Flora must have been bitter that I was supplanting her.

I pushed Kara into the clinic. The luxurious interior was all dark wood and dark stones, lit with a warm amber glow. Soft, ambient woodwind music added to the spa-like atmosphere. It was hard to believe this was a licensed physiotherapy center. I'd assumed anything remotely medical involved the color white, linoleum, and tiles.

I'd learned that money worked like a magic trick; anything was possible for the right price.

I rolled Kara to the counter, where a receptionist in a crisp black shirt was sitting, her gel nails wrapped around a glossy edition of a tabloid magazine. She looked up as I pushed Kara closer.

"Oh, hi. How's it going? Mrs. Harrington has an appointment to see a physiotherapist," I stated, realizing I didn't know her doctor's name.

Though Kara didn't speak, I could sometimes *feel* her disapproval. This was one of those moments. I swallowed compulsively.

"Absolutely," the receptionist said, her nails making an audible clatter as she tapped the keys on her keyboard. "Please have a seat. It will only be a moment."

I'd barely had time to find a seat before a man in a white coat appeared. He had a perfectly clean-shaven face, an almost blindingly white smile, and that same quality the Harringtons had, so clean you'd imagine dirt was incapable of adhering to them. Probably something he'd perfected to please his wealthy and exclusive clients.

Something I hadn't yet picked up.

"Good morning, Mrs. Harrington. What a pleasure to see you again," the man said, greeting Kara with enthusiasm. Then, he turned to me. "And you must be…?"

"I'm Anna Albright. Mrs. Harrington's companion." I surprised myself by hearing a hint of pride creep into my voice.

"Wonderful. You can wait here while I take Mrs. Harrington for her appointment."

"Oh," I said uncertainly. No one had briefed me on what to do in this scenario. I had assumed I'd be in the room with her. I glanced at Kara, who seemed lost in the movements of the fish in an aquarium on the other side of the room.

"I'm not sure, but I think maybe Kara would want me there?"

Just then, Kara tapped twice on her armrest. The man nodded. "There's your answer."

"I'm sorry? Usually, she taps if she needs to use the restroom…"

"One tap is yes, two taps no," he explained.

"Oh," I heard myself say. I couldn't think of anything better. Why hadn't anyone told me this? Flora had been so adamant that Kara's communication was limited to indicating she needed to use the restroom. Had Flora undersold Kara's abilities to make herself, as a qualified nurse, seem more valuable?

Did Colin know?

The physiotherapist left with a small smile, but he may as well have been shaking his head. How could someone who worked for Kara not know such a basic thing?

Wanting to crawl somewhere and hide, I sank into a chair in the waiting room. The receptionist who had been lazily flipping through her tabloid magazine looked up.

"He pretends to be her best friend, but Kara never pays him any attention," she said.

That made me feel a bit better.

"I guess it's good to know she's an equal-opportunity ignorer."

The receptionist smiled at me conspiratorially from over her magazine.

"*So*, what's it like working for the Harringtons?"

"Colin—Mr. Harrington—is nice," I replied honestly. "Although he's not around the house much."

"Pity. He's nice to look at, isn't he?"

I blushed and hated myself for it. "I haven't thought about it," I replied dishonestly.

The receptionist cackled. She leaned over her magazine still in her hands, eager for gossip. "I promise I won't tell Kara."

"Well…I mean, I guess," I admitted. Who was this receptionist going to tell anyway? She was clearly hungry for social interaction. I doubt the clientele here gave her the time of day. "He's like a walking fragrance commercial. He makes my ex look like Oscar the Grouch."

"That's *funny*. You know, I think I like you better than the last girl."

"I like myself better than Flora, too," I muttered.

"Was that her name? I don't remember. I've seen more than a few girls walk Kara in. They only accompany her for a few weeks. They never last long," she said matter-of-factly, folding her magazine on the desk.

I stared at her blankly. I'd assumed I was Kara's first companion, but that clearly wasn't the case. It seemed odd no one had mentioned the previous companions before.

"Do you think she's still in there? Kara? Do you think she knows what's happening?" the receptionist asked.

I remembered Kara's sharp gaze in the rearview mirror, full of venom. But then I thought about the moments of stillness and Kara's distant gaze. The way she seemed to go somewhere far away, where nobody could follow.

"I think so. At least some of the time."

Then, the receptionist said something unexpected.

"Good. I hope she is. The way she bulldozed over other women to get where she is now, she had it coming. It's only right that she has to suffer in silence."

I froze. The receptionist continued, evidently mistaking my shock for curiosity.

"You know, I had a friend who worked on a set with her once. She said Kara took a special dislike to her, being young and pretty. And the way Kara acted to my friend was just *awful*. And not just Hollywood-awful, but actually messed up. She said Kara was a real evil b—"

Before I was able to speak up, the side door slid open and the physiotherapist appeared, pushing Kara toward me. I thanked him and hurried Kara out of the clinic, disturbed by the casually malicious words. I heard the receptionist idly wish us a good day as we left before her eyes lazily flicked back to the glossy pages of her magazine.

It was a terrible and cruel thing for her to say, and I was not prepared for it. But beyond my disapproval, I had to wonder.

What could Kara have possibly done to deserve such a fate?

8

I'd thought the previous week was unbearably hot, but it was subarctic compared to the heatwave that followed. The sun blazed down relentlessly, heating up the asphalt on the streets which sent up distorting waves.

Even the advanced air-conditioning in the house struggled to keep up. I started keeping my lotions in the fridge. And despite the basement being the coolest and most secluded part of the house, I slept restlessly. I dreamed of Kara setting me on fire with her cigarette.

The week before, I'd sent my first batch of recordings to Micky but hadn't heard back yet. It was unusual for him not to respond quickly. Maybe he was still upset about his last visit, where he went on that odd rant about the Count and the Jester.

If Micky wanted me to forget about his speech entirely, I was only too happy to oblige and get on with the project. I had already begun recording the second batch, but this heat had put a stop to it. It was just impossible to concentrate.

Another annoyance was Flora. I'd never been late for my shift, but she always came looking for me a good ten minutes early, as if I were an unruly child that had to be shepherded. Recently, she had also started showing up at odd times, probably hoping to catch me doing something I wasn't meant to. Her abrupt appearances had kept me from listening to the mystery cassette tape during daytime hours. I couldn't chance her wandering in and questioning me about it.

I wandered to the basement fridge and dispensed a few ice cubes into my palm, where they instantly began to melt. I slipped them into my mouth, but it did little to alleviate the stuffiness I felt. I still had an hour before my shift, and I didn't know how I'd bear it.

I decided to risk it and try the Harringtons' pool.

I grabbed my only swimsuit—a skimpy turquoise bikini with criss-crossing strings over my bare stomach and back—and headed up the marble steps from the basement that led straight to the pool. Its sparkling surface rippled in the soft breeze, the sunlight reflecting in scattered silver crescents. Without hesitation, I tossed my towel onto a nearby lounge chair and dove into the cool, refreshing water.

Calling it heaven would be an understatement.

I broke through the surface of the water and swam toward the edge of the pool, where the ground dropped off to reveal a breathtaking view of the glittering city. Somewhere down there, I'd hustled from one desperate audition to another while someone, possibly Kara or even Colin, idly floated and gazed at the city that unfurled before them, its people like microscopic specs of dust.

"Hey, Anna."

I spun around to see Colin standing there in a fitted cotton suit, his handsome features framed by his tousled black hair.

"I'm sorry," I stammered. "I should have asked—"

But Colin waved away my apology with a smile. "What? You're welcome to use the pool anytime. It's a brilliant idea in this heat." I noticed his blue eyes perfectly matched the color of the pool.

"Honestly, I used to think those resort restaurants you ate at while submerged in water were tacky," Colin mused, "but now I think they may have been on to something."

"I've actually been to a restaurant like that," I admitted. "In Belize. On a family trip."

"Oh?" Colin raised an eyebrow. "And what was your verdict?"

I tried to remember the meal. I'd just turned eleven. I'd splashed around in the water, stuffing myself with watermelon and skewers of spiced pork, exhilarated by the idea of doing something that felt distinctly forbidden.

And my mom had been there. It was one of the few memories I had of her where she was laughing. Where she seemed happy.

"It was actually really great," I confessed with a smile.

Colin clapped his hands approvingly. "That settles it. Next chance I get, I'm ordering us dinner into this pool."

Us.

I couldn't tell if he was joking or not, but his enthusiasm was infectious. I'd missed Colin. He was the only person who seemed happy to have me around. Even the timid maid avoided me after I'd confronted her about moving my stuff. She'd stared at me as if uncomprehending, told me adamantly it wasn't her, and had stopped cleaning my room entirely.

But here was Colin, appreciating my presence and making me feel wanted. Ironic, considering he'd hired me to keep his *wife* company.

I wondered if I made him feel the same way. His wife wasn't exactly making *him* feel wanted, was she?

"There's actually something I've been meaning to discuss with you," Colin said, his smile fading. He crouched at the edge of the pool. My heart started to race. Surely, he'd noticed Kara wasn't warming to me as much as he had hoped. I was relying on the earnings from this summer job to pay off my debts and have some extra savings, but if he terminated my contract now, I wouldn't even be able to finish the project with Micky.

"I need your permanent address for tax purposes before paying you for your first month," Colin said. "I checked, but it doesn't seem to be included in your CV."

I tried to keep the panic off my face. Ever since I got kicked out, I didn't have a permanent address. It felt absurd to claim I was homeless when I was living in the lap of luxury in the Harringtons' house, but technically, I was. What would Colin think if he found out?

"I'll get back to you with that," I said quickly.

"Great, thanks, Anna," Colin replied. "I should..." He hesitated, sweeping his fingers gently through the water.

"...ignore my very important work and join Anna in the pool?" I finished his sentence for him, startled by my own boldness.

Colin laughed. "It would feel really good, wouldn't it?"

I couldn't help but grin.

"You *did* say it was a fantastic idea. And I've heard you say you always choose the best idea in the room," I teased.

"So you *have* listened to my podcast," Colin said with a wolfish smile. "Well, I guess I can't argue with my own logic. I better get out of these clothes then."

I watched him walk away and felt a rush of excitement. I adjusted the straps on my bikini and smoothed my hair down with some water.

What was I doing?

Colin returned shortly, and I had to fight the urge not to stare. He really looked sexy in his swim trunks, his long, well-defined torso peeking out from his opened cotton shirt. His dark hair was just slightly curled from the sweat and the heat. I swallowed as he pulled off his shirt and descended into the pool. It was hard to believe he was famous for a podcast when he could so clearly be a model.

Focus, Anna.

"You look like a merman," I blurted out without thinking. I instantly wanted to drown.

"This pool should pay you a commission," Colin joked. "That's the nicest thing anyone has said to me in a long while. If it's a compliment, that is."

"Oh, it's a compliment." Heat rose to my cheeks.

"I left my trident inside," Colin said, swimming closer. "Hope that's not too big of a disappointment."

"You couldn't. Disappoint me. I mean—" I ducked underwater to avoid finishing the rest of the sentence.

After just a moment, Colin dove underwater after me. His eyes looked even bluer in the bright water of the pool.

I hid my face behind my hands, but Colin gently grabbed my wrists, grinning, and pulled me up to the surface.

When we resurfaced, Colin shook out his hair, spraying droplets everywhere. A grin still spread across his face.

"Good," he said.

But before I could react, Flora's head popped up over the balcony above.

"Mr. Harrington. Mrs. Harrington has just woken up."

Colin, surprised, looked up. "Thank you, Flora. Please tell her I'll be right up."

Colin looked over at me and gave a rueful smile. "I guess the pool will have to wait. I'm happy to see it being used again. It's been a while since a beautiful young actress swam in it." With that, he turned around and headed back into the house.

Was he...flirting?

Despite the cool water, I felt hot all over, a pang of disappointment in my chest as I watched him go.

But before I could compose myself, I looked up and saw Flora staring down at me, her face a cold mask of disapproval. Without saying a word, she pulled her head back and disappeared.

I floated in the water, trying to hold onto the joy of swimming while feeling deflated by the interruption.

Flora had no right to disapprove. Colin himself said I could use the pool, and our interaction had been perfectly innocent.

Hadn't it?

9

Usually, I snuck my lunch from upstairs down into the basement where I felt less exposed. Let's face it, the kitchen was beautiful, but with so many glass and balcony views from above, sitting and eating at the counter made me feel like a test subject under observation.

But Flora's belittling remarks and her underhanded actions, like her trick with the seatbelt, were pissing me off so much I claimed a barstool in the kitchen and ate my superfood salad at the counter. It was almost disappointing when she didn't come looking for me before my shift as she usually did.

Five minutes before I was scheduled to start my time with Kara, I placed the empty glass container from my salad into the dishwasher and headed upstairs.

As soon as I entered Kara's room, Flora spoke up. She was packing away what looked like a blood pressure cuff and was dressed in her usual nurse's uniform, which I suspected she wore to establish authority. Her hair was somehow pulled back even tighter than before, almost as if compulsively tightening her hair would also maintain her hold on her job. Or perhaps me.

"I notice you ignored my advice," Flora said.

"With the avalanche of unsolicited advice you dish out, you'll have to be more specific," I replied, keeping my tone neutral. I saw a flash of surprise in her eyes at my disobedience and stood up a little straighter.

That's right. I bite back.

"Mrs. Harrington's wardrobe," Flora said curtly. "The one for her expensive designer clothes down the hallway. I was looking for a silk scarf and found the room in chaos."

I opened my mouth to defend myself, but then closed it, confused. I'd expected Flora to parrot her earlier advice of "remembering my place" and "not getting close to the family." She always scowled or tutted if she saw me interacting with Colin, as if I were the village leper jeopardizing him by my mere proximity.

But Kara's walk-in wardrobe? Sure, I may have spent more time than necessary admiring the beautiful gowns I could only dream of wearing, but I always made sure everything was put back exactly as it was before, down to placing shoes and bags back at the correct angles.

I would never have left a mess. I would never have been that stupid.

"Don't look so surprised. You know exactly what I'm talking about."

"I don't! I didn't—"

Flora shook her head, cutting me off. "Well, come on. Come see the damage."

It was clear that whatever I said didn't matter.

I glanced at the sleeping Kara, then back at Flora, and followed Flora reluctantly.

Flora led me out of the room and down the corridor to the wardrobe. As she swung open the door, my heart sank. It was a disaster. Expensive dresses drooped haphazardly from hangers, drawers for accessories were ajar, as if someone had quickly slammed them shut and they'd rebounded, and shoes were scattered everywhere.

Flora. For some reason, Flora has done this and is trying to make me look bad.

"You have about fifteen minutes before Mrs. Harrington wakes up," Flora said from behind me.

My blood boiled. "Is this because I went swimming in the pool?" I demanded, swerving around to face Flora. "Or because I'm taking Kara to physiotherapy now?"

"I've been working here for a long time. I've seen opportunists like you come and go. *Companions,*" Flora spat the last word, pointedly choosing to ignore what I said. "They were all unqualified and scared of Mrs. Harrington. Just like you are." She waved her hand at the mess.

"If you want to keep this job for however long you can handle it, clean up, and I won't have to tell Mr. Harrington about this mess."

"*Mr. Harrington* wouldn't be happy to hear that you sent his wife off to physiotherapy with an unfastened seatbelt," I retorted, instantly regretting it.

"Excuse me? Are you saying *you* didn't fasten Mrs. Harrington's seatbelt when *you* took her to physiotherapy? No, Mr. Harrington won't be happy to hear about that at all."

My throat tightened. I'd shown my hand too early, and now Flora had played me. I could see the barely concealed smirk tugging at her face.

Flora checked her watch, then glanced back at me. "Do you have your pager?"

"Yes," I said through gritted teeth. I *always* had my pager on me. Flora checking was just another way to belittle my competence.

"Then you will know if Mrs. Harrington needs you. I'll return later to give Mrs. Harrington her meds," Flora said and headed out of the room without another word, leaving me seething at the crime scene.

Cleaning up felt like admitting culpability, but I didn't know what else to do. I began to carefully rearrange the clothes and shoes, even though I was more in the mood to fling them across the room. How could Flora stoop so low to get rid of me? She must be even more unhinged than I'd realized.

But one thing Flora said was true: She had worked for the Harringtons much longer than I had. When push came to shove, who would Colin believe?

The way she'd walked away with her head held high, as if she'd backed me into a corner…

She really didn't know me at all.

When the receptionist at the physiotherapist's office mentioned previous companions staying with the Harringtons for short periods of time before being replaced, I assumed it was because of Kara. Let's face it, working as Kara's companion was about as appealing as working the night shift at a creepy wax doll museum.

But after today's events, I suspected Flora had something to do with the turnover as well.

I could not afford to lose this job.

I had to change my strategy.

So far, I'd focused on doing my job and staying out of Flora's way, but that only made me an easy target for her bullying. I had to get ahead of her. And I knew exactly how I'd do it.

I had to become the perfect companion for Kara.

Now, I know—that's why I was hired, right? But truthfully, while I did attend to Kara's needs and helped her with daily tasks like showering, I hadn't really played the best friend. Though I hated to admit it, Flora may have been onto something: Kara intimidated me. Her odd, absent gaze. The way I'd suddenly realize she was staring at me. The insistent tapping. And how things seemed to break or fall in her presence.

But I now realized that the truth did not matter. What mattered was how things appeared. Flora proved that when she framed me for upending Kara's closet. I hadn't done it, but it only mattered that it *looked* like I did.

From now on, I was going to make it look like I adored Kara, and there was nothing she could do about it.

And I was something Flora could never be.

A damn good actress.

I started enacting my new plan immediately.

"Good morning, Kara," I said chirpily, floating into her room. She was lying in bed, her eyes half-hooded from sleep. She craned her neck a little to check where the noise was coming from as I drew open the curtains to let in the light. Kara blinked.

I leaned over and gave the air on either side of her cheeks two light pecks. "Or should I say *Bonjour*. I heard you love Paris, so I started learning French. It can be our secret language!"

Kara responded with one of her most disdainful looks yet before her eyes returned to their default absent state. Despite how unsettling it was, I couldn't help but feel a slight twinge of victory.

What are you going to do now, Kara? Roll your chair over my foot? Drool on me?

"Anyway," I said as I changed Kara out of her pajamas and into one of her cashmere, beige leisure outfits, "I thought we would take a little tour about the house. Enjoy a change of scenery. How long has it been since you had a look at all your pieces? You love art, right?"

I slipped my hands under Kara's arms and lifted her onto her wheelchair. When I stepped back, Kara had tilted her head just a fraction and seemed to be studying me. Then she lifted her finger and tapped the armrest of her wheelchair, once.

That meant yes.

At that moment, I really had to suppress a grin. After a month with the Harringtons, was it possible I was finally *actually* getting through to Kara?

"Perfect. Who knows, maybe we'll venture out of the house one day and visit a gallery. Would you like that?"

There was no response. Still, I could feel her eyes on me. I reached into my pocket and held up for her to see, between my fingers, a pair of earrings I'd taken from the walk-in wardrobe.

"Let's add some color to your all-beige wardrobe. You are so beautiful, and you have all this lovely clothing and jewelry to accentuate it. Let's show you off a little, shall we?"

Kara may have displayed as much emotion as a stone statue, but I swear I saw a flicker of surprise on her face.

Just you wait, Kara. You haven't seen anything yet.

I spent half an hour styling and grooming Kara's hair and touching up her face with cosmetics. With a bone structure like hers, she didn't need much help, but a touch of corrector under her eyes and some blush and highlighter made her look healthier. Dewy. Less…ghostly.

Once she was all made up, I rolled Kara out of her room and down the hallway, stopping every so often at a piece of art. It had taken me a whole night, but I'd Googled every single piece of visible artwork I knew of in the house and made notes.

There were bold abstract paintings, geometric chrome sculptures, and even one painting a website had claimed featured a color that was utterly unique and impossible to identically replicate. I thought it looked like a grayish beige.

"You sure have an eclectic taste in art. I mean, there doesn't seem to be a single unifying quality to the pieces you have around the house. Except…" I started, unsure whether I should finish. Now that I thought about it, there *was* a unifying quality to the pieces. All of them were unsettling. I wasn't sure whether it was the color choices, or the shapes, or even the way some of the paintings had scratches or slashes on them.

It's not like she could talk back to me, right?

"They all seem kind of…depressing."

Kara's eyes washed over from me to the painting. I regretted saying anything and began to roll her back down the corridor.

Suddenly, Kara made a noise. It was halfway between a grunt and a sigh, like she was straining to project air from her lungs.

I stopped the wheelchair and circled to Kara. Was she feeling all right? Was she positioned uncomfortably in the wheelchair? But she seemed oblivious to me, fixated instead on the door we had just passed.

"Are you all right, Kara?" I asked, leaning over her.

Kara's gaze turned watery. I glanced sideways at the door, then back at Kara.

"Do you want something from that room?"

Kara did not react. But something was different about her. She seemed more haunted than I'd ever seen her before. Almost…possessed.

"Stay here," I told her, snapping on the lock of the wheelchair with my toes. I walked up to the door and wrapped my fingers around the handle, thinking back to how Flora had sped past the door. How her eyes had been fixed far ahead, how her steps quickened as she passed.

Kara made another sound, almost like a gurgle.

"It's okay," I reassured her, not sure who I was talking to—Kara or myself.

I turned the handle.

I half expected it to be locked, but the door swung open easily.

The room appeared to have once been an office, with a couch and a desk. The upholstery was a dark floral pattern I hadn't seen anywhere else in the house. The room had no windows. And unlike the rest of the house, this room did not intuitively light up upon my arrival. It just sat there in the windowless dim gloom, like it had been forgotten by the rest of the building.

I approached the desk, where a tape recorder sat. I was unsure if I'd ever touched a tape recorder, though the machine felt inexplicably, oddly familiar to me. I pressed the button with a symbol for eject, and the recorder clicked open to reveal an empty slot. No cassette inside.

Was this where the strange recording had been made? And if so, why was the tape hidden in the basement? Why would anyone record with an old cassette recorder in the first place, when the house had a fully equipped sound studio?

I stepped away from the desk…only to realize my fingers were coated with a thin layer of powdery dust. It seemed that the maid had neglected this room. How long had it sat untouched?

Just then, I heard a loud thump from the hallway.

"Kara!" I shouted, stumbling out of the room and back onto the landing. Kara was sprawled at the foot of her wheelchair, her long limbs tangled awkwardly. I crouched beside her and tried to haul her into a sitting position in the wheelchair, but she was like a dead weight, impossible to move.

As I struggled, I felt something wet on my knee and noticed that Kara's cashmere pants were now a shade darker. The smell of urine lingered in the air. Kara must have wet herself during the fall.

"Come on, Kara, help me out here," I said, gritting my teeth as I attempted to inch Kara back onto the wheelchair seat.

I heard footsteps and turned to see Colin bounding up the stairs.

"I heard a noise," he explained, glancing at the scene before him. I opened my mouth, unsure of what to say. It probably didn't look great, whatever it seemed like I was doing. Would Colin still believe I was taking good care of her?

But before I could say anything, Colin wordlessly came to my side and looped his arm around Kara.

"If you grab her feet," he suggested, and I did as he said.

"On three: one, two, three," Colin said as we both grunted, lifting Kara off the floor and back onto her wheelchair.

Once on the chair, Kara started tapping on her armrest with her finger.

"Thank you for taking care of Kara," Colin said. "I know it's not always easy." His eyes briefly registered the dampness of Kara's pants. "I'll go and clean her up."

"No, please. I can do it."

"I wouldn't want her to think I'd push her off on someone else." Colin shook his head ruefully. "I did think...well, I thought things had been improving lately. Kara's been getting better. It's been a while since we've had an incident like this."

I nodded in response, unsure of what else to say. I'd been working for the Harrington family for a month now, and unfortunately, Kara's condition had not improved as far as I could tell. I'd never tell Colin this, but if I had to guess, I'd say that Kara's condition was permanent.

I wondered what Colin saw in Kara that made him believe she was getting better.

Colin circled around to release the brakes on Kara's wheelchair. "Do remember to pay attention to her signals, though. At least in that, she is consistent."

I couldn't help but feel a sting. Colin assumed I had missed something, even though I always caught Kara's signals. She hadn't signaled this time.

Was it possible that her condition was *worsening*?

10

I couldn't remember the last time someone had texted me to ask me how I was doing. My phone constantly buzzed with notifications, but they were always just spam emails or newsletters from websites I'd forgotten to unsubscribe from.

My phone was a useless tether to a club that didn't quite include me.

The last message I sent was to Micky, to ask him if I could claim his address as my home address for whatever tax forms Colin needed filled out. He'd shot back with a simple: *Of course Anna. You owe me one!* I was relieved, but...it wasn't like we were friends. I had no idea what he did in his personal life, and he didn't know much about mine.

A year ago, when I had more friends, they would have been dying to know all about my life with the Harringtons. But now I neither had friends nor, I realized, much I could have told them.

That's what you get when you try to climb to the top.

Even after a month, a lot of my knowledge felt trivial. I'd become familiar with Kara's collection of beige and the moles on her cheeks, blurred out with foundation during her public appearances. And I'd learned about Colin's love for cotton shirts…and the musky scent he left in the gym in the morning.

True, I'd become accustomed to their quirks. But what did I *actually* know about the Harringtons?

Though I'd sworn off tabloid media to Colin in my interview, the first headlines that popped up when I searched for Kara's and Colin's names late at night in my room were from tabloid media. My fingers snagged against the chipped glass of my screen as I scrolled through the clickbait.

Hollywood it-couple RIGHT NOW…

How Kara Harrington ruined a franchise: EXPLAINED.

SOAPBOX with Colin Harrington: earworm or earsore?

Top ten controversial couples in Hollywood…

Top 10 celebrities who are difficult to work with…

Who are the highest paid podcasters?

How much is Colin Harrington worth?

I stopped, catching an intriguing headline, and clicked.

Acting careers ruined by accidents: Kara Harrington.

Kara Harrington's career was defined by PR mishaps, rumors of being difficult to work with and award-winning performances…until an accident that put a stop to her career.

I scrolled to the part detailing the accident and winced. A two-story fall. Kara had been taken to the hospital, and some documents had leaked, confirming a high level of alcohol in her bloodstream. I knew all this, but it still hit hard.

Reclusive life away from the public eye following devastating head injury.

There was an interview with Kara embedded on the website. I clicked play.

The video sprung up on my screen. Someone had made the artistic choice to film the video in black and white, and Kara was dressed casually, but even then, her beauty shone through. Her dark hair was pulled back in one of those buns that look messy but have been artistically arranged by at least two stylists. Her short nails were painted some dark color that showed as black.

With a pang of self-consciousness, I realized that, even understated, Kara's beauty was in a league of its own. Feeling slightly sorry for myself, I dug my other hand deeper into my bag of kale chips.

"Whether fairly or unfairly…You've gained a reputation for being difficult to work with. What are your thoughts?" the off-screen interviewer asked Kara.

"The constant media attention gives people the illusion that they know me. They hear one thing and fill in a lot of blanks," Kara answered levelly.

"Do you *care* that people seem to dislike you?"

"I care only about what a very limited number of people think."

There was a brief pause before the interviewer continued.

"What is the single best piece of advice you have?"

Kara thought for a moment.

"When I was younger, I was worried I wouldn't make it. But someone told me once that there is always room at the top."

"Meaning…?"

"Meaning that though there are a lot of reasonably talented people, truly talented people are rare. They'll always make it. That's why I'm not too worried."

The audience responded with scattered applause, perhaps unsure whether the comment was a joke. Kara's eyes twinkled.

"My final question," the interviewer began, "is about your breakthrough. You received arguably your biggest role after your husband's first wife, Mary Harrington, killed herself. Do you ever think…"

I held my breath. In the video, Kara impassively picked up a drink from the table beside her and sipped it through a long straw.

"Next question," she said.

I continued my investigation into the Harringtons by listening to Colin's podcast. It was early morning, and the sun had only begun to crest over the horizon. I'd left for a jog as soon as Flora took over. Soon it would be too hot to run outside.

The cords of my headphones bounced lightly against my chest.

"Welcome to *Soapbox with Colin Harrington*."

Colin's slightly raspy voice came through clearly in my ears, like a husky whisper. My cheeks flushed with heat at the sound, at the strange illusion that he was right next to me, up against my ear.

As I listened, my feet fell in a comfortable rhythm. My sneakers bounced off the clean, smooth pavement of the streets of the Pacific Palisades.

"It's easy to believe that tough times will never end, isn't it?" Colin was saying.

His guest chimed in, some electronic musician I'd never heard of before. "It's like a flaw in our design as humans."

"A design flaw, indeed," Colin retorted, his tone sharpening. "Is that the excuse you told yourself when you were caught stepping outside your marriage? That it was innate human fallibility rather than your inability to work through your problems?"

Ouch. I listened as the guest tried to fumble his way out of the situation. Having listened to several episodes of Colin's show, I wondered why guests with skeletons in their closets even bothered showing up. Maybe they really were blind to their own shortcomings and needed someone like Colin to point them out.

"But let me be clear," Colin was saying, "we can overcome anything —if we're willing to fight for it."

My shoes drummed against the street with more determination as I picked up my pace, feeling the jolt of impact in my bones. My old sneakers didn't offer much cushion from the road, but now that I'd claimed Micky's address as my own, Colin could finally pay me, and I'd invest in some new clothes. I had a free afternoon coming up, and I planned to spend it online shopping.

"Do you have any examples?" the guest asked, grateful the topic had moved on from him.

"I do. For example, my wife—"

I slowed down my jog until I almost came to a standstill. Colin continued in my ear.

"—my wife, Kara, suffered a terrible accident, as I'm sure most of my listeners know."

"A truly horrible accident," the guest echoed inanely. He still sounded shell-shocked about the grilling he'd received earlier.

"The doctors said she may never wake up. Never move or speak or walk again. Never act. But now, she has mobility in her hand. She can communicate, and do so much more. I truly believe that, with determination and my support, she will be able to walk again in a year."

A *year?* I came to a complete stop, disbelief flooding me. I'd seen enough of Colin to peg him as an intelligent guy, but this was delusional. There was no way Kara would be up on her feet and acting in a *year*.

"I will never give up on my wife. When I commit to someone, that's it for me. The only way it ends is if they give up on me."

"That takes dedication," the guest crooned, as though he believed Colin had achieved some yogi level of focus and concentration rather than just being a good husband. "And I can see you apply it in all areas of your life."

Colin laughed modestly. "I try," he said before directing the conversation to another topic.

I gulped down a complex cocktail of emotions as I spun around and started back toward the house. Sweat dripped down my forehead, streaking my cheeks like tears.

Unbidden, old memories bubbled to the surface. Memories of my ex screaming at me with such anger that I could feel his spit landing on my face.

Your career is over. We are over. I can't believe I ever loved you. What a mistake.

What a world of difference compared to how Colin talked about Kara.

Once I commit to a person, that's it for me.

I picked up my pace.

The only way it ends is if they quit on me.

What I would have given to have someone like that on my team. Someone who would stand by me, no matter what happened. No matter what I had done.

It was a pity that the quality that made Colin so admirable was the one that ensured he would never be available.

I was pretty sure it would take the death of Kara for him to move on with another woman.

11

When I returned to the house from my morning jog, I instantly spotted a stunning red Porsche parked outside. Its glossy paint job shimmered in the sunlight. My whole time here, I hadn't seen any visitors for Kara.

During my interview, Colin told me Kara's friends were leaving for the summer, and that was why she needed company, but now, I suspected she didn't have many friends at all.

Maybe I had been wrong. Had Kara's alleged friends returned to town?

As I walked into the house, I heard voices coming from the kitchen. There was an older man there, wearing an expensive suit and engaged in animated discussion with Colin. He had wrinkles on his face and slightly squinting eyes, as if he needed glasses but refused to wear any. When he saw me, his face instantly lit up.

"Oh, hello, dear! Could you grab me a cigar from the fridge?"

Before I had time to respond, Colin laughed.

"She's not the help, Luke," he corrected the man, who then turned to look at me with curiosity. "Anna, this is Luke, Luke Worthe. Luke, this is Anna."

"It's nice to meet you," I said, trying to keep my voice level. The man was a legend in Hollywood, and here I was, standing in front of him in inexpensive leggings and a sweaty crop top. "I'm sorry, I didn't mean to interrupt—"

"Oh no, it's fine!" Colin said, waving me in and turning back around to open a small fridge filled with cigars.

A cigar fridge? I should have known.

Luke reached over to shake my hand.

"Luke is here to record an episode with me," Colin explained. "He's one of the few people who prefers to drive here for it."

"Can't get these downtown," Luke said, gesturing toward the cigar Colin had withdrawn from the fridge. "Besides, I like to say hi to Kara every now and then." He winked at my starstruck expression. "Colin knows just about everyone."

"But Luke is a trusted ally. Real inner circle," Colin interjected.

Luke waved him off, refocusing his attention on me. "He flatters me. Now, who might you be?"

"I work as Kara's companion," I answered.

"*Oh*," Luke said, glancing sideways at Colin. There was something in the way he said it, an emphasis on that "oh" I couldn't quite place. Had Colin told him about me? Or was it more to do with the fact that companions never seemed to last long here?

"Anna is also a voice actress," Colin interjected, handing the man a cigar. I blushed a little, but Colin and Luke just gave warm chuckles. "Don't downplay your talents, Anna. She's incredibly gifted, and she's working on a really exciting new project. It's an adaptation of a cult classic."

"Always a pleasure to meet one of Colin's talented friends. I expect Colin to forward the project to me when it's done. I'd love to have a look," Luke said.

I couldn't believe what I was hearing. With just one introduction from Colin, Luke Worthe, one of the biggest producers in the city, was excited to have a look at my work?

I better call Micky—we need to get moving on the project, *pronto*.

Luke followed his statement with a laugh. "Though I must say, you must be mad having another actress wait on Kara, knowing how jealous she is."

"*Competitive*," Colin corrected him. "Kara was always very competitive. It's a valuable quality, don't you think?"

I wondered what someone as admirable as Colin had seen in Kara, who was almost universally reviled, despite her talent. Maybe he'd seen a side to Kara no one else had. Or maybe he just wanted to see the best in her.

"Not sure if the other actresses felt that way," Luke said with a bellowing laugh and pointed toward me with his cigar. "I'd watch my back if I were you."

Colin shook his head at Luke's response and turned to me. "We'll get out of your hair."

"It's your house," I reminded him.

"Yes, but your job is much more important," Colin retorted with a smile.

"Well, you sure know how to make your guests feel appreciated!" Luke said, although he seemed amused by the back and forth.

"It was nice to meet you, Anna. Eyes forward," Luke said, following Colin, who began to lead him down the stairs.

I watched them descend, then headed to the other side of the stairwell and began to climb upstairs.

I'd watch my back if I were you...

As I climbed the stairs, my mind was preoccupied with thoughts of Kara and what she'd been like before her accident. Had she really been as terrible as Luke Worthe insinuated? I wondered how serious his warning was. What harm could Kara possibly cause in her near-vegetative state?

At the top of the stairs, I was greeted with further evidence that Kara was not the imminent threat I needed to worry about.

"What are these?" Flora snapped as soon as I entered, pointing at a stack of books on Kara's bedside table.

Well, good morning to you, too.

"Books," I said. My relationship with Flora had been strained from the beginning, and the tension was only growing. Since giving short or monosyllabic answers seemed to irritate Flora, that was what I had begun to do. She could try to goad me into going along with her games, but I wouldn't make it easy for her.

"Why are they here?" demanded Flora.

"Some people use them for reading," I said innocently.

Flora's face turned red with anger. "Don't play dumb. You've been reading these books to Kara, haven't you?"

"Yes," I admitted. There was no reason to deny it.

Flora took a step back and nodded, victorious. "So you admit to reading these books to Mrs. Harrington? Even though these are the books to do with the role she never had the chance to play? The role she lost because of her tragic accident?"

My jaw dropped. "I don't—I didn't—"

"It is either immensely stupid or immensely cruel to read such books to Mrs. Harrington. Which are you?"

My face burned with the audacity of Flora's accusation. "I didn't know," I managed.

"You are meant to be her *companion*," Flora said, "But I wonder—do you know anything about her at all?"

"Those books were already there," I objected.

"So many excuses from you, Anna," Flora mused. "Will you ever take responsibility for your mistakes?"

I stared at the pile of books long after Flora had departed. I was so angry I could have thrown something.

Had Flora left those books there, knowing I would read them to Kara, so that she could accuse me?

I was getting sick of Flora. And soon I'd have to make a move before her machinations got me fired.

Flora may have been taking care of Kara for a longer time, but I was beginning to think she didn't know better. Sure, keeping Kara to her room was an easy solution, but even though I'd only been with the Harringtons for a little over a month, even *I* was getting stir-crazy from all the hours I'd spent up in Kara's room. Not to mention the more time I spent in there, the more haunted it felt.

I could only imagine how Kara felt. Sitting day in and out, trapped inside herself, in the same eerily still room. And coupled with Flora's hostile and patronizing attitude...

I couldn't live like that. I'd go mad.

But I guess, Kara wasn't *really* living, was she?

Despite our previous art outing ending poorly, I decided to take Kara out again. Not just out of her room, but out of the house entirely for a walk. There was a farmers' market not too far of a drive from the house, so I packed Kara in the van and drove us there.

I wanted Colin to see I was the best companion for his wife. And then, maybe, there wouldn't be much need for Flora. And a redundant Flora would be that much less likely to get me fired.

Who knew, maybe I'd be able to continue for a while beyond the summer and save up some money. That way I'd have a *real* chance at getting back on my feet.

Of course, that meant more time with Kara. But I'd cross that bridge when I came to it.

I parked the car in a lot and lowered Kara out of the vehicle. It was a bright, blazing day, but mercifully, a small breeze was wafting out from the ocean, providing some desperately needed cool air. I'd dressed Kara in her regular beige but mixed it up by grabbing a periwinkle blue top and scarf from her other wardrobe. Coupled with the delicate diamond earrings, a silver wristwatch, and a pair of Chanel sunglasses accented with mother-of-pearl, Kara looked quite elegant.

I, on the other hand, wore my only pair of tight jeans and a cheap white top, but I did borrow a velvet hairband from Kara's wardrobe to add a touch of sophistication. I figured if I was going out with Kara, I needed to look presentable. And having one expensive item in my outfit made the rest seem intentional rather than necessary. At least, that's what I told myself.

And it wasn't like Kara could tell on me, right?

I pushed Kara past the different stalls, stopping occasionally to show her one thing or another. As was customary to her, she barely reacted, but I liked to think I was offering her stimulation anyway. Even if it was just piles of organic zucchini or artichokes.

"The next outing will be an art gallery, I promise," I told her.

Just as we were at a stall selling extortionately overpriced flowers, I overheard a group of young women nearby. I had to do a quick double-take when I saw them.

You'd think my month with the Harringtons would have jaded me to meeting celebrities. But it still felt surreal seeing people I'd seen tons of times on screen here, in real life. I could name at least three of the women in the group by full name and was reasonably sure I could quote a full film one of them starred in, if pressed.

They were all perfectly tanned and dressed in designer activewear and giant sunglasses. Not a hair was out of place, and their lips were so glossy I could have caught my reflection in them. I suddenly felt like my one designer hairband was inadequate.

"Did you see the name of her new film? So pretentious," one of them was saying.

Another chimed in, "Have you seen that meme going around?"

They all laughed, but one added, "It's hilarious. I would have reposted it, but her fans would *ruin my life*."

"What's that nickname she's got for her fans?"

"Don't remind me. I want to keep this food down."

I concentrated on picking new flowers for Kara's bedroom while totally eavesdropping. I was determined to bring some life into the stuffy room—and also to identify the target of this gossip.

"Wait—is that Kara?"

I wheeled around just as the pack rounded on her.

"My gods, it *is*! I almost didn't recognize her," one of them said, eyes sweeping Kara up and down with barely concealed glee. One was already pulling out her phone.

"It's really brave of you to be outside," the one with a matching set of black activewear and shades said. "I remember that time at the Globes when you refused to have your picture taken because you felt like your stylist had messed up. But here you are, in casual wear! It suits you."

But from the way she said it, it sounded like anything but a compliment.

"Do you think we should get a photo with her?" one of them whispered to her friends.

They were saying nice things, but I'd been around bitchy girl-cliques enough in high school to recognize this for exactly what it was. These actresses hated and envied Kara and were relishing the opportunity to make her feel small.

"No photos, please," I said. "Although maybe an autograph could be arranged." I looked over to Kara as if confirming something. Then I shrugged at the women, as if disappointed for them. "Well, maybe later."

"I'm sorry, do you not know who we are?" one of them asked.

"We *know* Kara," another said.

"Oh, apologies," I said. "As Kara's companion, I have to remember her *A-list* friends, but there's just no way to remember *everyone* she knows. I'm Anna. What were your names again?"

Each woman's mouth hung open. The one in the middle grabbed her friends by their arms and dragged them off, muttering and casting glances over her shoulder.

"So rude…"

"There's *no way* she doesn't know who we are…"

"Well," I told Kara, "that should keep the vultures at bay for now."

And I could swear the corner of Kara's mouth twitched up in a tiny smile.

I parked the car in the garage and took Kara up in the elevator, giddy that we got away with the trip and Flora would be none the wiser. As we rolled onto the ground floor, we ran into Colin, dressed sharply.

Colin broke out in a wide smile when he saw Kara in her scarf and sunglasses. "Looks like you two were out on an adventure."

"Just to the farmers' market," I said, placing a bouquet of hot pink lilies onto the marble kitchen island. I glanced at Kara, who was idly staring at a saltshaker, and paraphrased the encounter with the actresses to Colin.

Colin burst out laughing. "Oh, to be a fly on the wall. You couldn't have hit them in a more sensitive spot than by having someone young and beautiful question their relevance. Well done, Anna."

My heart skipped a beat at the compliment. "It was my pleasure," I replied, lost in Colin's gaze, until I had the sense I was being watched.

I stole a glance at Kara. Had she stopped staring at the saltshaker, or was it just my imagination?

"Ah, Flora," Colin exclaimed, waving over my shoulder. "You're early!"

My pulse, already having picked up, tripled. I would have a heart attack soon with all these surprises.

Well, so much for keeping our little escapade secret from Flora.

"Anna was just telling me about taking Kara out."

"Out?" Flora asked pointedly.

"And I must say, it has done wonders for Kara. She's positively glowing," Colin added.

"Yes, Mr. Harrington," Flora replied, with the expression of someone being forced to sniff rotting garbage. I was enjoying this far more than I should have. There was no way Flora could complain about this trip now that Colin was so decidedly pleased by it.

"If you could take Kara up to her room, I need to go over some things with Anna," Colin suggested.

"Yes, Mr. Harrington," Flora repeated obediently. I suppressed the urge to give her a cheerful wave as she pushed Kara toward the elevator and disappeared.

"You've been doing a great job, Anna," Colin said. "It's so important that Kara has some…normalcy."

This was my chance to dig around a bit about Flora. I choose my words carefully.

"Flora doesn't seem to think it's a good idea to take Kara outside," I said delicately.

Colin's face fell slightly. "She's just...cautious when it comes to Kara. She's been here since...well, since before my first wife took her own life. That experience really rattled Flora."

It was such a forthright and painful sentence that I didn't immediately know how to respond. Though I'd come across less information about the first Mrs. Harrington, I knew that she, too, was in entertainment and had struggles with mental health before taking her own life.

I understood Colin better than he realized.

My mother had killed herself as well.

I'd been young—it was a long time ago—but those scars never heal. I knew she'd been sick, that it wasn't fair to blame her—but some days, it still felt like a crime. I was left with no one to hold accountable. No one to blame. But this wasn't the moment to bring it up.

"I'm sorry."

"Thank you, Anna," Colin said.

"I guess you trust Flora then," I said, "if she's been with you for so long."

"To be honest...I'm not sure how necessary she is anymore. I initially hired her to oversee my late wife's medication, and she came back after Kara's accident. In the beginning, Kara needed a lot of medication. Did you know she broke nearly ten bones in the fall?"

"No, I didn't," I replied, a bit faint. "No wonder she requires so much medication."

"She doesn't need it so much now. She's healing remarkably well. The doctors say the rest of her recovery is up to her. There don't seem to be any physical issues they can detect. I have faith that she'll pull through."

I didn't have the heart to tell Colin I disagreed.

"So...what are the injections Flora administers then?"

"Oh, those? Just some multi-vitamin shots. Muscle relaxers, on bad days. But those have been getting more and more rare."

I *swear* Flora had mentioned medication to me on multiple instances. It was one of those things she lorded over me, one of those things that separated her, a licensed nurse, and me, a companion.

But if I knew how to care for Kara, and if she truly didn't need any medication, then what was the point of Flora?

"And Anna...I've made sure the sum for your first month has been transferred to your account. Who knows, maybe we can bump it up a little more in the future...if you get more responsibilities."

...if you get more responsibilities.

I could tell he was thinking Flora may no longer be needed.

Like a coiled snake, Flora waited for me at the top of the stairs. I didn't even have time to open my mouth when words began to rush from hers in a low hiss.

"What are you doing with Mr. Harrington?"

Had Flora overheard the entire conversation? Had she been spying on us?

"What am *I* doing?" I lashed back. Now that I knew her position was on the chopping block and that I had Colin's favor, I was no longer cowed by her or her false implications of holding some kind of power.

"I took Kara outside. And as Colin said, it probably did her a world of good."

"Don't pretend like you care about her," Flora said sharply. "Your little act of playing friends isn't fooling me. I know you're just desperate to make yourself look good."

"And what about your act?" I fired back. "I heard the *super* important shots you give Kara are just vitamins. If all she lacks is company and light caretaking, I wonder which of us really is the best suited."

I had imagined the knowledge of Kara not needing her was the ace in my sleeve and had expected Flora to recoil when presented with it, the way bad guys stumbled in movies when the hero pulled out some magic weapon. But Flora did no such thing. Instead, she smirked at me.

"I asked around about you, and I found out some very interesting things. I wonder if Mr. Harrington knows what really happened between you and Mr. Berg?"

I froze.

How much could she know?

But a victorious glint played in Flora's eyes. Her hands were fidgeting with excitement.

"Do you want me to tell him?"

Panicked, I shook my head quickly.

"Then you won't entertain any more stupid thoughts about supplanting me," Flora hissed, pushing past, leaving me reeling.

How could Flora possibly know my secret?

And more importantly—how could I stop Colin from finding out?

12

Now that I finally had my first paycheck, I'd spent the late afternoon compulsively scrolling through pages and pages of online stores, trying to distract myself from the gnawing anxiety that had been eating away at me.

I clicked my way through websites, throwing clothes in and out of intangible, electronic baskets. After going through with the purchase, I immediately felt hungover from spending a large chunk of my hard-earned money. But at the same time, I was sick of wearing cheap, uncomfortable clothing. I wanted to look polished and put together when standing next to Kara.

The clothes arrived a few days later in a parcel. I opened the door to a young delivery guy and signed the slip as he waited. I could feel his eyes trace my blonde hair, glossy and soft from the hi-brand shampoo I'd found in the guest shower. He was probably wondering if he knew me from somewhere.

Maybe one day, he would.

In my room in the basement, I carefully laid out the clothes on my bed and appraised them.

In shots of Kara caught by the paparazzi strolling casually down the street, she'd had a habit of pairing simple, casual outfits with one surprising feature. Perfectly fitted jeans and a loose shirt with large diamond earrings. A simple strappy black satin dress and electric blue heels. A lace dress, almost translucent, with a leather jacket.

I couldn't afford to replicate such style, so I'd opted for close alternatives. Fitted black pants of quality material. Strappy tops in basic colors but made of organic cottons and silks, and which probably cost more than all the strappy tops I'd ever bought in my life combined. That part still made me wince a little, truth be told. I'd also splurged on jogging shoes.

And I'd bought a new swimsuit and some nice lingerie. You just never knew when you might want to look or feel your best. After all, just wearing a nice set could boost your confidence.

I slipped out of my clothes and tried on some of the new lingerie, checking myself out in the mirror, when my phone rang. I picked it up and felt a clammy sweat break out as I took in the caller.

My father.

I suddenly felt stupid. I quickly pulled on a shirt and answered the phone. There was no use prolonging the inevitable.

"Hi, Dad," I said, holding the phone to my ear.

"Anna Sophia," my father said. He was the only one who ever called me that. When I asked him about it once, he had told me that Sophia meant "wisdom" in Latin, and he hoped that by using it, the meaning would manifest itself in me someday.

He wasn't joking. My father did not joke.

"You didn't answer my last call," my father stated.

"I've been busy," I said. "Working," I added quickly.

"Oh? I thought work had run out," he said dryly.

"Well, I got the job! The one you told me about." I paused, trying to force myself to follow up with the obvious. "Thank you."

"Now you just have to keep it."

I bit my tongue. I'd landed a job—count on my father to manage to twist it into something to admonish me about.

"It's pretty perfect actually," I started, not able to resist the temptation. "I'm able to make money *and* do voice acting—"

"Do you know why I chose to not financially support you?" my father interrupted.

I'd heard this before. It went better if I went along with it.

"So I am not complacent."

"So-and-so," he replied. My father had a habit of providing evaluations on any given answers. "It was to see what your reach was. What you had a disposition for. I had no intention of artificially instating you in an environment for which you have no natural inclination."

"I'm not sure it's that black-and-white," I muttered, despite myself. "The industry is oversaturated, it's just objectively hard for anyone to make it as a voice actor. It takes time and luck—"

My father cut me off. "Wrong. One thing I have learned, Anna Sophia, is that there is *always* room at the top."

I frowned. Hadn't Kara said something like that in her interview?

I tried to keep my voice level. I could too easily imagine the disdain on my father's face if he realized I was on the verge of tears.

"You are saying that were I truly talented, I would make it. No matter what."

"Not *'no matter what.'* One still has to put in the work. If one is truly talented and puts in the work, there will always be room for *them*," he said. The line was quiet for a few moments. "You know, I lived and worked in LA for a while. With celebrities. I've seen what it takes to make it there. You have to be hungry, Anna. Sharp. You *must* be able to sustain the pressure of being pushed."

I could imagine him sitting behind his grand, polished wood desk in his study surrounded by books. Downstairs, his new wife Dina was probably preparing dinner, expertly dicing vegetables into perfect, symmetrical pieces.

She and I got along well enough, but I didn't think we'd ever understand one another. The last time I was over, I asked her if she'd seen *The Stepford Wives*. My father told me not to try to be funny.

According to him, I wasn't very good at that, either.

"I know, Dad."

"We teach our children this lie," my father began in his low, rumbling voice. "This lie that they can become anything. Do anything. But they really can't. No creature can. The best any parent can do is help their child recognize their limitations. So they can find the ecosystem befitting their level to thrive in."

"But I *can* do this," I objected, even though my voice was cracking and sounded weak, even to myself. My volume picked up as I went along. "I know I'm meant to be someone. I know I can make it here, I just need a little more time."

"Well, I suppose now is your chance to prove it. The Harringtons could take you places. If you play it smart. *If* you are good enough."

"I *am*," I insisted, wondering for the millionth time what it would have felt like to have a parent I didn't have to convince to believe in me. How different my life would be if my mother was still alive.

"Then I would *love* to be proven wrong."

The line went dead.

With shaking fingers, I put my phone down on the bed beside me. The clothing I'd just bought suddenly felt ridiculous and desperate. Like a costume. Like I was performing a version of myself that didn't exist.

But a small part of me refused to accept this defeat. I *knew* I was a good actress. Not just good, *talented*. If last year hadn't happened the way it did, who knows where I could be now?

My father had no idea how far I was willing to go.

How far I already had gone.

Just then, my pager went off.

Kara.

13

I made my way through the dark and quiet house. Small motion-detecting lights sprung up in my wake, bathing the rooms I'd barely occupied in a pleasant, if minimally comforting, wash of light. I made my way up the steps out of the basement and over the cool marble floors toward and up the steps to the upper story landing. Every shadow stretched endlessly along the floors before it was evaporated by a light that turned on automatically above me.

Kara had never paged me in the middle of the night.

I was sure she just needed to use the bathroom or maybe wanted a sip of water. That had never happened before, in the whole month I had worked at the Harringtons'.

Up the stairs I crept, over the landing, toward Kara's bedroom door. I stopped, as I swore I could hear a thump resound from somewhere in the house. Then, again, a muffled thump.

What was that thing I'd heard on the tape?

I have a feeling something terrible is going to happen to me.

Why did I know exactly what that meant?

I crossed the distance to Kara's room. My throat felt hoarse. I cleared my throat and tried to will myself to enter.

Despite every cell of my body screaming at me not to, I reached out and pushed open Kara's bedroom door. From inside, I heard nothing but deafening silence.

If something happened to me, no one would find me until the morning.

"Kara?" I called out into the dim room. My voice sounded shaky.

I could just barely make out Kara's figure in bed, tangled in her satin sheets as if she'd been turning. Her head moved jerkily from side to side. She glistened as if she was feverish, strands of her hair plastered against her forehead.

Was she having a nightmare?

I stood there for a moment watching her, but she seemed to be asleep. In the dark, her skin nearly glowed.

I'd never believed in ghosts, but if I didn't know better, I might have guessed Kara was a specter.

Carefully, I adjusted Kara's bedsheets and crept back out of the room, closing the door with relief. Was it possible she had simply knocked her bracelet against the frame of the bed while stirring, alerting me?

There is nothing to be scared of.

But just as I headed down the hallway, I noticed something strange. Outside, the front lawn lights were switched on, illuminating a dark silhouette standing at the edge of the property. It was still enough to be a statue. But I didn't remember a statue at that end of the front lawn.

Then the silhouette moved. It lifted up its arms, as if holding a camera, and seemed to focus directly on me.

There was a distant flash. I screamed in surprise.

Then the shadow dropped its arms and moved, crossing the few last paces into the darkness.

My hands flew to my mouth. It was a pointless gesture—I must have woken everyone in the house. Sure enough, moments later, Colin's voice called out for me. "Anna? Was that you?"

"I'm here," I called out hoarsely. Colin appeared shortly after, rubbing his eyes with the back of his hand.

"Are you okay?" Colin asked, looking me over, taking in my disheveled appearance.

"I'm sorry, I—" I began, and then swallowed my apologies. "There was someone out on the grounds. I think they took a picture. There was a flash…"

Colin cursed under his breath. "Damn crazy fans."

"Not paparazzi?"

Colin shook his head. "Even they have rules and regulations. They know a picture clearly taken from the grounds is a lawsuit waiting to happen. But fans…well, who knows what they'll do?"

My heart sank. A paparazzo was bad enough, but at least I could understand the motivation for money or professional advancement. A member of the public, though, felt more unpredictable to me. Dangerous.

"Has this happened before?"

Colin winced. "I do have a few persistent fans with no sense of boundaries. Some might refer to them as stalkers. I should have mentioned it sooner, but I didn't want to worry you. You *are* safe here. But I'll call my security company and have someone come over right away."

He glanced at Kara's bedroom door before turning back to me.

"You should go check on Kara," I suggested.

"Are you sure you're okay?" Colin asked, placing a hand on my shoulder.

"I'll be fine." His strong hand was more than comforting.

"Stay here. I'll be right back. I'll walk you to your room."

I waited in the hallway as Colin checked on Kara, my eyes wandering to a shelf lined with awards glinting in the dim lighting. I'd not paid them much attention after my first week, when I'd still gone around mentally cataloging every Hollywood artifact and memorabilia.

Aside from a few awards I recognized, a number of them looked like tiny ugly sculptures. I'd been disappointed to find that some of them were even plastic. Maybe from earlier in Kara's career.

I'd become accustomed to them. But now, at night, they looked different—more like relics of a forgotten civilization than modern accolades.

Then I noticed it. A tape tucked between two of Kara's awards. What was it doing here?

Should I tell Colin?

I glanced between Kara's bedroom door, where I could hear Colin addressing her in a low voice. I crept closer to the shelf and stood on my tiptoes to reach the tape. I pulled it back, turning the tape around in my fingers. Like the first tape, this one too was labeled: *Kara*.

I heard Colin walk up to Kara's door and quickly tucked the tape in the pocket of my pajamas. I felt it through the thin fabric, bouncing against my thigh, as I backed away from the shelf.

Colin closed Kara's door softly.

"Fast asleep," Colin whispered. "Now let's get you downstairs. You must be so tired. I'll stay up until the security guard arrives, so you don't have to worry."

"Thank you, Colin," I said as he led me downstairs.

"Don't worry about it," Colin said. "If you ever need anything, I'm here for you."

"I'll feel safer knowing you're keeping watch. I'm sure I'll fall asleep as soon as my head hits the pillow."

A lie. I knew that as soon as Colin headed upstairs, I'd slip into the sound studio.

I just *had* to know what was on this tape.

14

So, I know this sounds stupid. I know I sound paranoid. Everyone says I'm that. Paranoid.

The interviewer's question was an indistinguishable murmur in the background.

They think I'm not listening, or not paying attention. They can't really tell when I'm...here, or not. But I know much more than I let on. I know what they really think of me.

Another question. The female voice broke a little when answering.

I couldn't do it, you see. I just couldn't. No matter how much Colin tried to help. No matter how disappointed he is in me, I just can't seem to get it right.

Maybe it's that I go too deep into the characters, like my director suggested. Or maybe there's something just broken about me to begin with, that I don't know how to fix. But it's just too much. It's all too much.

The role. The work. The life. The husband. The paparazzi.

And sometimes I think to myself...could she handle all this?

Maybe I ended up in the wrong place, somehow. I can't help but feel like she would do this so much better than me. She was always so... hungry, even when we were young. So determined. Fearless.

The voice in the background murmured another question.

Who? Kara, of course.

The recording abruptly ended with a click and a hiss of rolling tape. I stared at the monitor in the sound studio, ignoring the time in the corner—past three a.m.—and pressed the rewind button. The cassette tape began to whir as the adapter rolled it back into starting position. I pressed play again.

While the conversation unfolded in the background, I revised what I knew. The voice on the tape hadn't been Kara at all but Colin's first wife. I closed my eyes and concentrated on the name. It only took a moment to recall. Mary. Mary Harrington.

I strained to remember what I knew about her. I knew she'd been an actress, like Kara, but had never reached the same level of success. After a breakout film and a few moderate hits, she faded into obscurity and eventually became reclusive.

That was the thing in Hollywood. You had to fight to stay relevant.

Colin had said that she had killed herself.

And then Kara inherited her role in a film. And her husband.

Had Mary willingly given all of that up?

15

It had been weeks since I last saw Micky in person, not since we drank cheap sour liquor in the sound studio and he got oddly aggressive about some of the characters. But after telling him about meeting Luke Worthe, Micky perked up a bit, and our communication seemed to be going back to normal. I was hopeful we could move past the awkward encounter and continue working on our project.

In the meantime, I'd been recording various sounds and vocalizations: short clips like "Look out!", "Help me!", "No way!", and "Yes!". Battle cries for when my character, the Countess, blasted enemies with her magic powers. Grunts. Gurgling. Sounds of her tripping over and stubbing her toe.

Let's be real, voice acting is not always that glamorous.

I had also been recording screams. There's a lot of different ways to scream, you know. Screams of terror. Screams of surprise. Screams of anguish.

I spent countless solitary hours in the late afternoons in the sound studio, screaming until my throat was raw. Thank goodness the space was soundproof and isolated from the rest of the house.

I had just finished another long, gut-wrenching scream when the door to the sound studio swung open.

I screamed again.

Micky poked his head in through the doorway and adjusted his glasses. "Did you get that one?" he asked through the intercom.

"I think so," I said, my heart still hammering as I paused the recording and slipped out of the booth. At least this time I didn't have to worry about having Micky in the studio; I'd checked with Colin beforehand that it was okay to bring someone in.

"Sure, Anna," Colin had said. "Just make sure they stay away from Kara, all right? You never know if someone might be an over-eager fan, and I don't want to burden her with any unnecessary encounters."

I'd promised to keep my guest confined to the basement. I'd told Micky to wait for me by the poolside door, but I guess he'd just shown himself in, like last time.

"Micky, you scared me half to death."

"Are you getting jumpy?" he asked as he dropped his bags on the floor and took a seat in one of the swiveling chairs in the studio. He spun toward me, facing the computer monitor.

"I can't help it," I admitted, absentmindedly chewing on my fingernail. "This script has so many creepy parts. And so much screaming."

I didn't tell Micky I suspected my jumpiness had something to do with the house, the odd atmosphere that permeated it. The sense that someone was always watching me.

"Perfect, you're getting into character," Micky muttered, focused on adjusting some settings on screen. "Why don't you go ahead and get back in the booth? Let's not let this atmosphere go to waste."

"Can we run through the scene one more time?" I asked.

"Sure," Micky said, pleased. He dug out his notes. While he was busy arranging his things, I pulled out a bottle and two glasses I'd left in the studio in preparation for the session. I poured each of us a drink and handed him one.

"I wasn't sure if you approved of drinks in the studio," Micky remarked, adjusting his glasses on his nose. "Especially after how I went on about the characters the last time. Maybe a bit too much…"

"No, I like to learn what you think about the characters. It gives me an insight into their minds," I said, clinking my glass against his. "To our project!"

"To our project," Micky agreed, knocking his glass back.

Truthfully, I had gone through the scene enough times that it was ingrained in my memory by now. Micky and I had also had numerous conversations about it. I was fairly certain I knew exactly what he wanted from me in terms of performance. But I let him ramble on, my mind drifting to the tapes I had discovered and the haunting voice on them.

Micky was a wealth of knowledge about Hollywood personalities. There was no way he wouldn't know more about Mary Harrington. But he didn't like to gossip. Which, normally, I'd find admirable. But if I just got him a little drunk, I was sure he'd share everything he knew. Maybe even what he didn't want to say about the Harringtons the last time.

Maybe I could have forgotten all about it. Focused on my job as a companion. I could have kept quiet and waited until summer was over, left with a nice bit of savings to set me up for the coming year.

But there was just something off about Kara. About Flora. About this *house*.

And for some reason, I felt like the tapes were the key to it all. That it all started with Mary.

I had to know more.

"Great, I think I've got it," I said, after about half an hour of Micky monologuing and a few more refills.

"Perfect," Micky said, his voice ever-so-slightly slurred.

I grabbed my script and water bottle and entered the booth, reprising some simple vocal exercises and stretching my neck. The door to the booth shut behind me with a click.

The world became muffled, and I could only hear Micky once he clicked on his microphone on the other side of the glass.

"Can you hear me?" he asked, his displaced voice sounding out from all around me.

I leaned over to my mic. "Yeah. You?"

Micky gave a thumbs-up. "Whenever you're ready."

"Okay," I said, glancing down at my script before closing my eyes and getting into character as Countess. Someone strong. Undaunted. Burdened by a dark past.

In my mind, she looked a lot like Kara.

"My love," I began, "I…don't know what to believe anymore. I don't know who to trust. Least of all myself. I know that together we have stood against the might of the Shadow Empire, but I am starting to get scared…"

Something began to nag at the edge of my mind, but I pushed it away, trying to concentrate on the performance. I drew a breath, trying to pace myself differently than I'd recorded before.

"I have a feeling something terrible is going to happen to me."

I'd rehearsed these lines a hundred times. But why did they feel familiar to me in a way I couldn't quite place?

Micky clicked on his microphone from the other side. "You nailed it, Anna. Just great. Can we maybe put some more emphasis on 'something terrible'?"

Where else had I heard that before?

"Anna? You there?"

"Oh, sure," I said, snapping back to reality. "I just need some air."

I opened the door and walked out to stretch my legs. I held out my glass for Micky, who refilled it and sat down next to me with a somewhat guarded expression.

"Um, I was just wondering…I've been thinking about what you said when we last talked. About how everyone loves the Count and overlooks the Jester—"

Micky waved his hand. "You should forget about all of that."

"No, I mean, I think you're right. The Count is charismatic, but why is the Countess with him instead of the Jester?" I continued.

Micky took another swig of his drink. "I think it's hard for her to imagine another way is possible for her. She's too stuck in her ways." He looked at me expectantly. "But you tell me. What do you think?"

I gulped. I wanted to steer the conversation in a direction that was favorable to Micky and his work on the script. But now it seemed like we were talking about something completely different. I decided to pivot.

"I guess she's too busy with other things to think about it too much. Saving the world from darkness and all that," I replied awkwardly.

Micky sipped his drink.

"I guess she's a pretty tragic character, isn't she? The Countess?" I pressed on.

"That's an understatement."

"You know, I didn't realize at first how much tragedy there is in *this* house," I waved my arms around, trying to maintain a light and curious tone. "First with Mary, and then Kara."

Micky had frozen, the glass halfway to his lips. An odd expression colored his face.

"It's a pity Colin won't talk about his first wife," I quickly continued. "I'd like to know what she was like. But he isn't open like that. Not like you."

Micky's eyes flicked up to mine. His expression was unreadable. I did my best to casually meet his gaze and reached for my glass. My fingers were shaking. Had I pushed too far? Was Micky going to storm off?

"Did you know…that Colin and Kara had something going on while he was still married to Mary?" Micky started.

My jaw dropped.

"Yeah. They were eyeing each other long before she was cold and in a casket. And did you know that Kara was her *friend*?"

"That's crazy," I said. *Tell me more.* "What happened to Mary?"

"She…I've heard she had a lot of ailments. Allergies, sprains, and she was on medication for her mental illness too. No one knows how much of her issues were…psychosomatic."

I inched just a tiny bit closer to Micky. "And?"

"They found her dead one night in her office, surrounded by EpiPens," Micky revealed. "They think she was hoarding them. She'd slammed half a dozen into her thigh, one by one. She died from a violent cardiac arrest."

"Oh my god," I exclaimed. "That's awful."

"Yeah," Micky agreed, looking faint. Maybe the drink was really beginning to hit him.

I reached out to touch his arm. In the same moment, Micky began to lean his face toward me. I quickly dodged out of the way.

Shit.

We sat on the sofa in awkward silence.

"Look, Micky, you're a really nice guy…"

"That stuff you said about the Count and the Jester before," Micky said, his eyes behind his glasses cold but unfocused. "You don't actually agree with any of it, do you?"

"I—"

"Were you trying to get me drunk to ask me questions?"

I shook my head, but I could see he was not convinced. He got up and grabbed his bag.

"Please, Micky, let's take it easy. Let's not let this affect the project—"

"It won't," Micky replied impassively, a strange note in his voice. "But maybe we shouldn't read lines together. Maybe you should rehearse with someone you like more. Like *Colin.*"

"I don't—"

Before I could finish my sentence, Micky got up, stormed out, and slammed the door behind him.

My heart sank.

Had I just ruined my chances with the project?

16

After Micky stormed out, I remained in the sound studio, slowly sipping on my liquor even though I felt little desire to drink. These late-night hours were typically when I was most productive, and I still had a load of lines to record, but after our disagreement, I couldn't focus. Did I even still have a role in the project?

It seemed drastic that Micky would fire me over one drunken disagreement, but I knew how fickle directors could be. And Micky had seemed bitter following my rejection.

Shaken by these thoughts, I forced myself out of the studio and made my way down the basement hallway toward my bedroom. As soon as I reached the doorway, I froze.

My bedroom had been ransacked, again.

But this time the intruder had not been subtle.

My new lingerie was strewn all over the bed and the edges of my bedside table, its delicate fabric twisted and torn. The swimsuit I had worn in the pool was tossed carelessly on the floor. My makeup had been taken out and dropped haphazardly, violently, so that my bronzer and blush had crumbled in dusty chunks on the floor. But that wasn't the worst.

Someone had scrawled *Whore* on the mirror with a tube of lipstick.

I stared stupidly at everything, shocked, as if it was an equation I was unable to solve. My hands began to shake. I'd been the target of vicious insults before, but this was different. Someone had broken into my space. Suddenly, I didn't feel safe sleeping in my own bed.

My heart racing, I suddenly thought of Colin and what he said to me when he found me in the hallway following my scream.

If you ever need anything, I'm here for you.

Colin would know what to do.

I nervously made my way through the house and knocked softly on his door. After a few moments, Colin opened the door, pulling a loose shirt over his well-sculpted shoulders. He blinked sleep from his eyes and looked me over, surprised, then instantly became serious.

"Anna? Is everything okay?"

"Someone…someone has been in my room," I said, struggling with my voice. I hugged my arms around myself.

Colin noticed my distress and pulled me into a comforting hug.

"Oh, Anna," he murmured. I gratefully leaned into Colin's shoulder, feeling an ounce better with his long arms wrapped around me.

"It's going to be all right."

"I'm scared, Colin. It's just so…malicious."

"Just give me a second."

Colin retreated into his room, and I could hear him rummaging through his things. He returned a moment later.

"Okay. Show me what happened."

As we walked down the hallway together, I scanned every corner, expecting someone to jump out at me. What if the intruder was still here?

"Easy," Colin whispered, sensing my anxiety. "I've got you." But from the way his shoulders were tensed and his fist clenched to his side, I could tell he was on high alert as well.

When we reached my room, Colin muttered under his breath.

"Jesus, Anna. I'll call security. Now. There's no way they should have got into the house."

I shivered. Colin had called security last time when the intruder had made it onto the grounds, but they'd discovered nothing. And now *this*.

The house was well-guarded: the imposing front door, the high-tech gate, and the numerous security cameras placed around the perimeter. Could it be possible for an outsider to get past all of that and *into* the house?

Would it not be more likely the person who did this was someone *inside* the house to begin with? I thought of Micky getting up from his chair and slamming the door on his way out. He'd been really angry. And the sound studio wasn't that far from my room…

And if it was Micky, what would Colin do if he found out I had let in someone who vandalized his house?

I swallowed hard. "Do you think…it could be your crazed fan?"

"Who else could it be?" Colin replied grimly. "Who else would have a motive to do something like this?"

I could think of a few people.

"Anna?" Colin asked gently.

I shook myself out of my stupor. "Sorry, what?"

"I asked you if you were okay," Colin repeated, softer.

"I'm fine, I'm just…" I waved my hand at the general space.

Colin shook his head to himself. "I'm sorry, that was a stupid question. Of course you're not fine. You should feel safe in this house."

"I do *love* this house," I reassured him. "It's like something out of a dream. I mean, I can't even imagine living in a place like this—"

"But you *do* live here," interjected Colin.

"Yeah, but you know, permanently," I said, and instantly regretted it. There was a moment of strained silence.

Did I just suggest Colin hire me on a permanent basis?

"I'm sure you can achieve anything you set your mind to," Colin said. "I wouldn't be surprised if you owned a house like this very soon."

"*I* would be," I replied, feeling a little better.

"Here," Colin said, gently taking me by the shoulders. Now I was feeling a *lot* better, his touch electric on my bare skin. He guided me out of the room and toward the basement bar where he sat me down on one of the stool chairs and stepped behind the counter. He quickly moved around, grabbing a shaker and a strainer, and began to make a drink. He laughed at my confused expression.

"I used to work as a bartender," he explained as he swiftly plucked an orange from a drawer that was apparently stacked full of them. "I make a mean old-fashioned. I figured we could use a drink right about now."

"I could definitely use one," I agreed. Just the thing to go with my cocktail of emotions.

Colin began to peel curved slices of orange zest into the drink, then conjured up a jar of maraschino cherries to top it off. He slid the glass over to me.

"On the house."

I picked up my drink. "You aren't worried the intruder might still be in the house?"

Colin shook his head, lifting his shirt to reveal his chiseled abs and the glint of metal tucked into his waistband.

"Is that…a gun?" I asked, taken aback. "You'd *shoot* the intruder?"

He dropped the edge of his shirt back down. "They wanted you freaked out, Anna. There is no knowing what a person like that might do."

"I guess," I said. As weird as it was, part of me felt touched that Colin took this so seriously. That he'd be willing to shoot someone who made me feel unsafe.

I took a sip of my drink to hide my smile. The bitters burned on my lips, but I enjoyed the sensation. Colin finished making his own drink and came around the bar to sit on a stool beside me.

Maybe it was the effect of the amber-colored lights of the bar, but there was something different about him tonight. Though he was as handsome as usual, he also looked tired.

"How are *you* holding up?" I suddenly realized I hadn't asked him.

"I think life throws challenges at us to see how we handle them," Colin replied with a halfhearted smile. "And the bigger the challenge, the more impressive the story of overcoming it, don't you think?"

My heart broke for him.

"Do you feel like you're facing a big challenge right now?" I asked, placing my hand on his arm.

Colin took another sip of his drink and ran his fingers through his dark hair. "Things haven't turned out like I've expected. My first wife, Mary, was very sensitive and troubled. I often felt like the world was too harsh for someone like her. But Kara…Kara was a fighter. I was so sure she would make a full recovery."

My heart skipped a beat. *I was so sure.* Past tense. Was Colin finally starting to see that Kara might be beyond help?

I took a sip of my drink, deciding it was too soon to bring up the sensitive topic of Kara's stalled recovery.

"I don't think I've seen many photos of Mary," I said, trying to steer the conversation away from Kara.

"Let me show you," Colin said, digging his phone out of his pocket. After a moment of scrolling, he handed it to me. "Here."

I leaned toward him to look at the picture on the phone. It seemed to be from their wedding. In the foreground was an undeniably handsome Colin with his arms wrapped around a smiling, petite woman with wavy, sandy-colored hair cascading down her shoulders.

Mary had a delicate build and a rounder face than Kara's, which was more chiseled and defined—high fashion model material. On second thought, Mary looked a lot like me: the same round face, delicate features, similar blonde hair and curved up nose. We could have passed for sisters.

I wondered if Colin had ever had the same thought.

But then, I noticed something else in the photo.

In the blurry background were a few guests, their faces barely in focus. But as I squinted my eyes, I realized with a shock of recognition that one of them was Kara.

I remembered Micky saying Mary and Kara had been close friends, so it wasn't surprising that she had been at their wedding.

What was shocking was Kara's expression. She was staring not at her friend, but at Colin, with a fixated gaze.

Pieces began to click into place.

Kara, staring at Colin from the background of his and Mary's wedding picture. Mary's certainty on the tape that something terrible was about to happen.

A lump formed in my throat. Had Kara stolen Colin from Mary? Or... had she had something to do with Mary's death?

No, that was absurd. I had clearly gotten too immersed in my fantasy horror script. This was real life. People didn't *murder* their old friends to steal their husbands. And besides, Micky had made it clear—Mary had taken her own life.

But could Kara have driven her to it? Made her life unbearable, taken what she wanted until Mary had nothing left?

I felt a wave of guilt for even considering it, but maybe Kara wasn't the innocent victim in all this. Maybe her accident had been some kind of karmic payback. Maybe it was for the best if Kara never fully recovered. Maybe she needed to stay far, far away from Colin—and from anyone else who might end up in her way.

I hadn't wanted to, but I now knew I had to address the issue of Kara, even though it might be overstepping my boundaries. It couldn't wait. I took another gulp of my drink for courage and turned to Colin.

"I know you want Kara to get better. We all do," I lied. "But even if Kara is physically here, she may be...not quite here mentally."

Colin peered at me. "What are you saying?"

"There are a lot of good care homes." I tried to tread lightly. "Places where they could give Kara everything she wants and needs."

"Like the care home your relative is at?"

I nodded. "They aren't prisons. They are really homey places where the staff can constantly keep an eye on the residents."

And make sure they don't do anything crazy.

"I'm not the kind of man to give up, Anna."

"But maybe *Kara* has already given up."

"I won't let her."

"But it may not be up to you," I pointed out.

Colin stood up abruptly, clearly angry. "We're finished here."

Surprised, I watched as Colin walked off.

"You deserve to live your life too," I called out after him, but I wasn't sure if he heard me.

I stared at Colin's abandoned glass on the bar counter and, horrified, processed what had just happened.

I had essentially told my lovely, devoted boss to send his sick wife away.

I had *really* screwed up this time.

17

The whole following day, I was racked with relentless anxiety that clawed at my constricted chest and throat like a small, rabid animal. I half expected Colin to barge in and terminate my position, but he remained conspicuously absent.

Even if he wasn't going to fire me straight away, there were no guarantees I'd keep this job. I knew I needed to step up my game or risk losing it all. I remembered how pleased Colin had been after I'd taken Kara on the trip to the farmers' market, and I decided it was time for another expedition, regardless of Flora's objections.

Besides, I was eager to get out of the house. I was desperate to escape its suffocating walls for just a few hours. And my afternoon shift with Kara would be more bearable anywhere but here.

I dressed Kara in an outfit accented with what I knew to be her favorite colors—cool blues and deep purples and reds—and loaded her into the van.

After researching some potential locations, I found a nice restaurant nearby known for its beautiful, enclosed, vine-covered patio. Expensive enough to be exclusive, it seemed like the perfect place to take Kara without attracting unwanted attention. I could easily see why celebrities secluded themselves in gated communities, where they were safely tucked away from the rest of the world.

I parked the van on the street and rolled Kara into the establishment, where we were seated at a lovely table on the patio. The vines created a natural ambiance, wrapping up around the banisters and drooping down around us like a light green veil.

The other patrons were stylishly dressed, sipping their mid-afternoon drinks. A gentle murmur of conversation and clinking cutlery made pleasant background noise. There'd been a few exchanged whispers when I'd pushed Kara in, but no one was coming over to pester us. In a place like this, celebrities were commonplace. I'd chosen the place well.

The waiter handed me my menu.

A few months ago, these prices would have made me faint, but after our previous expedition, Colin had given me a credit card to cover any expenses for future day trips with Kara. I felt a pang, thinking about Colin. He had looked so angry when he'd stormed off, and there was a hint of something in his expression I had never seen before. Disappointment?

If I wanted to keep Colin and this life of luxury in any capacity, I needed Kara to like me. I needed everyone to believe I wanted her to get better, despite my growing doubt about that being a good thing.

The waiter appeared to take our orders, and I tried to push away my thoughts.

"Can I please have the kale Caesar, the langoustine bisque, and two citron pressés?"

"Excellent. Anything else, miss?"

"Could you also please bring a straw?"

"Of course, miss."

I felt pleased with myself. After spending almost two months with the Harringtons, I had changed in more ways than one. The expensive haircare and satin pillowcases had helped tame my frizzy hair, which I now wore in a stylish new cut that complimented my face, thanks to a recent trip to the hairdresser. My new high-quality clothes fit perfectly, their fabric cascading in flattering waves. I'd even borrowed a pair of sunglasses from Kara's closet, completing the outfit and my new, expensive look.

I deserved to live the sort of life they lived, wear the sort of clothes Kara did.

I wasn't just playing dress-up anymore. I *belonged* in this world.

The waiter returned with a straw for Kara's drink, and I reached over to offer her some, the ice clinking against the rim. I had equipped her with oversized sunglasses for her comfort, to hide her from prying eyes, but it made her expressions even more elusive than usual. So far, I had no idea what Kara thought about being here.

"Since we'll have to wait for the food, I brought this along." I pulled a tabloid magazine out from my bag. "I picked it up at the hairdresser." I flipped through the pages until I found the article I was looking for.

"Look, this is one of those women we ran into at the farmers' market. Sophia Bellamy? 'Actress Sophia Bellamy's dress *disaster* pre-wedding. Uncannily similar to an Amazon steal!'" I leaned over to show Kara the accompanying image, then inspected it myself, frowning.

"It really *is*. I guess money can't buy taste, huh?"

I couldn't say for certain, but I felt like a little smile was forming in the corner of Kara's mouth, and I smiled too. Surprisingly, I was having...fun?

Maybe we had more in common than I'd realized. After all, we were both ambitious actresses. We'd both sacrificed a lot to get ahead. We both found her husband dreamy. And to an outsider looking in, there was no way to tell I had simply been hired to keep her company. I'd already seen a few patrons glance our way, trying to identify the glamorous young actress lunching with Kara Harrington.

And that suited me just fine.

I went on to read aloud almost half of the salacious tabloid magazine as we waited for our food. Kara tilted her chin toward me, and I noticed her hands were resting comfortably on her handrests instead of twitching or fidgeting impatiently. If I had to guess, I would have said she was enjoying the gossip too. Certainly, she was concentrating much more on my reports of other actresses' missteps than the literary fiction or autobiographies of old-Hollywood actresses I'd found on her bedside table.

This was what really held her attention—the messy lives of the people in our world.

Suddenly, my phone rang, the blare interrupting my thoughts like an aggressive alarm clock. I picked it up.

"Hi, it's Anna."

An aggressive voice blasted at me from the other end, so abrasive I instinctively recoiled from the phone.

"Where *are* you?"

It was Flora. She sounded livid.

I quickly retracted the phone further, enough to read the time in the upper corner, and my blood ran cold. It was ten minutes past the time when I was supposed to hand Kara over to Flora. I had completely lost track of time.

"We're at…" I faltered. For a moment, I considered lying, but I knew it wouldn't work.

"We're having late lunch at Lila's in Santa Monica. We can start heading over—"

"*What*? You took Mrs. Harrington that far away from the house?" Flora's tone was incredulous.

"It's really not a big deal—"

"What if Mrs. Harrington had a medical emergency? Stay there, I will come pick her up."

"Why don't I just—"

"STAY. THERE."

Flora hung up. I placed the phone on the table, my heart pounding in my ears. The table next to us resumed their conversation, which they'd paused for the duration of my call.

I felt humiliated. Now everyone knew I didn't really belong here. I wasn't really Kara's friend, I was her…servant.

This was just like Flora. Trying to convince me everything I do is horribly wrong.

My hands trembled despite myself as I flagged down a waiter to bring the check. I didn't want Flora to show up at the restaurant and cause a scene.

I'd taken Kara to use the restroom, so by the time I rolled her out to the sidewalk, where we took shelter in the shade of the building, it only took about ten minutes for a taxi to pull up and Flora to step out.

She was still in her crisp white uniform, her hair pulled back in a painfully tight bun. She strode over and made to grab Kara's wheelchair, but I held out a hand.

"Flora, calm down. Let's all just go over to the van—"

"Step back. I will take Mrs. Harrington now," Flora replied, sharp and authoritative, and practically pushed me off the wheelchair. I stumbled back, and anger swelled in my chest.

"Flora, you're overreacting! I don't see anything wrong with taking Kara out for some fresh air—she shouldn't be locked away like some dark secret!"

"It is not your decision to make. You are an outsider. Your position is temporary. You know *nothing* about this family," Flora spat, wheeling Kara around.

"I'm just doing what I think is best for Kara. Isn't that what you should be doing, too?"

"She is *not well enough.* And how would you know what is best for Kara? You are not a qualified nurse. In fact, I don't think you have any experience caring for a disabled person like you claimed on your resume," Flora continued, her voice dripping with disdain. "And let's not forget about your past. You are a fraud and a liar, sneaking into this household, and—"

Before Flora could finish insulting me, she let out a shrill shriek.

She had moved so quickly and was speaking so animatedly that before either of us knew it, the handles of Kara's wheelchair had slipped from her grasp.

Flora's hand groped out desperately after Kara's wheelchair as it jostled down the sloped pavement, beyond her reach. A cacophony of blaring horns struck up as Kara rolled right off the curb—and straight into traffic.

18

I didn't have time to calculate trajectories, so I did the only thing I could.

I lunged after her.

Without thinking, I sprinted headlong after Kara, grabbing the handle of her wheelchair. Horns blared and tires screeched as cars came to sharp and sudden stops around us. My arm shook with the strain of yanking the wheelchair back from its intended trajectory. I wasn't entirely sure the bones in my shoulder were still in their sockets.

"Oh my god." I breathed frantically, adrenaline pulsing through my body. "Oh my god."

Kara had only rolled about five feet but straight into a busy lane, and at least three angry drivers were now sticking their heads out of their cars and yelling at me. Some of them were also yelling at Flora.

Flora's mistake had been miraculously timed. A few seconds earlier or later, and Kara would have been toast.

I pulled her back onto the sidewalk and locked the brakes. Flora, for once, was silent. I kneeled over beside Kara.

"Are you okay?"

If I needed any reassurance that Kara was truly out of it, here it was. Kara's reaction to practically being roadkill was…to not respond. She simply gazed off into the distance, like a wax puppet.

Possibly, there *was* a wax sculpture of Kara at a Madam Tussauds. I would have wagered that you could have switched the two, and no one would have been the wiser.

Flora seemed to have regained her function of speech, although she still looked very pale. "It is unacceptable…totally unacceptable, your lack of oversight…"

I was not having it.

"Flora, don't you dare," I hissed, rounding on her. "This was on you! *You* nearly got her *killed*!"

Shaking my head, I pulled out my phone. Flora reached out a hand to slap my arm down.

"What are you doing?"

"Calling Colin, of course," I said. Irritated that it had to be spelled out. "We need to let him know what happened."

"No!" Flora exclaimed, pushing my hand away. For a moment, her eyes moved about wildly, as if she was a trapped animal trying to figure out a means of escape. But then she seemed to think of something and gathered herself.

"And why would you want to tell Colin that you pushed Mrs. Harrington into traffic?"

Heat rose to my face. This was by far the most audacious of Flora's attempts to gaslight me.

"Don't you dare attempt to twist this. You practically tore Kara away from me and then *you* were too busy reprimanding me to keep her safe. Colin should—"

"I'll tell Colin everything about you and Mr. Berg," Flora said quickly. "*Everything.*"

I inhaled sharply. Flora had pulled out her trump card, and she knew it. I could see the color return to her cheeks. She held out her hand.

"The keys to the van, now, please."

Reluctantly, I handed her the keys. She snapped them up, then reached over and tugged Kara's wheelchair handles out of my fingers.

"I'm being very gracious by not mentioning this gross oversight to Mr. Harrington," she said, holding her back straight and the usual patronizing tone creeping back into her voice. "You should count yourself lucky."

"Uh-huh," I murmured through gritted teeth.

I watched Flora roll Kara off to the parking lot. She didn't turn around to see if I was following.

I didn't follow. I stood on the sidewalk, seething, sick to my stomach that Flora had triumphed again.

A desperate thought crossed my mind—maybe *I* could tell Colin first and get a jump on Flora. After all, he clearly thought she was no longer necessary. A few days ago, I would have easily wagered that he preferred me to Flora.

But would Colin take my side, now that he was angry with me?

19

An hour later, I returned to the house after walking off the frustration and calling a cab. It felt strange to arrive at the Harringtons' on foot again rather than gliding up and down the driveway in the black van. Even though I wasn't the one to blame for Kara's near miss, it looked like I was slinking back to the Harringtons' with my tail between my legs.

Maybe that's how Flora had wanted it to look.

I waited for the gate at the upper end of the driveway to slide open, trying to shake the memory of someone watching me from Kara's bedroom window on my first visit. Could it have been Flora, taking me in, assessing the competition? Perhaps already making plans for how to undermine my work and get rid of me before I could challenge her position.

But when I looked up, there was no one there. No one following my every move as I made my way to the house, cataloging my failure.

I didn't want to linger in any common areas of the house, afraid of running into Flora any sooner than necessary, so I retreated directly to the only room where I felt completely comfortable: the sound studio.

But to my surprise, someone was already inside.

"Oh shit," I exclaimed as I swung open the door, interrupting Colin mid-sentence, leaning over a microphone. I gestured toward the door, taking a step back. "I'll just—"

"No, please, Anna. Stay," Colin said with a reassuring smile. "I'm just finishing up."

"Oh…okay," I replied, caught off guard by his suggestion. I awkwardly made my way over to one of the office chairs by the monitors and sat down, crossing and then uncrossing my legs. Colin turned back to his microphone and continued his previous sentence.

"So remember, life throws mountains and canyons at us to test us. What do we do? We smack them in the face and move on. We keep climbing. Remember, there's always room at the top! Until next time!"

Colin waited a few seconds and then flipped off the record switch. He quickly began cutting the audio, adding his freshly recorded take to cover the tail end of the one I had just ruined.

"We're almost there…"

Colin ran the stitched-up audio through a few software programs, occasionally making small adjustments. "You aren't sending it to an editor?"

"Nah. I want it to sound candid. Honest. That's what my listeners enjoy about my podcasts." He continued to click a few more options on the monitor. I watched the abrupt spikes of the audio on the monitor flex and retract.

"I just make sure there's no distracting peaks, add a bit of reverb, and..." he clicked a button, and a small loading bar appeared on the screen. "Done."

"Done? That's it?" I was surprised—in all my previous projects, sound engineers and producers would spend a significant amount of time—and money— perfecting the audio. Creating Colin's podcast seemed like a much simpler process.

"Well, one last thing," he said as the loading bar reached completion and stopped. "Could you hand me my phone, Anna?"

I reached over to where Colin had pointed and handed him his phone. He opened up his notes and entered a passcode into a prompt that had sprung up on his screen.

"I can never remember my passwords," he explained sheepishly.

"Oh, I'm the same," I said. It was a lie. I practically had a photographic memory when it came to numbers. But Colin flashed me an appreciative smile that made the little white lie feel worthwhile.

"What happens now?" I asked.

"After I verify the upload, my host automatically distributes it to all major podcast apps: Spotify, Google, Apple, et cetera."

"So, it's just out there now? There's no middleman?"

"That's right. Freshly served! But in all seriousness, it's not always this easy. Sometimes I have guests who have no control over their voice, or the audio is messy. Or we want to add effects, clips, or songs or connect shorter bits. But sometimes it's easy. Natural." He smiled at me.

"Damn. I chose the wrong profession," I joked.

"That's what Kara used to say," Colin replied with a sad smile.

My laughter died down. "Colin, I'm sorry—"

"No, please, Anna. I'm the one who's sorry." Colin brushed the hair out of his eyes and let out a sigh. "I pride myself on discussing tough issues on my podcast, on tackling challenges, but when you brought up Kara, I ran away instead of facing the conversation."

"Of course, it's a difficult topic," I swiveled my chair a little closer to Colin, tempted to grasp his hands supportively. "I had no right to impose my opinion. You know what's best for Kara."

Colin rubbed his neck, looking thoughtful. "The thing is, I really don't. I haven't even looked into care homes for Kara. I didn't want to consider the possibility that she may not fully recover. She's always been so resilient, has exceeded every expectation. When the doctors said her physical injuries were healed and that whatever was holding her back was mental…I couldn't accept the idea that she wouldn't rehabilitate."

"So you think her condition is just…all in her head?"

"Brain injuries are difficult to diagnose," Colin explained. "In Kara's case, specialists couldn't distinguish between what might be a brain injury and what might be a psychological condition."

"And she's really not on any medication?"

"That's right," Colin confirmed.

"Flora *specifically* told me not to touch Kara's medication…" I said, hoping Flora's deceit would call her position here into question.

Colin laughed. "Flora takes her job *very seriously*. I've even told her she doesn't need to wear the uniform, but she won't have it. I've met presidential bodyguards who have looser standards than Flora."

"Presidential bodyguards?" I asked curiously.

"I haven't actually met any," Colin laughed. "But I'm sure if I did, they'd be comparatively easy going."

The last time Colin and I discussed Kara's "medication," I hadn't yet known how to leverage that information. But now, surely he'd realized how redundant Flora was. In addition to the deception, if he knew what happened earlier, he might be moved to take action. To cut the dead weight.

I opened my mouth, on the verge of telling Colin what had happened earlier that day, but then stopped myself. Even though Flora had made such a big mistake, I couldn't risk her exposing my secret.

Instead, I shifted the conversation toward Kara's recovery.

"I'm sure Kara did her best to recover," I said. "But it may not be up to her."

Colin clenched and unclenched his fists. I could see this was difficult for him.

"You don't have to say anything," I added quickly. After how he reacted last time, I was desperate not to be too pushy.

"I had this...whole idea in my head of how Kara would make a comeback," he sighed. "She'd show everyone what a fighter she was. A survivor. She had been punished for her actions in the industry, but people love a good comeback story, you know? They would have finally seen her worth and truly loved her."

Colin paused before continuing. "She always envied Mary for that."

"Oh?" I asked, trying not to sound too curious. I thought back to Mary's voice on the tape.

I can't help but feel like she would do this so much better than me.

"The audience loved Mary, *loved*, but public opinion was against

Kara. I don't think Kara ever really got over Mary's success. Right before the accident...we fought about her."

As I listened, an image of their past formed in my mind. Mary had been popular with audiences but troubled and paranoid, causing her to lose roles and eventually take her own life. Kara was jealous of her popularity and, by all accounts, was generally envious and competitive.

It didn't seem like a stretch to think she might have wanted Mary's life and saw an opportunity when tragedy struck. Colin would have been devastated. He may have even blamed himself. Miserable people are so vulnerable; Kara would have offered him a shoulder to cry on, and soon he'd have been eating out of her hand.

"Kara raged about Mary. She was drunk. I don't think she'd been happy for a while. Trapped in Mary's shadow."

I thought back to the art Kara had collected throughout their house and how it seemed to have a dark undertone connecting all the pieces; it made sense now. Kara had been depressed. Perhaps she had thought marrying Colin would have automatically afforded her the life Mary had, but rather than improving, her public image had plummeted. And while the depressed Mary had killed herself, Kara had turned to alcohol.

And then, it had just taken one fall...

"Anyway," Colin continued, jolting me back to the present. "You have someone close in a nursing home. How is the place?"

I thought back to the Green Village care home. I hadn't been in a while, and I had received no further calls.

"It's nice," I answered truthfully. "Feels homey, in an opulent sort of way. And the staff, it feels like they care."

Colin paused for a moment, and I thought he might actually say he'd decided to send Kara there. That it sounded perfect.

"Thank you for being here, Anna," Colin finally said, placing his hand on my arm. "Kara is so lucky to have you."

"Thanks," I said softly.

I'd be lucky to have you.

We stared at each other, Colin's hand still on my arm. Seconds passed, my heartrate spiking. Eventually, Colin averted his eyes.

"Now," Colin said, clapping his hands together as if dispelling the strange moment we'd just shared. "Since you helped me with something earlier, I should do something in return."

"Help? I just handed you your phone," I said with a laugh. "And if you'd remembered your password, you wouldn't have needed even that much help."

"Look, Anna, I *never* remember my password. So you see, checking my phone for it is an integral step in the process of publishing my podcast. You definitely helped!" Colin insisted with a mischievous glint in his eye. "And that merits me doing a favor in return."

"Well...you could help me practice some lines."

"Ah," Colin said. "I used to do that with Mary. In this very room, actually."

"Oh." My heart plummeted. "I'm sorry I suggested it, please forget all about it."

"No, you misunderstand me," Colin replied with a small smile. "I've missed it. I've missed being useful like that."

"Oh. Okay. I'll just grab my script from my room?"

"Take your time."

With a mix of emotions, I got up and walked over to the door, glancing behind me. I was almost worried that after making up with him, he'd now somehow disappear.

Back in my room, I quickly brushed my hair and checked my face. I'd been practically makeup free when I started at the house, but I'd slowly amped up my makeup routine. Just little subtle touches here and there.

I swiped on a smudge of red lipstick and blurred it with the tip of my thumb. Sure, it may have been a shade I'd borrowed from Kara's cosmetics. But the shade was perfect on me. I'd promised myself I'd return it…as soon as Kara asked me to.

Confident with my appearance, I grabbed the script and tried not to skip down the hallway.

But when I walked through the door of the studio, I found the room empty. My hand fell to my side and the script hit my thigh with a thud. Did something come up? Was Colin called away urgently?

Or was he feeling guilty about spending time with me?

Suddenly, I heard Colin's footsteps behind me as he entered, carrying a bottle.

"Wine?"

"Yes, please," I replied, giddy with relief and excitement. Colin collapsed on the comfortable sofa, and I joined him, suddenly very aware of how close our legs were.

I rifled around my script nervously while Colin poured us glasses.

"Okay, how about we…start with this part?" I suggested.

I leaned over to hand Colin the script. He accepted it and reclined on the sofa, crossing his legs and bringing his foot dangerously close to mine. I swallowed hard.

"Oh, do you mind if I record this?" I asked. "It helps to have a reference if something works."

"Sure." Colin moved his blue eyes up to me from behind the page as I fumbled on my phone to the voice recording app and pressed the comically large red button that sprang up on screen. He gave me a small smile before becoming serious. "Are you ready?"

My heart raced and my cheeks burned. This wasn't even an audition, but I felt incredibly nervous. I definitely wasn't ready.

"Okay, go for it," I said.

Colin cleared his throat and began reading. I'd chosen a passage where the vampire Countess was attempting to seduce the Count and convince him to join her in undeath.

Yes, it was exactly as gothic as it sounded.

At first, I was incredibly nervous, but I soon got caught up in the scene. The Countess was sultry and seductive, and I relaxed as I eased into her character. Colin took a bit longer to get there, but he was used to talking for a living: His deep voice and slight rasp suited the character of the Count. A few pages in, and I was in a flow state.

"Do you truly think you can resist me, Count?" I whispered, putting on the slight accent I'd honed for the Countess. "You've loved creatures like me before. Even now, your blood burns for me."

"Perhaps. But I've also dealt with women like you before. I know what is necessary." Colin wasn't putting on an accent, but to his credit, he was really selling it. "I had no choice but to kill my first love, and I'll do the same to you if you won't obey me."

I laughed, or rather, the Countess laughed—a beautiful, melodic cackle. "You can deny it all you want. But the hunger in your voice gives you away."

In the moment, I hadn't realized I'd chosen such an erotically loaded scene. To be fair, most interactions between the Countess and Count were like this, a game of cat and mouse. Even knowing I was playing a character, heat rose to my cheeks. Colin fixed me with a smoldering look. I was sure he was just putting it on for his performance.

Wasn't he?

"You underestimate me," he growled, raising his voice. "I watched the light die from her eyes. I'll happily watch it die in yours."

"You know that's not what you truly want, Count," I murmured, leaning forward. "You want me close enough to feel my breath on your skin and hear my voice in your ear. Tempting you to surrender."

Colin leaned forward across from me, matching my gesture. He leaned close enough for me to smell his cologne. Cedar wood and musk.

"Try anything," he threatened, his voice husky. "And I'll grind you to pulp. I'll wipe you from this earth. There will be *nothing* left of you. And I'll laugh as I watch you die in agony."

"Then let the dance begin, Count," I countered, unfazed. "Let's see who truly holds the power here."

We stared squarely at one another. We were close enough for me to count his lashes. I bit my lip, despite myself.

"And...scene," Colin said, flopping the script down on the sofa between us. We both looked at each other and burst into laughter.

"That was amazing!" Colin exclaimed after the laughter had subsided. "And very, *very* dramatic!"

"It's based on a video game," I explained, apologetic. But only a little. I hadn't had this much fun in a long time.

"You were really great, Anna."

"Well, you make a pretty saucy Count," I teased, and we both succumbed to another fit of laughter.

"But seriously," Colin said, wiping the corners of his eyes. "You have something special. Trust me, I've seen a lot of Hollywood types. Raw talent is rare, and it should be nurtured." He tilted his head, studying me. "You should be getting more opportunities, but here you are, working as a companion for Kara. What's up with that?"

I could still feel the recent strain of laughter on my face as my expression died down from a smile.

Was this the moment where I needed to come clean?

I drew a deep breath.

"Well…I was doing well for a while. Or at least, I was booking more and more work. Then I met this fairly big director. Marcus Berg. He had a role he thought I'd be perfect for. Only…" I faltered for a moment, feeling Colin's eyes on me. "When I showed up for what I thought was an audition for the part, he had something else in mind."

Colin nodded, encouraging me to continue. I gulped, wondering if disclosing all of this to my new boss was a good idea after all. Still, Colin's steady gaze encouraged me to keep going.

"He made advances toward me, thinking I would sleep with him to get the role. I didn't, of course. I guess I hoped he still thought I was the perfect fit for the part. Well…not only did I lose the role, but somehow word spread that *I* had made advances toward *him* to get the part, and *he* turned *me* down. So he looked like the good guy, and everyone thought I was trying to sleep my way to the top. Shows me, huh?

"After that, people started spreading rumors about me, and I became a pariah in the industry. Only total sleazeballs gave me any attention, thinking I'd do anything for a job."

Colin shook his head. "I'm so sorry, Anna. They had no right to treat you like that."

"And the worst part of it...my fiancé." I smiled sadly at Colin. "He believed the rumors. He left me and said a lot of nasty things as he did."

"That's not right. A partner should stand by you, no matter what." He drew a deep breath. "I would never leave my partner. Never."

"Never?" I asked. "Not even if they did something objectively horrible? If they messed up really bad?"

"If they messed up, I'd try to set them back on the right path. No, I wouldn't leave them. I would only ever accept if they wanted to leave me."

Can a heart leap and sink at the same time? I stared at Colin, absorbing the impact of his words. *I would never leave my partner.*

I thought about how easy it had been for my fiancé to leave me. Kara was so lucky, and she surely didn't even realize.

How different would my life have been if I'd had someone like Colin on my side?

But then I thought of the final thing Colin said. That he would only accept separation if his partner wanted to leave him. Did that mean he would stick by Kara until the bitter end?

"There are different ways of leaving," I said softly, thinking of Kara—how she was physically fit but mentally gone. She could be present, but she would never be truly here.

Whether consciously or not, hadn't Kara *already* left Colin?

I looked up at Colin, terrified of a backlash, of him storming off like he had before. But he was staring at me steadily.

And I could see he understood.

Suddenly, my phone chimed, breaking the moment. I cursed inwardly as I withdrew it and saw Micky's name on the screen. Time had flown by; he was due to arrive any minute now.

"It's my director," I explained. "He's coming here for the end of my session…"

"I won't keep you then," Colin replied as he got up to leave. "You've got important work to do."

"Thanks," I said, even though at that moment, our project felt a little less important than it usually did. Colin walked out of the room and closed the door, leaving me a little emptier, somehow. I already knew it would be impossible to amp myself up about working with Micky tonight.

I distracted myself by uploading the audio I'd just recorded onto the sound studio computer. I cut mine and Colin's lines into separate audio tracks and exported the one containing mine. I'd play it for Micky once he arrived. He might have some good feedback.

After a moment's hesitation, I exported the track with Colin's lines as well. Plugging in a pair of headphones just in case Micky was about to barge in through the door, I pressed play.

"I've dealt with women like you before," Colin purred in my ear. "I know what is necessary…"

I closed my eyes and allowed the sound of his voice to wash over me. It didn't matter that he was reading lines; the content of his words was secondary. It was the intensity of the voice. The focus. More intimate than his podcast. More passionate.

And he'd been speaking just to me.

20

It was well past eight p.m., but the vibrant colors of the sunset had painted the sky a beautiful pink, and the sun slipping behind the horizon had drenched the separation between earth and sky a rich amber. The sight reminded me of the cocktail Colin had made me back when he'd been showing off behind the downstairs bar just a week earlier.

The fact that we'd settled our disagreement following that night had eased my anxiety a little, but I was still tense as I headed upstairs to check on Kara. A smug Flora had bossed me around all week, confident in the knowledge that she knew my secret and could lord it over me. I may have told Colin my side of the story, but I didn't know what version Flora would tell.

It wasn't quite time for my shift with Kara, but I saw Flora descend the stairs with her bag. Some days, if I was lucky, she'd simply ignore me. Tonight, she barely flicked her eyes in my direction as she passed by. I took that as a win and jogged up the stairs to Kara's room.

As I approached Kara's doorway, I heard voices.

Peeking my head in, I saw Colin propped in Kara's bed next to her, light dancing over them from the television screen on the opposite wall. Kara's eyes were closed. Colin glanced my way, smiled, and waved me in. I turned to see what he was watching, and my stomach sank as I took in Kara in white, in Colin's arms, on the dance floor at their wedding.

He was watching their wedding video.

I tried to smile, as if I thought it was sweet, but my blood boiled. I resisted the sudden urge to walk over to the DVD player, rip out the stupid disc, and break it into pieces.

I knew I was being irrational. He was *Kara's* husband after all, not mine.

But still.

"Oh, I don't want to intrude." I made my voice amiable.

"Nonsense!" Colin said. "It's just about over anyway." He sat up, reaching for the remote, and paused the video. The frame froze on Kara staring into Colin's eyes.

"Actually," he said, glancing at his watch. "Why don't you go relax for a while, and I'll get Kara set up for the night?"

"Okay, no worries," I said and closed the door behind me, fuming.

I walked down to my room, where I flopped face-first onto the bed.

What would compel him to do that? To watch their wedding video, knowing I would be coming in any minute. After our last conversation, I'd thought we were on the same page with Kara's…status. Had Colin changed his mind? Was he still convinced she should stay in the house, that she'd get better? Or was he sending me a clear sign that he was irrevocably married, that I shouldn't get any stupid ideas?

Whatever the reason, I didn't like it.

In her bedroom, Kara was asleep. Her eyelids fluttered slightly as I gazed down at her. I adjusted her covers, then crept back out of the room, closing the door quietly behind me.

After my previous experience with someone sneaking around at night, I felt uneasy moving about after the sun went down. I didn't even feel safe in my room.

Following it being trashed, I'd been convinced the most likely culprit was a drunken Micky. But then, after my heart-to-heart with Colin, Micky had come over for a recording session and been perfectly professional and congenial. Was Micky only pretending? Or was someone else responsible?

It was most likely someone in or with access to the house. My next guess was Flora. But what if it wasn't her *or* Micky? The idea of a stranger silently watching me, while I was oblivious, made me sick to my stomach.

As I made my way down the now darkened hallway, something caught my eye. The light was on in Kara's walk-in closet, the one Flora had messed up and blamed me for.

I approached cautiously. It wasn't like Flora to leave a light on. She was uptight about things like that. Like Colin had said, she took her job way too seriously. Seriously enough to *seriously* try to get me fired.

Glancing over my shoulder, I half expected to find evidence of Flora setting up some kind of trap for me. Maybe a hidden camera to record incriminating footage of me leaving the wardrobe. Something Flora could take to Colin: *Look, Mr. Harrington, Anna can't stop rifling through your wife's stuff!*

It was true that I'd borrowed something every now and then. But I *always* returned it. Or at least, intended to return it.

The point being I'd never be stupid enough to leave a mess.

But there was no camera set up behind me, and the inside of the closet was perfectly organized: expensive haute couture red carpet gowns and the lines of designer shoes, all arranged in neat, perfectly spaced rows.

Maybe Flora *had* forgotten to turn the light off. She must've been *really* rattled by what transpired earlier.

As she should be. I still couldn't quite believe she had lost control and endangered Kara like that. For all of Flora's faults, it was hard to believe she'd neglect Kara's health and safety. But I guessed she'd finally found something she aspired to more than making sure Kara was taken care of—making sure I wasn't around.

Having confirmed this wasn't some kind of setup by Flora, I allowed myself to enjoy the room. I darted in and quickly shut the door behind me.

Being inside Kara's walk-in closet was like being in a candy shop, except that the candy was excessively expensive designer clothes. I was sure just one of Kara's Hermes bags would have set me up for a year.

Kara may have been determined and ambitious and competitive, and Mary beloved, but something in their nature had prevented both of them from appreciating the enchanted life they lived.

If I had this life, I would never take it for granted.

I reached out to stroke the fabric of one of Kara's dresses. It was sheer and layered with hints of glittering navy cloth. I'd never worn anything like it.

Before I could think better of it, I stripped off my own clothes and carefully wrangled the dress off the hanger. I stepped into it, wincing as I pulled it up, forcing it over my hips.

Zipping up the back was a nightmare. But once I was done, I couldn't help but admire myself in the wall-length mirror.

The dress was asymmetrical at the top, leaving one of the shoulders bare, with a straight, deep neckline that revealed my collarbones and just the very top of my chest. It bunched up around my waist, pooling onto the floor.

Sure, Kara had freakishly long legs and arms, as proven by the excess fabric around my feet and wrists. But despite not being a perfect fit, the dress was *gorgeous*. And dare I say, I looked great.

Just as I was considering going for broke and trying on some earrings, I heard a loud thumping coming from down the hall. From Kara's bedroom.

I froze. Was that a sound I'd heard before? The night the stalker had breached the grounds?

And there it was again. The repeating thump at steady intervals.

Someone was in Kara's bedroom.

Forgetting all about the dress, I sprinted toward Kara's room, almost tripping on its train as I ran. I swerved left into the hallway that led me straight to Kara's bedroom, mind racing with thoughts of intruders and what they could want.

Compromising shots of Kara? To rob the place? A way to get at Colin?

Whoever it was, I didn't want them slipping away like they did last time.

I burst into Kara's room and stopped in the doorway, panting, glancing around the room to spot any intruders. There was no one. Just Kara, in bed.

And speaking of Kara…

She was staring right at me with a fierce, keen expression on her gaunt face. In the dim gloom of her bedroom, her eyes seemed almost colorless, like a shark's. Her skin glistened with beads of sweat. And in her hand, something sharp glinted when it caught the dim light pooling from the hallway behind me.

"Kara?" I cautiously called out. I'd spent hours, sometimes days at a time in the company of a completely dazed out Kara. This sudden, unbridled focus made my insides feel like solid ice.

Kara's eyes flicked up and down, taking in my dress. Her grip tightened around whatever she was holding—something reflective. I could see her fingers were bleeding. Small, dark stains were already blooming on the satin bedsheets.

"Kara, it's okay. It's just me. Anna." I edged closer to her, willing myself to remain calm. Kara's arm twitched. Her fingers clutched the thing tighter, drawing more blood.

"Kara, please, calm down," I begged, slowly reaching for her hand. She flinched, and as she did, I felt a sudden sharp pain as the razor-sharp edge of the reflective shard cut into my forearm. Up close, I recognized it as a broken piece of a DVD.

I grabbed Kara's wrist to steady her hand and made out her and Colin's names written in black marker on the DVD shard.

Their wedding video.

"Kara! Just calm down!" I struggled to pry her fingers off the broken shard. They came away with deep cuts on each finger. I managed to loosen her grip enough for the shard to fall onto the floor with a clatter.

Lines of red dripped down Kara's fingers. I looked around for something to stop the bleeding on her hand. Kara was shaking slightly, but her eyes remained narrowed and fixed on me.

"How did you get this?" I muttered, wrapping her fingers around a small hand towel.

Kara remained silent. Her eyes pierced me with the same expression she'd worn when I came through the door in the dress: judgment and disgust. Just the force of her gaze was almost enough to make me recoil. Was Kara cognizant enough to recognize I was wearing her dress?

Just then, I heard someone rushing down the hall. Colin called out.

"Anna? Is everything all right?"

Shit. There was no way I was being discovered in one of Kara's gowns. There was just no way I'd be able to explain myself. In a panic, I clawed at the zipper in the back and wiggled out of the dress.

21

I had just bundled up armfuls of fabric and stashed them under the bed when Colin rushed into the room. He was wearing nothing but a pair of boxer briefs. His eyes were wide.

"Anna?"

"Kara's hurt," I explained breathlessly, my heart hammering rapidly in my chest. After stripping off the dress, I was left in my underwear with smudges of blood over my arm. It must have been quite the sight.

Colin looked from me to Kara. "I'll call Flora," he said.

It only took five minutes for Flora to arrive. Colin's call had clearly woken her up: her usual nurse's uniform was replaced with a loose gray sweater that had lost its shape, and her hair was tied in a haphazard ponytail with strands sticking out here and there. If I didn't hate her as much as I did, it would have almost been relatable. She glanced at my state of undress, and I saw her mouth purse into an even thinner line than usual.

"What happened?" she asked, pushing past me forcefully to reach Kara's side. She quickly inspected Kara's fingers and pulled out her kit, withdrawing some disinfectant and gauze.

"It was a...what did you say Anna?" Colin asked. He was pacing back and forth.

"A piece of a DVD," I said. I was suddenly aware of its position on the floor, by the edge of the bed. Anyone bending down to snatch it would inevitably see the dress I'd stashed under the bed. I grabbed it and offered it to Colin.

He took it, his eyes taking in the names on the disc.

Colin and I watched Flora wipe disinfectant on Kara's fingers in silence. She wrapped strips of gauze around each finger.

"Luckily, the cuts aren't deep enough to warrant stitches. They should heal with proper care."

"Thank you, Flora," Colin said, pausing his aimless pacing.

"It's my job," she said, with a little more emphasis than necessary.

"Well," Colin said. "Much appreciated."

Satisfaction crossed Flora's face, and suddenly I realized.

Wait. Did Flora manufacture this accident to hold on to her job?

"The question is, how did this incident happen in the first place? How could Mrs. Harrington have had access to such a sharp object?"

I'd been too slow. Flora was already getting ahead of the narrative.

"I had just checked on her, and she was sound asleep and didn't have anything in her hand." I tried to defend myself.

"Did Mrs. Harrington page you for help?"

"No, I—I heard something. A noise. I thought there might be someone in Kara's bedroom."

"You thought there was an intruder in Kara's room?" Colin asked, surprised.

"You heard something all the way from the basement?" Flora asked, suspicious.

"No, I'd—" I paused again. What reasonable explanation could I give for why I was standing in Kara's bedroom in my underwear? I was desperately avoiding glancing at the edge of the bed.

"Perhaps," Flora suggested, "you returned to Mrs. Harrington's room post haste in your state of undress because you remembered she had access to something she shouldn't."

"No," I said, furious at Flora's implication.

"Easy, Flora," Colin said. "That's quite an accusation. Let's not jump to conclusions. I think it does Anna credit that she rushed here as soon as she heard something."

"Look," Flora continued, undeterred. She turned to Colin, practically turning her back to me. "I have to be honest, just like I have for previous companions. I don't think Anna is suited for this position."

It wasn't at all a surprise that Flora could say something like that, but the words still stung like a slap. I balled my fists at my sides, trying to stop them from trembling. Half-naked, I felt even more vulnerable than usual to Flora's berating.

This was her plan all along. To discredit me.

And now, Flora was making her move.

"Oh?" Colin asked, looking from Flora to me curiously.

"It's clear she doesn't know how to handle critical situations like this."

"I mean…she just disinfected the cuts," I started, knowing I had to correct any and all accusations, *now*, before Flora could convince Colin to fire me. "*I* could have done that. And yesterday—"

"But you didn't," Flora cut me off. "You had to call *me*. And let's not forget…" Flora drew a deep breath. "Yesterday she put Mrs. Harrington's life in danger."

"That's not how it happened." My voice was shaking following Flora's words. I was not going to let her make Colin believe it was *my* fault Kara had rolled into traffic. "It was *Flora* who let the wheelchair slip—"

"Oh, *I* let it slip now? Come on, Anna," Flora interjected, shaking her head at me as if I were a little child making up nonsensical lies.

"It's true!" I said, turning to Colin for reassurance, willing him to see past Flora's ridiculous charade. "I had to pull Kara *out of traffic* after Flora let her slip away!"

"And what about the seatbelt incident?" Flora continued relentlessly. "How do you explain *that*?"

"That was Flora too," I continued, keeping my eyes on Colin. His eyes were darting between Flora and me, his expression unreadable.

"And what about your little habit of stealing things from Mrs. Harrington?" Flora asked. "Was that also my doing?"

"I haven't stolen anything." I felt the borrowed lipstick burning a hole in the pocket of my bag.

"And…" Flora drew a breath, as if ready to present her final, most powerful argument. "Did you know she has a reputation for trying to steal her bosses from their wives?"

"Anna has informed me of the rumors surrounding her," Colin stated firmly. I almost cheered. I'd made the right call confiding in Colin and getting ahead of Flora.

"But did she tell you he suffered a suspicious *accident* after the accusations? After they'd been alone in a room, just the two of them?"

Colin paused, looking at me. An appraising look. A *why has she not told me any of this before* look.

My mind scrambled for an explanation, but Flora kept going.

"She is *not* who you think she is," Flora hissed at Colin.

"That's enough," Colin said with finality. He glanced between the two of us, exchanging venomous stares. I trembled with adrenaline. "This has gone too far."

"But it's not true, Colin," I said, trying to keep my voice level. "I *am* who you think I am."

Colin studied me intently but said nothing. Both Flora and I opened our mouths, but he raised his hand, requesting silence. We stopped short. I bit my tongue. Now I really wished I would have gone to Colin about the wheelchair incident right after it happened rather than letting Flora spring it on me.

"The only accusation here that matters is whether someone has put Kara in danger. Now Flora, you claim that Anna lost her grip on the wheelchair, sending it into traffic? And left a seatbelt undone?"

Flora sniffed. "Yes, that is what happened."

"No, it isn't," I started, but Colin gave me a warning look.

"And Anna, you say *Flora* was neglectful with Kara and left a seatbelt undone?"

Flora shook her head. "Yes," I said, with emphasis.

"You know, this doesn't come as a complete surprise to me. Do you know why?"

Flora and I both stared at Colin. I shook my head while Flora shook hers vigorously.

Colin pulled out his phone and tapped on the screen before showing it to us. The headline read:

KARA HARRINGTON'S NEAR MISS! Hollywood star disrupts traffic.

"Did you really think there wouldn't be paparazzi?" Colin asked, turning the phone back to himself and scrolling through the article while Flora and I stood in stunned silence. "Why I had to find out this news from a tabloid rather than the two of you, I do not know. Now, from this image it's clear that Anna jumped into traffic. But what happened just moments before the paparazzi took these pictures?"

"Flora—" I started.

"How dare you?" Flora cut me off.

"Only one person can say," Colin said loudly, cutting us both off. He turned to Kara in bed.

"Kara, darling. Please. Is there someone here who makes you feel unsafe?"

There was an awkward pause. I couldn't say for certain, but Flora must have been thinking what I was thinking: There was no way Kara was lucid enough to testify for either of us. But Colin was our boss, so both of us fell silent, indulging him.

I turned to look at Kara. She was propped up on pillows, her bandaged fingers pointing up at the ceiling. The sheets around her were still soiled in blood. In the dim half light of the room, she looked haunted, like a ghost painted into one of those creepy mirrors in a haunted house. I wondered how long we'd have to expect her to do something.

Kara's eyes met mine and I recalled her expression before, when I'd stumbled into her room in her gown: judgment. Hate. Envy?

I recalled her piercing eyes on Colin and me whenever she saw us together.

Her steady gaze when I'd emerged from the wardrobe during my first week.

The sharp cut from the broken DVD that I was even now cradling with my other arm.

Colin's director friend's comments about her being jealous. The physiotherapist receptionist's comments about her terrorizing younger women on set.

Had Kara been able to express herself, there was no way she would have favored me. No way.

Kara's eyes held mine.

And then she lifted a trembling finger, just inches above where it had rested.

She pointed at Flora.

"She doesn't mean that," Flora said quickly as I stared wide-eyed at Kara's finger, undeniably pointing at Flora. Since when had she been so responsive?

Flora continued desperately. "She means—"

"I know what my wife means," Colin snapped, turning back to Kara. "Did Flora do everything possible to keep you safe before these photos were taken?"

Kara lifted her finger and brought it down in two sharp taps. *No.*

"My third question. Did Flora neglect to fasten your seatbelt?"

One tap. *Yes.*

"Please, Mr. Harrington, I beg of you. I need this job. My baby boy…" Flora pleaded. I watched as Colin ignored her. I'd never heard her mention a baby before…

"Was Flora responsible for you rolling into traffic?"

There was a pause. Then Kara lifted her finger and brought it down a singular time.

Yes.

"Mr. Harrington—" Flora began. She looked like she was about to cry.

"Flora," Colin said, turning to her. "You are fired. Pack your things. And get out of my house."

22

Flora had packed and was dismissed within the hour. I watched from Kara's bedroom window as she walked up the driveway and got into a cab. She looked so small from up here.

I tried not to feel sorry for her. After all, she had been after me since day one. After what she had said the night before, I was convinced she had manufactured the departure of all the previous help in a desperate attempt to hold onto her job. But she hadn't managed that with me.

I watched the cab drive away into the night and supposed this was the last I'd see of her.

Victorious, I slipped into Kara's bathroom, took out my phone, and tapped in a number. I waited, listening to the familiar jingle, before a familiar receptionist picked up.

"Green Village care home, how may I help you?"

"This is Elsie Wyatt," I said, my voice echoing ever so slightly in the tiled room. "I wanted to check if there were any updates?"

"Hi, Elsie," the receptionist replied. "Let me see…no, I don't think we've flagged anyone to call you regarding his condition. He's stable, and all his vitals are normal."

"Thank you," I said. "Well, that's all. I'll visit again as soon as possible."

"I'm sure he would appreciate that."

I ended the call and slipped the phone in my pocket, then unlocked the door and stepped back inside the bedroom. Kara was in bed, deep asleep, her mouth lolled open just a bit, and her breath came in and out in long, wheezing drones.

The door opened just a fraction, and I saw Colin in the hallway, peeking in. Glancing once more back at Kara, I dodged through the doorway and closed the door behind me.

"She's asleep," I told Colin in answer to his unspoken question.

"You're hurt!" Colin exclaimed, looking at my forearm. The blood on the cut had already turned tacky, and the skin around it was smudged with drying blood.

"Oh," I said numbly. "I forgot—"

"Follow me," Colin said. He led me to his bedroom where he sat me down on the edge of his bed. I waited, suddenly aware of our state of undress, while he fetched some bandages and disinfectant.

"I'm uh, sorry about—" I started.

"Don't be," Colin said as he gently picked up my arm and inspected the cut. "And don't worry about having to cover for Flora's shifts. We'll get someone to come in soon to give you a break."

I winced at the sting of the disinfectant. "No, really, I'm so sorry for not telling you about what happened with Kara and the traffic. But Flora—"

"You were worried I wouldn't believe you," Colin said. He gently began to wrap a bandage around my arm. His fingers grazed my skin, and a shiver went through me.

"Well…Yes. Flora has been around a lot longer. I thought you might trust her over me."

"Sure, Flora was around a lot longer. But sometimes you need some new blood, to shake things up a little bit, don't you think?" Colin asked with a familiar grin. I smiled too. Losing this job would have been a gut punch, but the idea of Colin thinking less of me physically hurt.

Colin finished tying a bandage around my arm and released his hold on me. "Look, I've thought of a way to thank you. For being here for me. For dodging into traffic to save Kara."

"Oh? Are you giving me a raise?"

"I wasn't going to, but sure. I'll give you a raise. You deserve it." I beamed, and Colin chuckled at my reaction. "But no, I'm thinking of something else. Anna, I want you to be a guest on my podcast."

My mouth dropped open. "A—what now?"

"I've thought about it, and it's the perfect way to thank you."

"Not to sound ungrateful but…aren't your guests usually well-known?"

"They are typically famous because I interview my friends and people I admire, and I tend to be surrounded by famous people," Colin explained. "But it's *my* podcast, and I choose who to interview. And I'd like to interview you."

"And um…this is your way of thanking me? You know, I would have settled for dinner."

"Think about it, Anna. My podcast has a huge following. Millions of people listen to it. This is your opportunity to share your side of the story. Get ahead of the narrative. People love a good underdog. You are cast out of the community now, on your last leg, working to get by and to sustain the dream. You've been beat down, but you are still going at it."

I'd been biting back another joke, but it slipped away as I looked at Colin. He was *serious* about this. Could it be this was actually a good idea? That like Colin said, it was a chance to present my version of the story?

I suddenly thought back to what my father had said when I'd told him about landing the job. That the proximity to the Harringtons could take me places. *If I played it smart. If I was good enough.*

"I mean…It's maybe not a bad idea. A terrifying idea. But a good idea?"

Colin laughed. "The best ideas often are a little intimidating, but that's how you know what's worth going after. The smartest, most successful people I know taught me that." Colin leaned over a little. "Look, I have to warn you. I'm going to go tough on you. I don't want it to look like I'm paying you any favors; it will backfire. I'm always honest, remember? That's what my audience loves about me."

I squared my shoulders. "That's okay. I can take it."

Colin smiled. "I know. You're tougher than you look."

23

Colin made good on his promise a few days later. He'd hired someone from an external agency to take over my responsibilities and watch over Kara while I was away. The replacement was cool and impersonal when we introduced ourselves. In his black suit, he looked more like a security guard than a nurse. But I supposed it would be all the same to Kara.

I left the temp in charge of Kara without a second thought as I headed down to the sound studio, unsure what to expect.

Sure, I'd listened to Colin's podcasts before. I knew his mannerisms: the way he paused before asking difficult questions. I knew Colin prided himself in digging deeper and getting to the real meat of the matter. His approach wasn't too combative, from a listener's perspective. But it always feels different, actually being in the hotseat.

Now, sitting across from him, I nervously adjusted my microphone, tucked and untucked loose strands of my hair.

"Anna," Colin said, breaking me out of my nervous trance.

"Hmm?" I looked up to see him smiling at me. "I've never been interviewed for a podcast before. Actually, now that I think about it, I don't remember recording anything in my *real* voice."

"It's going to be all right," he said. And the way he looked at me, it was hard not to believe him. Then he pressed record.

"Welcome to a live episode of *Soapbox with Colin Harrington*," Colin began, leaning into his mic. "And tonight, we have a very special guest with us—emerging voice actress Anna Albright."

"It's great to be here on your show."

"Anna, you are a relatively new friend of mine, but when I heard what you were working on, I was immediately impressed by your talent. Your ability to capture the essence of a character through voice alone is truly impressive."

A surge of pride washed over me.

"Thank you, Colin," I said, feeling my voice steady as my nerves washed away. "That means a lot, coming from someone like you."

Colin chuckled softly. "Oh, please. We're not that different, you and me. I used to be a small-town boy. But then I found a group of like-minded people who helped me realize my full potential. Who pushed me to be the best version of myself. And now I am trying to pass on the favor."

He gave me a wolfish grin and a quick thumbs-up to check how I was feeling. I gave him a thumbs-up in return. This felt good—no different to having a regular conversation with Colin.

"Now, Anna, tell us a little about yourself. What are you working on at the moment?"

I went on to explain the project I was working on with Micky, trying not to make it sound too much like a sales pitch. Colin listened with interest, occasionally interjecting with questions. Micky had better be pleased: I didn't think we'd find a better platform to promote our upcoming crowdfunding than this. With Colin's gigantic listener base, the project was practically *guaranteed* funding.

"Regular listeners will know I frequently feature high-profile guests on my podcast. You might be wondering what Anna is doing here. But you see, what truly captivated me about you, Anna, was not just your talent, but your journey. What happened to lead you here," Colin said, his blue eyes fixed on me with an intensity that made me shift in my seat.

"It's been quite a journey for sure. I'm from a small town—"

"I'm not talking about how you ended up in LA, Anna. That story is almost always the same, with just a few minor variations, don't you think? Taking a chance to chase a dream, and so on, right?"

"Right."

"No, I mean you've had your fair share of challenges and obstacles along the way, haven't you?"

Straight to the point, then. I'd spent days preparing for this moment, but now that it was here, I struggled to find the best way to approach it.

"You are right. There have been a lot of challenges. And I've definitely been naive. When you want something so badly, you believe every opportunity might be *the one*. The one that helps you break out and become a star..."

"There was an opportunity like that for you, wasn't there? Tell me what really happened. The rumors are everywhere."

"Yes." I took a deep breath. "I met a director. His name was Marcus Berg. He promised me a role in his project. I just...didn't realize there'd be strings attached."

"What happened then?" Colin asked.

"Well...I refused. And he retracted the offer."

"We don't shy away from the details here, Anna. What exactly did you refuse?"

"I refused to sleep with him. But that didn't stop him from spreading rumors about me..."

Colin paused, looking intently at me for a moment.

"But that's not the whole story, is it, Anna?" He glanced at a paper he had in front of him, then back at me, his eyes boring into me. "You know, I have to do a lot of research for these podcasts. Fact checks. And there are pictures, Anna. Of you and Mr. Berg out on the town. Dinners. Hotels."

I'd known Colin would be tough on me, but I hadn't known how far he'd go. And I hadn't been able to prepare for how it felt to hear him say those words in the moment. My mouth went dry. I suddenly went cold.

Colin checked something on his paper. "The project Mr. Berg almost cast you in was *Serpent Blade*. Huh. Great series, won numerous awards." He glanced up at me. "Does it hurt to hear that?"

"Yes," I said blankly, still trying to wrap my head around the situation. How long had Colin known all of this? And what was he planning to do with the information?

"True, this was before he announced the casting, so some part of your story may be true. Evidently, you didn't get the role. But did you refuse Mr. Berg's advances? Or did you, in fact, encourage them?"

His eyes, which usually had such a bright and charming twinkle, were two vats of impermeable steel. The air in the studio suddenly felt light, as if it was devoid of oxygen.

Colin knew. He knew what I had done to try to get ahead.

And soon, so would the rest of the world.

"Yes, Colin," I admitted softly, my voice barely a whisper. "I did encourage his attention. I...I thought if I did what he wanted, I'd secure the role. You have to understand, I was young and naive, desperate to prove myself. I'd worked so hard and wasn't getting anywhere. But it was wrong, and I regret it."

Colin's eyes narrowed slightly, a flicker of disappointment passing over his features before he quickly recovered and cast me an understanding smile. "It must have been a difficult position for you, Anna. To have something you want dangled in front of you, but to get it, you must do something socially unacceptable."

My hands fidgeted in my lap as I struggled to find the right words. "I...I regret hurting someone. My ex-fiancé." I clenched my fists tighter, nails digging into my palms. "But I refuse to be defined by it forever."

"But it *has* defined you in the sphere of your industry, hasn't it? You've lost a lot of opportunities over this." Colin was staring at me.

"I have." I matched Colin's gaze. I'd been scared before, but now I was starting to feel enraged. How dare he do this to me? How dare he set me up like this? And for what? Drama for his listeners? To prove some kind of point?

I laughed bitterly. "I made a mistake, yes, but how long will I be punished for it? Is one misstep going to dictate my entire career? And besides, if I *had* gotten the part? Well, would it have even been a mistake? I would have proven my talent to everyone, no matter what I may have done for the opportunity."

"Do you really think you're talented, Anna?" Colin asked, leaning further toward his mic. "It seems to me that if some felt they needed to sleep their way into a role, they must not truly believe in their talent."

He was beginning to sound like my father. My father, who never believed in me. I suddenly remembered all the faces of my former friends and colleagues, turning away from me. Shying away at events. The emails and calls that had gone unanswered following my scandal.

"I *know* I'm good at what I do," I said forcefully. "And a lot of people in the industry are. The thing is, the same people who judge me have done the exact same thing, only *they've* gotten away with it! I wasn't punished because they're better people. I was punished to make everyone feel better about *themselves*. To allow them to draw some kind of line of separation between my actions and theirs. But we're not any different. All of us in this city have gone to low places to get to higher ones."

I took a breath.

"So, what would you call me, Colin?" I concluded, staring at him over my mic. "Did you bring me on this podcast to be a cautionary tale for young actresses? Or simply so you could have a little scandal?"

To my surprise, Colin grinned.

"I brought you on this podcast because you are ambitious, Anna," he said, his voice laced with sincerity. "And that ambition backfired for you. But it shouldn't have. You are absolutely right: Hollywood is a ruthless place. And a hypocritical one. We're all trying to get ahead here."

He paused. "But I don't just see your ambition; I see your *resilience*. Despite the setbacks and the whispers behind your back, you're still here. And that's *inspiring*."

I blinked in surprise, his words sinking in slowly. Was it possible Colin saw beyond the scandal and the tarnished reputation that followed me like a second shadow? Could he truly believe in my ability to rise above it all?

"I wanted to give you a chance to speak your truth, Anna. Not as how you think you should be perceived. But as you are."

I was still stunned into silence. Colin registered my expression and laughed. "I think that's all for this episode. What do you think of Hollywood's hypocrisy and Anna? Let me know!" He turned to me. "And thank you, Anna. For sharing."

"Thank you, Colin," I managed to say. Colin leaned over and pressed a button to stop recording.

We sat for a moment in silence, Colin observing me. He had a contemplative look on his face.

"I'm not sure I was ready for that," I said quietly.

"I'm sure it was a shock, Anna. My style often is. But you were amazing. You held your own."

"I'm not sure I feel that way. I've dealt with the rumors and whispers in my circle for a year now. With that episode out there, won't I just have to deal with it…well, everywhere?"

"No, Anna," Colin said, moving forward and placing a reassuring hand on my knee. "Don't you see? You've never *owned* the narrative. The thing is, you can be anything in Hollywood as long as you own it. And now you do. You took ownership."

I relaxed just a little. It was true: I *had* taken ownership of the story. It wasn't just some ambiguous dark cloud following me. I'd named it. I just didn't know what would happen now.

"You know, Anna. When you said treating you to a nice dinner would suffice—how would you feel about heading out for a meal? The temp can look after Kara a little while longer. I think you deserve it."

"Sure," I said, the heady rush of adrenaline fueling me on, now that I had come to terms with what had happened. Maybe Colin was right. Maybe this was necessary to move past the scandal.

"I *really* need a drink."

Colin grinned. My stomach did a little cartwheel.

"I think that can be arranged."

24

Colin called a cab that drove us to the restaurant he had chosen, a lavish place in the penthouse of a skyscraper. After a brief negotiation with the Maître d', we were seated at a table with a gorgeous view of the last of the sunset. We took it in as the waiter served us wine.

"It's a gorgeous skyline. I could look at it forever."

"You could. Have you seen the skyline painting in Kara's room? I know the artist—he's exhibiting at Art Basel this year."

"Colin..." I almost laughed out loud. Colin was by far one of the most grounded celebrities I'd ever met, and even he forgot not everyone was made of money. "I can hardly afford to buy art."

"You don't always have to *buy* art," Colin said mischievously. "Someone can gift it to you."

I laughed, although I wasn't entirely certain he was joking. "The piece in Kara's bedroom. You bought that for her as a gift?"

"No, actually. Mary did."

"Oh?" I supposed it did make sense—the piece seemed different from the rest of the art around the house, the art Kara had chosen. Less creepy. More hopeful? But considering what had transpired between the two, I was surprised Kara had kept the painting in her bedroom. "They were...good friends, weren't they?"

"Very," Colin said. "Which perhaps...complicated things. But life rarely goes as neatly as we wish. Love often arrives at the inopportune time or with the wrong person."

My heart skipped a beat.

Colin shook his head, as if to distract him from his thoughts, and smiled at me.

"But we are not here to talk about my past. Let's enjoy this time together."

While Colin browsed the menu, I checked my phone. It had been going off incessantly since Colin's live interview aired, to the point that I had to silence notifications. I scrolled through the most recent comments on my social media accounts.

So brave and honest

Your life and come up is honestly crazy

Unapologetically one of a kind

Obsessed with you

Just finished listening to the interview...I need the sequel!!!

Girl you got me, I'm a fan

"Good?" Colin asked with a sly smile.

"Great," I said. I felt like a million bucks. Colin had been right; I needed to get my story out there. And I had to *own it*.

"Then we have cause to celebrate," Colin said, flagging down a waiter. He consulted with me on my preferences and then ordered almost triple the amount of food I had requested.

"Are you trying to win me over with food?" I asked, astounded that the waiter had barely blinked at Colin's disproportionate order.

"I want you to try everything," Colin explained.

Just as I was about to respond, a sharply dressed man in his thirties walked by and stopped when he heard Colin's voice.

"Rhett!" Colin exclaimed, standing up to greet him. "Great seeing you, man. Rhett, this is—"

"Anna Albright," the man finished for him, extending a hand toward me. It felt surreal that he'd known my name, as I knew exactly who he was: Rhett Vaughn, one-half of a directing duo who'd been helming many big franchise films in recent years.

"Such a pleasure to meet you," I said, recovering from his sudden appearance. "I'm a big fan."

"Likewise," Rhett laughed. "That interview of yours was something else. Well done, Colin," he said, shaking Colin's hand. "Listen, Anna, once you're done with your current project, give me a call. We've got a few upcoming projects that will involve robots…"

"You're going to have to get in line, right after Luke Worthe," Colin interjected playfully.

"Luke?" Rhett exclaimed, slightly annoyed. "Shit, you know, get Colin to give you my number. My *personal* one. Give me a call when you can."

"I will," I said, bewildered.

"Eyes forward." Rhett winked at Colin. Then he walked away, leaving me in a state of shock as we sat back down at our table.

"This doesn't feel like my life. It feels like a parallel universe. Like a dream."

"I'll take that as you approving of my choice of restaurant." Colin smirked.

I *did* approve of Colin's choice. The courses soon began to arrive, each more exquisite than the last. There were caramelized scallops, served still sizzling on a hot griddle; cuts of lamb drizzled in herbs I could not name but was determined to look up; Santa Barbara uni on toasted brioche; and wagyu beef tartare. By the time the waiter arrived with a rich dark chocolate ganache tart topped with gold leaf, I had ascended to heaven many times over.

"This is incredible," I murmured. "I want to elope with the chef."

"We can't have that, can we," Colin laughed. "Come on, I need to get you out of here before we get accosted by another director." He looked around until he spotted a man he evidently knew working behind the bar. Colin excused himself to go exchange a few words and returned, smiling.

"I've got another surprise for you." He held out his hand for me.

"And separate me from this ganache?" I asked, even though I'd scraped the dish clean at this point. I probably would have licked the bowl if I was in private.

"It will be worth it, I promise," Colin smiled. "You may even prefer it to the ganache."

"Don't make promises you can't keep," I mumbled. Colin guided me by the arm, one hand on the small of my back. Maybe it was the many glasses of wine, but I could feel myself leaning closer to him, my sense of personal space eroded by the alcohol.

Colin guided me through a door behind the bar and down what looked like a hotel hallway until he eventually located a door that he pushed open.

"What do you think?" he asked, closing the door behind us.

It was nothing short of breathtaking. Colin had taken me to a pool nestled high up in the skyscraper with glass walls offering an unobstructed view of the city lights below. The water shimmered under the soft glow of the moon beyond the floor-to-ceiling windows. The room was only lit by the ethereal moonlight pooling in, and the only sound apart from our breathing was the gentle lapping of water.

"This pool is officially closed, but I pulled a few strings. Seeing as our last swim was interrupted, I thought I'd make it up to you." He swiped his hair out of his face, as if he was abashed recalling that moment so clearly. I bit back a grin.

"Help me with my dress?" I asked, turning around and glancing at him over my shoulder. Colin stepped closer and began to unzip me. I could feel his hands working with the zipper through the thin fabric of my dress. Unzipped, it slipped off over my shoulders and dropped around my feet.

I turned back to face him. For a brief moment, Colin seemed frozen as he took in my appearance.

"Your turn," I said softly, backing to the water. I watched as Colin stripped off his clothes and left them on the floor one by one. I tried not to visibly gulp. To hide my expression, I dove, all the tension in my body swallowed up by the warm water.

I surfaced in a rush of bubbles, pushing back my wet hair. Meanwhile, Colin descended into the pool, his eyes fixed on me. He slowly waded over, the reflecting light from the pool glittering on his bare skin.

"This is the best night I've had in a long time," I told him.

"I'm glad," he said. "You deserve it. For everything you've done for us. And for being you."

My heart sank a little at the implication of Kara, and of my job. Kara was out there, somewhere, and tomorrow I would just be her companion again, shuffling around her house and stealing sideways glances at her husband.

"I wish this would never end," I whispered.

"I did mean what I've told you, Anna," Colin said. He was swimming so close I could almost feel his breath on my face. The city lights outside painted his face and neck a shifting shade of gold and silver. "I think you'll have this life, one way or the other."

I couldn't help but grin. "You really think so?"

"I do. You've got it. Whatever the elusive 'it' is. You have it."

"What makes you so sure?" I asked, leaning in closer.

"It's just…something about the way you talk. The way your eyes light up when you speak about your work. The way you move. The way you burn with determination," Colin whispered, his voice now husky. In the dimly lit room, his eyes looked darker than usual. Hungry.

"God, Anna," he whispered. He reached out a hand, brushing a stray strand of wet hair away from my face. His touch sent shivers down my body, and I found myself leaning in even closer toward him.

"What?" I whispered, my voice barely audible.

"You are infuriating."

"Infuriating? Me? After the stunt you pulled today?" I asked, but my voice was still low. I was almost murmuring every word against Colin's lips, almost close enough to touch them.

"When I'm around you, I just can't help myself. I can't help but imagine…"

"Imagine what?"

"You know what," he said with a knowing smile. "But we can't."

"You're right. We definitely shouldn't."

"Even though I desperately want to," he added.

"Even though I'd do anything," I whispered back. "Anything to—"

Before I could finish my sentence, Colin pulled me close, his fingers tangled in my wet hair. I pressed my lips against his in a hungry, urgent kiss.

25

We didn't get back to the house until the early hours of the morning. I'd passed out in my room and slept a deep, deep sleep until the early afternoon hours, when I groggily opened my eyes and blinked away the last of my dreams. I'd dreamed that I had kissed Colin—

Oh, wait. That had really happened.

I groaned as I remembered the night before.

Mercifully, Colin had booked another temp to cover my morning shift while I recovered from the hangover. And possibly from the embarrassment of what ensued after our kiss.

After the kiss, Colin had gently withdrawn and shaken his head. I was still catching my breath, the world around me hazy from the wine and the endorphins.

"I'm sorry, Anna. I can't. Kara…"

"Oh," I'd said, feeling a lump in my throat. "I mean, of course. I understand. I'm sorry—"

"No, Anna. I'm sorry. After what you went through with Mr. Berg, I don't ever want you to feel like you are not wanted. But Kara—"

"It's okay," I'd said, putting on a false chirpiness that sounded poorly acted even to my ears. "It's nothing serious, right? We just let it get a bit too far."

"If it weren't for Kara," Colin whispered regretfully.

If it weren't for Kara, Colin and I could be together.

If it weren't for Kara, Colin could introduce me to all his Hollywood friends.

If it weren't for Kara, Colin and I could live in the giant, beautiful house that would be perfect without Kara's oppressive presence.

If it weren't for Kara...

"If it weren't for Kara," I'd echoed, forcing a smile.

The taxi home from the restaurant and the pool had been...well, not exactly awkward. Heartbreaking would be more accurate, though I didn't want to admit I was that desperate.

I rubbed sleep from my eyes and patted the mattress around my head, searching for my phone. I found it and grimaced at the time, then remembered I was relieved from my shift. Would Kara notice I was gone? Would she be curious what happened to me?

After a quick shower and a change of clothes, I padded two stories upstairs. One of the temps was sitting in front of Kara's room on a chair, with earbuds in, watching something on his phone.

"Is she sleeping?" I asked. The temp removed an earbud and looked up at me.

"Resting," he said, returning to his phone.

I slipped inside Kara's bedroom. She was propped up in bed, all changed into her regular, unremarkable beige loungewear. A tabloid magazine had been laid out for her.

"Good afternoon, Kara," I said. "How was yesterday? I hope you didn't wonder where I went. I just took an evening off."

Kara continued staring at the page, idly scratching away at it with the tip of her nail.

I turned to have a look over the room. Beside Kara's bed, a vase held wilting flowers I'd forgotten to replace; a box of accessories I'd scavenged for her from her walk-in wardrobe down the hall sat untouched. On the far side of her wall, across from the bed, was the painting of the sunset over the city skyline.

"I heard Mary got this for you." I spoke softly, mostly to myself. "I wonder why you still keep it up."

I stared at the painting. There were so few elements in the house that felt somehow tethered to Mary. The sound studio, where she had read lines with Colin. Kara's awards for the role Mary had lost to her. In the vicinity of both of those, I had found a cassette tape—a tape that revealed more about Mary and her dangerous paranoias. If that was what they were.

On a whim, I carefully lifted the painting an inch off the wall and reached out behind it, brushing against the rough surface of the wall. Then my fingers found something.

I traced the edge of the tape with my fingertips and pried it from the wall with my nail. I pulled it out from under the painting. The plastic case was yellowed with age.

I traced the faded label with my index finger.

There it was. The same label. *Kara.*

I quickly glanced over my shoulder. There Kara was still, idly staring and scratching, oblivious to what I was doing. I tucked the cassette tape in my pocket and walked over to Kara.

"What are you reading? Anything good?"

Kara ignored me. I leaned over to look—and froze.

It took me a moment to understand what I was looking at. It was hard to recognize the scene from a different perspective. On the tabloid spread, I could see myself, diving into traffic to grab the handles of Kara's wheelchair. I could see a panicked Flora. I hadn't realized she was holding her hands in front of her mouth, bracing to scream. This must have been the article Colin had read, how he'd learned about the close call.

But that wasn't all.

The part Kara had been idly scratching at, over and over again, was my face. I could only recognize myself from circumstance, from the headline blaring about Kara's near miss, from my clothes. The rest of my features had been rubbed to a pulp.

I instinctively recoiled, but as I did, Kara's hand suddenly snapped around my wrist. The movement took me by surprise, as did the tightness of Kara's grip. She opened her mouth as if to speak and hissed.

"Maihn…"

"Kara, let go," I commanded, yanking at my arm.

"Maihn…" she repeated.

And then I realized what she was saying.

Mine.

Colin is *mine*.

"Kara," I whispered. "Please let go…"

I felt her nails dig into me. Her eyes locked onto mine, two dark pools of venom.

"*Mine.*"

Then her skeletal fingers creaked open. I pulled my hand away, and I ran out the door.

26

I sped down the stairs, my breath coming in short gasps.

Kara hated me. Somehow, Kara knew something was going on with Colin and me. Kara wanted me gone.

But there was only so much she could do.

Kara was deeply unwell. Who knew how much of what she said or implied she actually meant? Like Colin had said, we did not know the extent of her brain damage.

But a tiny voice in my head would not let it rest. What if Kara was more cognizant than she let on? What if she was fueled by jealousy, vengeance, and possessiveness? What if she was simply biding her time?

I gripped the tape tighter in my fingers. I had to know what had happened to Mary.

I withdrew into the sound studio, located the cassette adapter, and powered up the computer.

I held my breath and pressed play. Mary's familiar, strained voice came through the speakers.

I think I know what's happening now. I think my whole marriage has been some kind of sick test. I think I've been watched the whole time.

Her voice grew more urgent. *And I've failed. I don't even know when, but somehow I failed, and now I'm being replaced.*

A barely audible murmur on the tape.

Kara is not my friend. She's in on this. You're all in on this. You're all plotting against me.

Mary's voice picked up a notch. *You've been in on it too, haven't you?*

Another, more assuaging murmur.

I don't believe you. He wants me replaced. He wants me out of the way for a new, better wife.

There was a sudden crash, as if a glass object had shattered against a wall or the floor on impact. The interviewer's protests were drowned out by Mary's high-strung voice.

Don't lie to me! I know it! I know it...

The audio cut off; the rest of the tape was just static.

I sat there for a long time, taking in the contents of the tape. It was not at all what I had expected. Mary had seemed delusional, paranoid, believed that anyone could be out to get her.

Was Mary saying...*Colin* was responsible for her death?

27

As I sat in the sound studio, lost in thought, the door swung open, and a familiar figure stepped through. It was Micky, wearing his usual cardigan and his glasses slightly askew on his nose.

"Thought I'd find you here," he said, standing rigidly with his arms crossed by the door.

"Micky!" I pushed myself back from the table, retracting the cassette from the player. Micky wasn't paying attention to that; instead, he continued to stare me down with a serious expression. In all the time I'd known him, I didn't remember him ever entering a room without a humorous quip. But now all traces of the easygoing Micky were gone.

"We were supposed to record last night, remember? But you weren't here."

Shit. I had completely forgotten.

"Oh, gosh, Micky. I'm sorry. But listen, I don't know if you heard my interview? The response has been fantastic—"

"Anyway, I wanted to tell you," Micky interjected. "I don't think this is going to work."

I paused, shocked. All I managed was a single, strained word. "What?!"

"You're just...not the right fit for the role, like I thought you would be."

"But, Micky," I said, getting up from my chair. "We've already recorded the whole pilot. We've recorded *far beyond* the pilot. You said we practically had it in the bag. And *now* you're firing me?"

Micky seemed unmoved. "You'll be reimbursed, of course."

This was insane. I took a step toward him, propelled by the injustice of it all.

"Is this because I rejected you, Micky? You know how important this chance is to me!"

Sleep with them, don't sleep with them. It made no difference. At the end of the day, they would do what they wanted and discard me without a second thought.

"No."

Then he suddenly took a step forward. I instinctively retreated.

"Get out of here, Anna. You're done. You don't need the studio anymore. *Go home.*"

"Back off, Micky," I whispered, even though my heart was racing in my chest like a rabbit's. "I've worked too hard to give this up. I belong here."

"With Colin?" Micky asked, his eyes darkening. "Do you think you really know him?"

"Colin is—"

"What about me?" Colin asked, his voice ringing out from behind Micky.

28

Micky and I both turned to see Colin standing in the doorway of the sound studio.

"Colin," I said shakily. "This is—"

"I know Micky," Colin said, his eyes flitting between the two of us, trying to gauge the situation.

"You...you know each other?" I asked incredulously, glancing between Colin and Micky. Micky's face was a stone wall, revealing nothing.

"Yeah. We've been friends for years, since we both moved to LA. He told me you'd worked together, put in a good word when I hired you —" Colin paused, regarding Micky quizzically. "Wait, it's your project Anna is working on at the moment, in the studio?"

My head was spinning. Micky didn't only know *of* the Harringtons—he actually *knew* them, and he'd kept it from me all this time.

"Why wouldn't you tell me you were in the studio? You know I love to see you working on projects here," Colin said.

I had so many questions. But there was one thing I instantly fixated on. The reason I'd been so desperate to land the job with the Harringtons in the first place.

"Excuse me, what?" I asked, my voice rising a couple octaves within the span of a single sentence. "You've been allowed to use the studio this whole time?"

I expected Micky to offer to explain. Surely, there was a reasonable explanation for this.

But he said nothing, merely looked between the two of us with a dark expression.

Colin finally answered for him. "Yeah, he's got keys and everything. He's been using it for years."

Colin's initially confused expression hardened.

"Look, there's obviously something going on here I'm not privy to. Care to explain?"

"Micky…Micky fired me off his project after I rejected him," I said.

After what Colin had said about him and Micky being friends for a long time, I was worried he wouldn't believe me.

But Colin proved me wrong. He walked to my side and put his hand on my shoulder.

I expected him to ask Micky if this was true. I expected him to mediate some sort of conversation, to try to figure out why there had been a misunderstanding.

"Get out, Micky." Colin said. "And don't bother showing your face around here."

Wordlessly, Micky picked up his backpack and made his way toward the door. It was strange to me that I'd ever found Micky dorky, even pitiable: His eyes were dark now, a cold rage in them I'd never seen.

"Good fucking luck," Micky hissed at me as he passed, and then he was out.

My heart still hammered wildly in my chest.

"Anna?" Colin asked carefully. "Are you okay?"

"No," I said. "Can we…make sure he is gone? That he can't come back?"

"You've got it," Colin said, leaving the room. I had my arms wrapped around myself and was just wiping away some wayward tears when he returned, five minutes later.

"To hell with Micky and his project," Colin said, clasping me by the arms and gazing at me with passionate sincerity. "I'll help you. You've got what it takes, Anna. The sky is the limit. You only have to reach for what you want, and you'll get there, I promise."

"It's not just that…Colin…I think there's something really strange going on."

"What do you mean?"

"I mean, Micky hired me under false pretenses…someone has been messing with me, scaring me and vandalizing my stuff…" I wiped my eyes again. "And I don't know…how much do you really know about Mary's death? You said she killed herself? What if she didn't…what if someone was out to get her?"

"Hey, hey," Colin said, lifting my chin so I met his eyes. "Anna, easy. I'm here for you."

"I'm just really scared, Colin."

"I'll protect you. I'll take care of it." Colin pulled me into a hug, and I sank against him, tears welling up in my eyes. "Trust me."

It felt so good to let someone take care of me. To call the shots.

"Everything is going to be okay," Colin breathed in my ear.

"You promise?" I asked, nuzzling against him.

"Anna…" he whispered, pained. "We shouldn't…"

I looked in his eyes. "We *should*."

His breath caught in his throat and his eyes lowered to meet mine, his mind scrambling to make a choice.

Was he going to push me away like before?

"Anna…you are going to be the death of me," he whispered. And then he kissed me. We backed, kissing, until we collided into the desk. With one smooth motion, he lifted me on it. We kissed hungrily, desperately, as if there was nothing or no one else in the world.

He wouldn't push me away this time.

29

There was a whole new reason the sound studio was my favorite room in the house.

After we'd started, Colin had asked me if we should move to his bedroom. I wasn't sure. I felt comfortable in the soundproof studio, underground, a world away from the rest of the house. I felt like taking this somewhere other than a secluded downtown pool or an underground room would make us more…vulnerable. That some power intent on destroying what we finally had would find us.

But maybe I was being paranoid. I knew Colin would protect me.

I followed as Colin led me by the hand to his bedroom. By the doorway, he picked me up and carried me to his bed, where we fell right down into the tangled satin sheets and lost ourselves in them, in each other.

That night, when we curled into one another in the dark, I told him about my mother.

"How old were you?" Colin asked. He was tracing lazy circles on my back. The touch of his fingers against my bare skin made me shiver. I still couldn't believe this was really happening. That Colin Harrington was here. With *me*.

But I was willing to suspend disbelief a little while longer.

"Twelve. She'd been depressed for a while, from what my aunts told me. But I guess I didn't really understand that then. I just thought she was tired."

"I'm sorry, Anna," Colin said, kissing my shoulder. I smiled, leaning my head against his.

"I guess I should feel sad whenever I think about my mom. But most of the time I just feel angry. Angry she left me with my father, who didn't even seem to want me."

"I'd never leave you," Colin whispered.

"Then don't," I said, so quietly I wasn't sure if he heard me.

Colin continued running his finger along my back. "You know…I told my friends about you, Anna."

I couldn't help but smirk. "You've told your friends?"

I could feel rather than see him smile. "They can tell I'm crazy about you. But they're not…as sure yet. They are undecided."

"Oh," I said, a little disappointed. "Undecided how?"

"They think you're promising, but…" He paused, his fingers running up my back and along the side of my neck, his touch feather-light. "They're waiting for something, I guess. A gesture. A sign of loyalty. Something that proves that you're worth…"

Leaving Kara for?

He searched for the right words. How do you delicately ask if someone is worth leaving your sick wife for?

I supposed I could understand. It wasn't personal. His friends were just looking out for him.

He turned my face gently sideways, so his eyes met mine. "You are serious about this, aren't you?"

"Of course I am, Colin."

"And you'd stick by me?"

"I'd do anything for you."

He grinned and pulled me in for another kiss. I soon forgot everything else.

I woke up in the early morning to Colin quietly getting dressed. He leaned over, his unbuttoned cotton shirt grazing my cheek, and planted a kiss on my forehead.

"I need to go into town, Anna. To take care of some things."

"Are you sneaking out?" I murmured.

Colin tilted his head. "I'll make it up to you. Dinner here, tonight. I'll make sure your shift is covered."

"You can't always bribe me with food," I murmured before falling back asleep.

When I woke up again, the sun had cast long bars of orange light over the bed, over my naked skin. It was almost noon.

I pulled on my clothes, sneaking through the house, praying I wouldn't run into a maid or any of Colin's other staff. But I got downstairs and into the safety of my room without any incident.

That's when I noticed there was something waiting for me on my pillow.

It was a cassette tape. I stared at it for a moment, confused, convinced that despite her adamant insistence of her innocence, the maid had gone through my things again and left it as a warning; but when I checked the previous tapes, they were still safely tucked away in the hiding places I had found for them. No, this one had been left for me.

Again, it was only distinguished by a small label, in the same handwriting: *Kara.*

There was no question now: someone had meant for me to find these tapes. But who? And why? What purpose could they possibly serve?

Whoever had left them obviously had access to the house.

Mary had been scared, and she wasn't sure whether it was paranoia or whether she had reason to be. I wasn't sure either. I wanted answers.

I slipped into the sound studio.

30

Really...I never thought my life would be like this. So seemingly perfect, and yet so terrible.

You would look at me and think—she has everything.

But you wouldn't understand. Nobody would.

I don't have it in me to withstand this life.

I know they have feelings for each other. I heard them whispering the other day. I heard Kara say she wishes she met Colin before I was there. She is taking him from me, just like how she took my role.

This is the only way it can end.

Because when she wants something...she gets it. That's how it's always been, as long as I've known her.

This is the story of how I die.

That was always what this was, wasn't it?

31

It was clear now, following the last tape. Kara had to go.

I was going to bring it up with Colin over dinner. Which was why it was important he was in the best mood possible.

My fingertips grazed the silk of the dress I was wearing. It was a rich, complementary shade of blue. It had waited for me on my bed, the fabric cascading over the crisp white sheets. Alongside it, Colin had left a box of jewelry. I clasped the necklace around my neck, where its cool weight settled into the grooves of my collarbones. I doubted Colin just had a necklace like this lying around. Had he bought it for me, or had it belonged to Kara?

I assessed myself in the mirror. Who would have thought that a few months ago I was a frizzy-haired, unemployed, homeless, un-hireable actress? Now I was the talk of the town. I knew famous directors on a first-name basis. Dressed like this, I could pass for Mrs. Harrington.

I ascended the staircase and found Colin in the dining room, where a twinkling vista unfolded through the giant glazed windows under a velvety violet sky slowly dimming into darkness.

He stood by the table in a tailored suit, lit in the soft glow of the overhead lights, his pale blue eyes appraising me. A man behind him was working in the kitchen, juggling multiple pots and pans, and the scent of searing spices emanated from them.

"Anna, you look stunning," Colin told me, directing me to sit down.

"Thank you. I got a little help from a friend."

"He must have quite the taste," Colin said with a grin.

"Eh," I said, raising my hand to the diamond-encrusted necklace and feigning disappointment as I followed Colin to a seat by the giant glass table. "It will have to do."

"I've hired a private chef for us," Colin said as he pulled out my chair, indicating the man behind the counter who gave me an odd look and a tense smile. Was the look because he knew who I was, or because he didn't?

"Don't worry," Colin added as he leaned over my ear. "I'll dismiss him by dessert."

"Don't you dare," I murmured.

"I'm not taking any chances," Colin smiled, then circled around to the other side of the table where he seated himself. "Because tonight is about us, Anna."

"It is?" I watched as Colin deftly uncorked a bottle of wine and poured us glasses.

"It can be, if you want it," Colin lifted his glass. "Let's toast to…"

"Limitless potential!" I suggested. It was a term Colin repeated often in his podcast. He caught the reference and laughed.

"For those who have the nerve to see it through."

We drank. The hallowed silence was only punctuated by the chef moving about the kitchen, chopping things violently and efficiently on a cutting board or shuffling ingredients on the pan. A moment later he emerged with the first dish, a grilled piece of fish.

"Your arrangement," the chef announced, placing the dishes in front of us.

Why not call it a dish? I exchanged a look with Colin, who grinned. It reminded me of the jokes we'd shared at the expense of pretentious Hollywood the first time we met, at my interview. I looked down at the delicious meal and dug in, my fork piercing the white flesh of the fish.

I didn't care what it was called, it tasted heavenly.

"You know, Anna. Regarding our toast. My mentors always say that 'ambition' has been made a bad word, even though it drives all human progress. They believe it is worth celebrating. That societal rules are ultimately suggestions."

I smiled. "Like sneaking into an off-limits pool?"

"Sometimes you have to bend or even break a few rules to get ahead," Colin replied, smiling.

"Would you say you've done that, with your podcast?"

"Among other things." He gave a conspiratorial wink.

I took a sip of my wine.

Colin was staring at me, as if looking for the perfect opening.

My heart skipped erratically. Could this be the moment? Would Colin tell me he was sending Kara away? I wondered silently what expression would be appropriate for when he revealed his plan. Shock? Sympathy? Lust?

"Anna. There's something I need to ask you."

I held my breath, waiting for Colin to say the words.

I am sending Kara away. You don't have to keep looking over your shoulder anymore. We will live here together, and our life will be perfect.

"I've held onto hope for so long…hope that things would change with Kara," he started. "That I'd be able to help her realize her full potential. But now, I've lost that hope."

I nodded, encouraging him to continue, nervously fidgeting with the stem of my wine glass. "I'm so sorry. You really have done all you can. It's out of your hands."

"I hate losing," Colin said. "Unless there's a way I can transform a loss into a victory."

That felt like an odd way of phrasing it. But I supposed it was on brand for Colin to try to find the silver lining.

"Then…you'll put Kara in a care home?" I asked, my voice hopeful.

Colin's hand found mine. He rubbed it with his thumb as he continued his contemplation.

"It was the same with Mary, you know. She was so talented. Who knows how high she could have gone, if she wasn't so fragile? If she was willing to fight for her right to be at the top?"

"I…don't understand." Colin's words felt strange. "It didn't seem like she was in much condition to fight. She was sick. She needed help."

"Oh, she had a lot of help. So many people tried to help her. There were so many opportunities for her to do or not do things to get ahead."

His blue eyes, rimmed by those dark lashes, searched mine. His hand gripped me tighter.

"But *you*, Anna. You're not like them. You have what it takes, don't you?"

I had clawed my way up from my small-town roots and dirtied reputation to this position, and with Colin by my side, I could do anything.

"Yes," I said confidently. "I have what it takes."

"Good." Colin gave me a wolfish smile. "Then there's just one thing I need you to do."

Our conversation was interrupted by the gentle approach of the chef, bearing the second dish. It was as beautiful as the last and smelled even better, but I had lost my appetite.

I felt like Colin was dodging my questions. Why was it so difficult for him to admit that Kara needed to go?

Colin's face lit up at the sight of the food. "This looks absolutely fantastic," he exclaimed, his voice filled with genuine appreciation as he beamed at the chef. "You've really outdone yourself."

"Thank you, Mr. Harrington. More wine?" the chef asked.

"Not for me. Anna?"

"Yes, okay," I said, trying to push intrusive thoughts out of my mind. I wanted to enjoy the evening—Colin had obviously put a lot of thought into it.

The chef smoothly poured a current of wine into my glass.

"This wine tastes interesting," I said. I didn't want to say *bad,* because I appreciated what Colin had done here, but there was definitely something wrong with it. Cork taint?

"It's non-alcoholic," Colin explained. He exchanged a look with the chef, who smiled and retreated into the kitchen. I wondered if the chef had messed up somehow, failed to provide the right wine.

Colin eagerly dug into the food, evidently satisfied. I moved my own food around with my fork and tried to locate the source of my discomfort. Was it that the promise of sending Kara away hadn't yet materialized? Was it that I felt like I was missing something? Or that Colin was?

At least someone had their eyes on Kara.

"How long is the temp staying to watch Kara?" I asked Colin. He took a moment to swallow and wipe his mouth, neatly folding the napkin on his lap after he did.

"I sent the temp home an hour or so ago. Kara is asleep."

"No one is watching her?" I asked. For some reason, I felt uncomfortable with the thought of Kara being unsupervised, and my heartrate picked up.

"Relax. She's sleeping. She'll be taken care of shortly, anyway."

"I just really feel like she shouldn't be left alone, Colin. The other day, she vandalized my picture, and—"

"Anna, please. We are supposed to be enjoying our time together. I am going to need you to *relax*."

I stopped talking and took a sip of wine, my nervous gesture almost causing the wine to slosh out of the glass. Was this what Colin wanted when he said I needed to do something for him?

Was this a test?

32

But I just couldn't let it go. Not after hearing the tapes. And not after Kara grabbing me like she did. No matter how pushy I was being, I had to make Colin understand.

"Look, Colin. To tell you the truth, I've found some cassette tapes around the house…"

A slight look of surprise flashed over Colin's face.

"They were Mary's…I know it was an intrusion to listen to them, and I know a lot of what Mary said on them was probably tinged by her paranoia…but I'm scared. *She* was scared. Of Kara stealing her life. Micky told me the rough details of her death, and I just feel like… maybe it wasn't an accident. That maybe Kara had something to do with it."

"That's quite a theory, Anna," Colin said, unfazed. He was still chewing his food, as if I'd just made a comment about the meal, or something just as trivial.

I decided to press on. I *had* to make him understand.

"Look, there's something very strange going on. I'm worried about Kara. I know you think she is harmless, but I can't shake the feeling something is going on that I can't quite piece together, something she's plotting. I don't feel *safe* with her around, Colin. It's like she's always watching, waiting for the perfect moment to strike."

"You don't need to worry, Anna. I have everything under control."

His reassurances did nothing to alleviate the knot of unease that had taken root in my gut—quite the opposite. Something was wrong. Very wrong. But I couldn't understand what was going on. It was like being presented with a complicated equation: My mind was straining to solve it, but I desperately needed more information to fill in the blanks.

Meanwhile, the chef circled around from the kitchen and laid our final course in front of us: an immaculate chocolate flambé. He placed a spoon beside my portion, the metal clinking gently against the glass table. Colin's face lit up with delight.

"This looks divine. You are free to leave for the night. Thank you for making this evening so special."

The chef gave a little bow. "It was my pleasure, Mr. Harrington." Then he turned to me. "I hope you enjoyed the meal as well, miss?"

I forced a smile, even though the muscles in my face felt strangely uncooperative. "It was wonderful, thank you so much."

"I do hope you feel much better soon." The chef smiled at the both of us and took his leave. I watched him go, a part of me longing to call out and beg him to stay, although I didn't know why. I heard his footsteps recede and the distant smart door close with a barely audible hiss. Then Colin and I were utterly alone.

Colin picked up his spoon. "You know, I'm curious. What have you heard about Kara's accident?"

I swallowed. I wasn't sure I liked how Colin was leading these conversations. "I…I heard she was drunk. That she fell off a balcony?"

Colin hummed noncommittally, dipping his spoon into his flambé, coating the silver in a glossy chocolate sheen. "She did. You know that most accidents happen in the home, don't you, Anna? Especially in a house like this. So angular. So full of steep drops. You notice a distinct lack of railings, don't you? The architect suggested that they broke up the façade unpleasantly. I have to agree."

"Colin, please. I don't know what this has to do with anything. I need you to take me seriously…"

"I take you *very* seriously, Anna. I'm always serious about my prospects." Colin leaned back in his chair, fixing me with a penetrating stare. "Look, if you don't want to talk architecture, let's talk about something that *will* interest you. I want to think about your future. About the life you could have here, with me."

Despite my confusion, my heart skipped a beat. A life with Colin was everything I'd ever wanted. A chance to be someone. A chance to live this enchanted life.

But I pushed those thoughts aside for the moment.

"Of course I want that," I breathed, my voice barely above a whisper. "But Kara…I can't just ignore what's happening, Colin."

"Well, maybe you don't have to. Maybe we can solve your problem."

I breathed a sigh of relief. *Finally.* "So, you'll send Kara to a care home?"

Colin smiled. "No. You will take care of her."

"As a nurse…?" I whispered, feeling like my voice had left me. But I knew that wasn't what he meant at all.

"Anna, please. You're not an idiot. You know exactly what I mean."

I did and I didn't. Despite all the things Colin had said that night, I didn't want to accept he meant what I thought he meant.

But Colin continued relentlessly.

"I need you to kill Kara. And then I can give you the life you have always wanted."

33

We sat for a moment in tense silence. It was only interrupted by the sudden buzz of my pager. I reached for it instinctively.

Colin's hand shot out, gripping my wrist with a force that made me gasp. My eyes desperately glanced about the room, cataloging doors and exits. All too far away.

"Colin, let go. You're hurting me." I tried to wring my arm back, but Colin's grip was like a steel vise. Unyielding.

"Ignore it," he commanded, his voice low. "Kara can wait. This moment is about you and me, Anna. About *your* future."

My mind raced as I stared at Colin, trying to reconcile the man I thought I knew with the person before me. The familiar warmth and easy charm that radiated from him had vanished, replaced by a chilling decisiveness that made me sick to my stomach.

"But you asked me about the care home," I said, scrambling to make sense of it all. "Where my relative is. I thought…"

There was something lupine about the way he shook his head, his eyes never leaving me. Slow, considered, like an animal with its prey cornered.

"I never intended to send her away, Anna. Kara is *my* project. *My* failure. And she will remain under my watch for as long as she draws breath." He tilted his head slightly. "Which hopefully won't be too much longer."

My project? My failure?

My heart hammered in my chest as I began to understand.

"Mary was right. She was so scared you wanted to replace her…and you did. With Kara. And now you want me to replace Kara? Why?"

Colin released my hand. "You could be so much, Anna. I knew it from the moment I saw you. I know exactly how to manage you."

I pulled my hand to myself and rubbed my wrist, feeling a bruise forming. "Like you managed Mary and Kara?"

Colin scoffed and dipped his spoon into his flambé. "It wasn't my fault. Mary was so loveable, but she was meek. She lacked the will to compete and couldn't handle the stress of the maneuvers we did to make her get ahead. And Kara, well, she was competitive, I'll give her that. Ruthless. She never had a problem playing dirty. But at some point, she grew a conscience. It started bothering her that people hated her. She was depressed, and mopey, and she lashed out, and the press got worse. It was a vicious cycle. And then came the drinking…"

Colin shook his head. "I thought of it as a challenge at first. How could I reign her back in? What would make Kara popular and beloved? Well, my question was answered one day. She'd have to suffer something deeply traumatic and emerge victorious. Something terrible enough that it would absolve her of all her sins, make people feel sorry for her. It would endear her to everyone."

"You…you manufactured Kara's fall? To make her *popular*?"

"We helped her, even if she couldn't appreciate it. Once her bones healed and doctors didn't find anything physically wrong with her, I thought it would be just a matter of time before we could relaunch her career. But now that she has failed to snap out of it, she has proven herself as useless as Mary."

"We?" I asked.

Colin licked his spoon and set it down on the table, ignoring my question.

"And sadly, as useless as you, it seems," he continued.

My heart stopped. "Colin, please…"

Colin gave a great sigh. "You know why I hired you? Why I hired any of the companions? I thought of it as a final ditch effort to motivate Kara. She was always the jealous type. Proud. I thought—well, if a pretty young thing paraded in front of her won't motivate her to get up and prove herself, nothing could."

I swallowed. My mouth tasted strange. Was that a symptom of fear?

"But then I saw how you sabotaged that CV following our interview," Colin continued. "And yes, I had an investigator look into your past, so I know what you did to Mr. Berg."

He nodded appreciatively. "I'm not talking just about the seduction, but the fentanyl you snuck into his coke after he failed to give you the part you'd earned."

My hands shook. I felt like I might be sick.

"That showed *drive*. And it worked, didn't it? He's comatose in a care facility now."

Colin wiped his lips with the napkin and pushed his meal away.

"But I've presented you multiple opportunities on a silver platter. You could have supplanted Flora much earlier and with much more ease. You could have pressured me to move Kara to a care home or maybe manufactured a little accident. Hell, Anna, you didn't even have to do anything—just let her roll out into traffic when you had the chance." He shrugged a little sadly. "They warned me this might happen. I insisted you had it in you. But I suppose I was wrong about you. You don't quite have what it takes. You're not *really* willing to fight for me."

They warned him? What was he talking about? I closed my eyes, willing myself to wake up from a bad dream. But I couldn't. This was happening.

"*Why* are you doing this?" I asked weakly.

"Don't you see, Anna? I'm good at helping people. It's who I am. You should have let me help you too."

I felt nauseated. I felt lightheaded.

"Now that you've rejected this life, I'll have to find someone better. Someone deserving. And I can't have that if you are around to ruin it."

I was finding it difficult to concentrate on Colin's words. The whole room seemed to be slowly spinning. Through the blur, I could see Colin at the end of the table, still talking.

"Your death would be suspicious. But Kara's? She's so helpless. How could she defend herself against the jealous companion who envied her life? Who had a hopeless crush on her boss?"

"No," I murmured. "No, no…"

"Kara's death will be on you, Anna," Colin continued, ignoring my distress. "The inept companion who lied about her proficiency to secure a job she was unqualified for. Who manufactured evidence against her colleague, a qualified nurse. Flora will be only too happy to testify."

He shrugged.

"I still haven't figured out how you'll do it. Do you give her too many painkillers? Do you smother her with a pillow?"

I shook my head again. It was growing hard for me to piece Colin's words together into sentences that made any sense. "You won't—I can't—"

"Or maybe you shoot her?"

At this, Colin withdrew a gun and rested it against the table. The same gun he'd shown off to me when there had been an intruder in the house. The same gun he had sworn to protect me with.

I froze, staring down into the barrel across the table, aimed at me.

"Well, I guess you'll find out soon enough," Colin said. "Now, Anna, you're going to do exactly what I tell you…"

The whole world was growing hazy, the edges of the room softening, as the drug Colin had slipped in my wine slowly but surely circled my veins. I knew I didn't have long to act.

So I did the only thing I could.

I stumbled out of the chair and ran.

34

I ran. I stumbled. I crawled.

My eyelids were drooping. My limbs had never felt this heavy.

I couldn't get away.

Colin's echoing footsteps trailed me slowly, confidently, as I hopelessly stumbled down the hallway away from the kitchen and toward the front door. I tried to hold onto the cool walls to steady myself, but my body betrayed me, and I stumbled, bringing down a painting in my wake. I heard its glass shatter to my side.

"Anna, be careful," Colin chided me. "That's an original O'Keeffe."

I wanted to tell him to fuck off, but my tongue was glued to the roof of my mouth.

By some miracle, I made it to the front door. I clawed at the smooth metal handle, which I'd pushed down a hundred times before. But this time, it wouldn't budge.

"I suppose you don't have your smartkey in that dress," Colin mused, closing in on me.

"Open," I hissed at the door. "Let me out."

Nothing happened.

"I should tell you, I changed your access priorities for the door and the gate. They no longer recognize your voice." Colin chuckled. "I confess, I was eager to see your reaction."

I tried the door again. "Please," I whispered.

"Here, let me help," Colin said, and I felt his arm grip my waist, hard, yanking my hand off the handle. The cold metal of the gun lodged against my stomach, freezing me into place. I thought to clumsily grab for it in his waistband.

He laughed. "Oh, Anna, now's not the time for fooling around. We have work to do!"

He pulled me along like a rag doll, my feet dragging along the hard marble floor. He pulled me back past the kitchen and down toward the stairs to the basement.

"Down we go," Colin said, hoisting me into the stairwell.

My feet slammed against each cold stone step. I weakly clawed at Colin's arm. I felt like I'd heard that somewhere once: that you should claw your assaulters. Something about nails and DNA. I couldn't keep my thoughts straight.

Finally, Colin released me, and I stumbled down the rest of the stairs, painfully dropping in a heap at the foot of the steps.

"Let's see." Colin mused as he walked over to the bar, gun raised in one hand, and began rummaging around for bottles with his free hand. "You kill Kara in a drugged haze, then retreat downstairs to drink some more. Maybe out of guilt, maybe out of habit."

"You won't…" I slurred.

"...get away with it? Not very original, Anna." Colin pulled out a bottle, pleased with his choice. He walked over and lazily opened the bottle, unceremoniously sloshing me with its contents.

"I told the chef we were celebrating the decision to send you to rehab. He was very sympathetic. I don't think the story of your relapse will be a big surprise. Up-and-coming actress with a dark past, intoxicated by her newfound attention. I expect his testimony of the night will corroborate my timeline."

Then he grabbed me and began dragging me to the sound studio. I knew I should have put up a fight. I should have flailed and screamed. But I didn't have it in me. Even focusing my eyes was a herculean effort.

"It's going to be so much easier to find my next protégé without Kara looming around," Colin said as he opened the sound studio door and hauled me inside. "To be honest, she freaks people out."

Mustering my strength, I pushed myself into a sitting position with shaking arms, my hair falling over my face, and stared at Colin with as much venom as I could muster.

He looked me over and licked his lips. "God, I really wish you'd had it in you."

This time, I regained control of my mouth.

"Fuck you," I hissed.

"You already did, darling. Now, if you'll excuse me, I need to go attend to my wife."

Colin closed the door, leaving me in silence. Even if I'd had the energy to scream, it would have been futile. The room was utterly soundproof.

I crawled across the plush carpet, my fingers digging desperately at the fibers.

Come on. Come on.

I hauled myself up to the soundboard, my fingers scrabbling across the dials and buttons for the keyboard. The computer woke up with a melodic chime that bent and distorted in my mind, barely hanging onto consciousness.

I had to try something, anything.

Come on, Anna. Come on.

Think.

35

THE PAST

KARA

I think I fell in love with Colin the first time I saw him.

That was three years ago. It was April. I was standing on the lawn, smoothing my dark blue dress, doing my best to avoid eye contact with the waitress who was buzzing around, incessantly offering a tray of treats that individually eclipsed my daily calorie quota. I was just wondering how long I was obligated to spend there —surely turning up was enough—when I saw him.

He had that head of slightly curled dark hair, that wide, boyish smile, and those bright blue eyes rimmed with dark lashes. In Hollywood, there are plenty of men people might describe as "attractive." For heaven's sake, the male lead in my current project had been named Sexiest Man Alive by at least half a dozen women's magazines, an accolade he unironically mentioned far too often.

But Colin wasn't just attractive. He was magnetic.

My gaze followed him as he made his way across the lawn, stopping here and there to talk to the well-dressed wedding party. I watched him brush the hair out of his eyes, the way he flashed his white teeth when he laughed.

I watched the generous way he navigated conversation. I was close enough to hear bits and pieces. I noted how he had the ability to say even offensive things with an innocence and frankness that was hard to be offended by. I watched him slip in and out of conversations and incorporate himself effortlessly in every company, like a minnow weaving in and out of the stream, a perfect natural.

I admired that. Maybe because I envied it. Hollywood hadn't yet decided I was the devil incarnate, but a number of executives, directors, and coworkers had already let it slip that I was *difficult,* and I was beginning to feel the ramifications.

And he was wearing a suit because he was getting married to one of my oldest friends.

I watched Mary steer him over and rearranged my face into an expression of cool indifference, sipping my flute of champagne. It wasn't hard; people told me it was my default expression. But even as I stared levelly at the advancing couple, my pulse quickened in my chest.

"Kara! You came!" Mary exclaimed as she arrived, a little breathlessly. Mary had always been remarkably short, and Colin was notably tall, so she'd most likely had to stride twice as fast to keep up with him. But she smiled brightly, unable to hide the pride in her expression as she looked from me to Colin.

Mary looked so beautiful. Joy radiated on her dewy, pink-cheeked, doll-like face. I leaned over and gave her a kiss on the cheek.

"Congratulations, *corazón.*"

"I'm so grateful you could make it. It means a lot, you being here. I know it must have been a nightmare with the shoot…"

"Production gave me hell for it, and I'm off the director's Christmas cake list, but I think I'll survive," I quipped. "Mary, *nena*, you look stunning."

Mary gave a little twirl, then turned around and placed her hands on Colin's chest. "Kara, I'd like you to officially meet my fiancé, Colin."

"You're going to have to get used to calling me husband in a minute." Colin extended a hand over as Mary beamed. "I've heard a lot about you, Kara."

"I don't know anyone who hasn't," I replied coolly. "All terrible things, I know."

"Ah, I don't listen to gossip," Colin waved his hand, dismissing the idea of Hollywood hearsay as if swatting a fly. "I've heard everything worth knowing from Mary. Besides," he added, leaning over a little conspiratorially, "sometimes, you have to bite back."

Something purred in the pit of my stomach. I concealed any reaction by taking a sip of champagne and turning to Mary.

"Brave girl. Don't people think it's unlucky for the groom to see the bride before the wedding?"

"I trust my luck," Mary said sincerely. "After all, I met Colin, didn't I?"

Colin smiled at her fondly.

"You two sicken me," I said with a small smile. "Go off and get married or something."

"It was great to see you, Kara. Don't be a stranger." Mary gave me another small hug. "I need you," she whispered.

I didn't think much about that whisper as I watched them recede to the altar set at the end of the lawn, as the guests took their places and the ceremony began, as I slipped out and took a taxi back to the airport, thinking about why I'd gone through all the effort to attend in the first place. Probably out of some kind of guilt or obligation.

After all, Mary and I had been close friends. Once upon a time, when we were both broke and unknown. But now we were older, competing for the same roles. Chewed up by the same publications when we either played it safe or tried too hard or didn't otherwise play by the million unwritten rules that governed how to conduct yourself in the public eye.

I didn't think about that whisper when Mary killed herself, or a little less than a year later, when I married Colin and moved into the house that had belonged to her, thinking I'd finally made it to my dream life.

I only thought about that whisper much, much later, after the fall. When I was lying on the pavement under our second-story balcony, trapped in my broken body, on the periphery of consciousness.

Somewhere far, far away, rang the siren of an ambulance. And beside me, through the haze of shock and pain, Colin's leather shoes at my eye level, pacing back and forth. His heels crunched against the broken glass.

I tried to speak. But the words came out from between my lips as a froth of blood.

Colin was on the phone to the paramedics.

"Yes," he was sobbing. "Yes, I think she's still breathing…please, please hurry."

Like me, he was a really good actor.

36

Almost a year following Mary and Colin's wedding, in the tail end of spring, I arrived at the Harringtons' household. I paid the cab driver and walked down the driveway, my leather Chanel travel bag hanging from the crook of my arm.

I wasn't sure what I should pack with me. What do you pack when your old friend's new husband sends you a distressed email practically *begging* for you to come visit her? Telling you her mental health issues have flared up? That it started right after she lost a role to you? That she needed her oldest friend? Two cashmere sweaters, a jade roller, and a 300-dollar jar of night cream?

I found the whole situation hard to believe. Our past, along with Mary's depressive and manic swings, seemed like ancient history. Not this charmed present, where she lived in a house like this with a husband like that.

She had much better resources now than when we'd been young, broke actresses, struggling to make rent and dealing with shitty boyfriends and roommates. Now she had money to hire expert psychologists and afford medication.

What did she need *me* for?

I faltered in my steps as I recalled the film. Mary had already been cast and the casting announced when it became apparent she was not well enough to continue prep. They'd called the runner up. They'd called me.

Or maybe I'd called them and emphasized just how available and eager I was to do the film once I'd heard Mary was having trouble.

I shook my head to clear any lingering guilt. It was a cutthroat industry, and this was the name of the game. If Mary truly hadn't managed to convince the producers she was well enough for the film and she'd taken the loss of the role so hard, then maybe she wasn't cut out for this.

She was a beautiful young woman living in a multimillion-dollar house. She'd get over it. She'd be fine.

Even though Mary Harrington was not exactly a household name, she had an adoring fanbase nonetheless that did not take kindly to her recasting. So when I'd told my producers and agent about taking a few days off to visit Mary in the middle of preproduction, they'd been unexpectedly supportive, even insistent. My agent told me to take pictures, if I could. Something to demonstrate there was no bad blood.

I didn't want to believe that constituted the reason I was here. I wanted to believe I was better than that.

I barely made it to the door when Colin opened it. He must have been following my progression from the street down the driveway. I hadn't seen him in person since the wedding, although his presence had increased exponentially since we'd met, and he was everywhere. I'd convinced myself I'd be jaded to the effect he had on me by now, but it was different, seeing him in person. He was still as breathtakingly handsome as ever. Even if he looked very tired.

We exchanged a brief, stiff hug.

"Where is she?" I asked.

I shouldn't have bothered to ask. Right at that moment, there was a resounding crash that echoed from further in the house.

"Are you ready for this?" Colin asked.

I stiffened, but nodded sharply. I wasn't the type to run from problems. It was one of the traits I was most proud of in myself.

That didn't mean I was ready for what we found in the kitchen.

Mary was surrounded by broken glass and ceramic. She had been progressively dropping glasses and dishes from the cabinets and shelves. She must have demolished half the tableware. From the efficient way she was proceeding, it looked almost like a performance art piece rather than real life. Rather than an old friend.

She swerved around when she heard our approach and froze when she saw me. It's shocking how much one person can transform in a year. Rosy-cheeked, smiley, bright Mary had been replaced with shifting, narrow, suspicious eyes, hollowed cheeks, lank hair, dark circles under her eyes. If I hadn't seen her hit a low before, I wouldn't have recognized her.

"Mary," Colin began carefully. "Kara has come to stay with us for a little while."

Mary flicked her eyes from Colin to me, then vehemently shook her head. "No, Colin. Stop."

"Mary," Colin started. "You need to—"

Mary lifted the plate she was holding above her head.

I glanced at Colin and mouthed: "Go."

"Are you sure?"

I nodded. "I'll call if I need you."

Colin glanced between the two of us, then retreated out of the room to a nearby study. I was sure I didn't hear the door close entirely. He must have been keeping an ear out. I didn't blame him. We had a hysterical woman standing in a sea of sharp shards. Colin didn't know me; for all intents and purposes, I was a stranger talking his wife off a ledge.

But there was a reason Mary and I had become so close back in the day. Yes, people found me harder to approach, pricklier, blunt. But I also had something none of her effortlessly easygoing friends had.

When Mary had begun smashing plates in our apartment and cutting herself, I was the only one who didn't run. I'd stepped over the plates and held her tightly by the wrists until she'd stopped writhing and dropped them.

I stared at Mary, barefoot, standing in the middle of her sleek, sharp-edged kitchen. Framed by wall-length panes of glass and scattered, shattered glass by her feet.

Suddenly, I'd been transported a decade into the past.

Wordlessly, I stepped over the shards and grabbed Mary by the wrists. She instantly dropped the plate, which cracked sharply against the marble floor, and began sobbing.

"He *hates* me," she hissed. "He thinks I'm a disappointment. And I am. I'm a disappointment to everyone."

"Shh, Mary." I hadn't flinched from the falling plate; I was holding Mary's face by the temples and staring her in the eyes. "It's going to be all right. Everything is going to be all right."

"I'm worthless. I'll never be good enough. You all want me gone," she cried.

I pulled her into a hug and felt her tears dampen the fabric against my shoulder.

"I just want to go," she whispered feebly. "I just want to go."

I'd led Mary carefully out of the kitchen and to her bedroom where I'd tucked her in bed and kept her company. She was curled up in bed, staring mutely ahead, and I'd had a hand on her as if I could somehow anchor her to me, stop her from slipping away into whatever delusions she was harboring. Eventually, her eyelids began to droop, and she'd slipped away into uneasy sleep. I crept out of the room and ran into Colin, who was waiting on the landing outside.

"So?"

There was no point in sugarcoating it. I crossed my arms and leaned against the wall. "It's a lot worse than I've ever seen."

Colin rested his head in his hands. I felt the urge to bridge the distance between us and rest a hand on his shoulder. Such a natural gesture, but something stopped me. Guilt? I was too self-aware of the fact that I found him attractive.

"I don't know what to do, Kara. I've tried everything…"

I tapped my fingers against my arm. An idle habit, but I'd noticed people interpreted it as me expressing displeasure or impatience. Just last week, I'd inadvertently made an intern cry by doing it. She thought I was going to get her fired. I guess that's what reputation does to you; the story spins out of your control, and it becomes its own creature and starts living its own life.

I forced myself to stop the motion and tucked my hands behind my back, pushing out all other thoughts. My career could wait for a moment. I had to concentrate on Mary.

"Does she have professional help?"

Colin nodded. "We have a nurse, Flora, who comes to check her vitals, gives her meds, and keeps tabs on her allergies."

I nodded. Mary was notoriously allergic to, well, everything. It was one of the things that had made her an inconvenient roommate.

"And a...we call him a reprogrammer. Comes in twice a week."

"Her psychologist?"

"So to speak."

I arched a brow. Hollywood was brimming with experimental and pseudo-spiritual psychological treatments. Where Mary was generally more open-minded about that sort of thing, I ranked on the more skeptical side.

Colin must have seen my doubtful expression. "He's the only person she doesn't get aggressive around. She's noticeably more...herself afterward."

I was too hung up on the first sentence to concentrate on the rest. When we'd lived together, I'd seen Mary go up and down. I'd seen her teeter from highs to lows and even entertain dark thoughts. But aggressive? That was new.

"She's dangerous?"

"Not really. Only to herself. But you got her to calm down, didn't you?"

"Sort of. I just did the same thing I used to do back when we lived together. It won't always work, Colin. And it's never been as bad as this."

Colin nodded thoughtfully. "She's usually calmer after those sessions. But it's the time in between. I'm finding it...difficult. There was one time when she drank half a carton of pineapple juice. You know she's allergic, right? If I hadn't found the EpiPen, and if—"

I bit my lip. This was bad. Back when we were living together, Mary was very careful about anything that might prompt a reaction. EpiPens were expensive, and we'd been broke. Now she could afford as many EpiPens as she could possibly need. But this seemed…reckless.

"Won't you stay?" Colin fixed his bright blue eyes on me. The gaze was so intense, so pleading, that it almost physically hurt. I had to look away.

Stay with the Harringtons? It had been bold of him to suggest it. But it seemed impossible. I was knee-deep in work, not to mention my inappropriate attraction to him.

"I don't know, Colin. This is very inconvenient for me. I'm shooting a film—"

"Ah. Of course."

I paused. There was no accusation in Colin's voice, yet I felt a tinge of guilt. Here I was, the inheritor of Mary's role in a coveted blockbuster, and I couldn't find the time to help her. Not that many years ago, I would have been at her side, no hesitation.

I thought back to when we'd been inseparable. Back before the industry had done its best to pit us against each other, whisper forced comparisons, and tear us apart. She'd been a friend, maybe the only real friend I'd had. The truth was, it hadn't been easy for me back then, and I'd been determined to do anything it took to succeed so I'd never have to feel like that again. I'd fought tooth and nail for my place, taken roles I wasn't proud of, and burned bridges along the way. Even the bridge to Mary.

I wasn't sure I wanted to remember how ugly that desperation had made me. But now, seeing her like this...

Would Mary have dropped everything to come spend time with me, were the situation reversed?

I already knew the answer. She would have. And she *had*, countless times—been there for me when I was on the verge of giving up, coaxing me back with her gentle humor and heart.

Now it was my turn to repay her. And somehow, I'd have to find a way to ignore my attraction to her husband. I had to.

"Well..." I started. "I'll still have to go to the studios for prep. I can't say for how long, but I can stay."

"Thank you," Colin said, wrapping me in a hug. I tensed against him, against this sudden display of affection, but Colin didn't seem to mind my awkwardness. "Thank you, thank you," he repeated. "That's all I can ask."

37

I ended up staying with Colin and Mary for three months.

I hadn't intended to, and it wasn't easy. The days on the shoot were long and hard, and when I returned to the house, I was often confronted with an unstable Mary. Sometimes she vowed that she was glad I took her place in the film, that I was the right person for it, that I deserved it. I'd brush her tangled hair and spoon her to sleep until the nurse, Flora, checked up on her and liberated me.

One afternoon, on a good day, Mary surprised me with a present: a giant panorama painting of a sunset over downtown LA.

"Mary, *nena*, where did you get this?" I asked, admiring the piece. It wasn't exactly my style. It lacked any…gravitas. But it did have a sort of charming naivete to it. Nothing experimental, no layered meaning, no rich context: a simple appreciation of a beautiful sunset.

"I took a little trip to a gallery downtown," she mused. "It reminded me of the sunsets we used to watch. Back when we first met."

That day, she'd done her hair and dressed herself: She was bright, and energetic, and lively. Looking at her then, you'd have no idea she spent most of her days lying in bed, moping around her room, or pouring her heart out to whatever stupidly named expert Colin had insisted on hiring.

Colin…

I tried to shake him out of my head. I was here for Mary, not her husband.

"Well, I appreciate it," I said, leaning the painting against the wall. "Although you didn't have to get me anything."

"And you didn't have to come here. But you did. I appreciate that," Mary said. Then she sat on her bed. I sat down beside her, and she leaned her head on my shoulder.

"You know, I don't hate you for taking the role. You were always better suited for this. I should have been an actress in a small, quirky theater somewhere, on the brink of bankruptcy."

"It's not too late for that," I said with a wry smile.

"But he *hated* it. He hates it when I lose roles," Mary started. "Losing is unacceptable to them, and I must be punished for it…"

I'd stopped stroking her hair. I'd assumed now that Mary was having a good day, her delusions would be on pause as well, but that didn't seem to be the case. She still thought everyone was out to get her. She still thought Colin and I hated her. I'd spent enough time with Colin by now to know he was a good man. Not just a good man—a great man. A man I'd pursue in a heartbeat, if circumstances were different.

But if Mary was having delusions like this about her perfect husband on a good day, how far gone was she, really?

Mary drew a long, deep breath, steadying herself.

"I'm imagining it all, aren't I?" she whispered.

"Yes," I told her, relieved, softly resuming stroking her hair. "Yes, you are, *corazón*."

That was one of the better days.

But more often she waited for me, wild-eyed, rambling on and on about how she was caged, surrounded by enemies watching her, trapped. She accused me of colluding with the enemy, of wanting to replace her.

I never knew which Mary I'd get.

Inevitably, I returned to set the next day tired, irritable, and snappy. The PAs knew to start avoiding me. Rumors of my petty tantrums began to spread in tabloids, despite strict confidentiality clauses written into the crew's contracts.

It was after a particularly rough day that I found myself dealing with the more unreasonable version of Mary.

"Why won't you let me leave," she was wailing. "I just want to go. Please."

"Mary, you are not well. Please, we just want to take care of you…"

"No, you don't. You hate me…I'm not crazy. I'm not. I'll prove it."

"You are sick, Mary. But you can get better." I held her hand in mine. "We are both here for you."

Mary snapped, as if I'd slapped her. "Colin hates me. He wants to kill me."

I shook my head, willing myself to calmly repeat the same thing I'd told her a thousand times. "No one wants to kill you. Colin loves you and wants to take care of you."

Mary sniffed. "You don't hate me?"

I pulled her into a hug. "I don't hate you. *I am on your side.*"

She ate the sleeping pill I offered her from the palm of my hand like a pet. I pulled the covers over her and stared at her, willing her to sleep.

"I'm not crazy," she murmured. Then, eventually, her eyes drew shut. I could finally breathe a sigh of relief.

I just wanted one moment of peace. I wanted to find Colin and share a glass of wine and forget this terrible afternoon.

Not for the first time, a small part of me wondered if it would be better if she never woke up. If Colin were free of her. And if both of us were free…

Like always, I told the voice to fuck off. But I'd thought it, all the same.

I found Colin talking to an older man in the foyer, who wordlessly dipped his head to me and proceeded down the hallway with a faint limp. I'd seen him around the house now and then, when he led Mary inside her office for one of their sessions. We'd never spoken.

"Has Robocop made any progress?" I asked as the man closed the door behind him.

"Reprogrammer," Colin corrected me, not for the first or last time. "And yes, I believe he has."

"Good," I said, although I was unable to muster much conviction into my voice.

From what I'd understood, the man's methods boiled down to listening to Mary talk and recording the conversations on a cassette recorder, which sounded an awful lot like therapy, except with needlessly outdated technology. Although, I supposed the cassettes made it hard to disseminate whatever crazy things she said during her sessions, which was probably for the best.

Still, I couldn't help but feel like Colin was getting swindled by someone offering a trendy rebranding of standard psychological practice. At least it didn't seem to be doing any harm. And Mary was more mellow after the sessions.

"How is Mary?" Colin asked, placing a hand on my shoulder. I was acutely aware of the weight of it, the warmth of his fingers seeping into my skin through the fabric.

"Having a bad day." Since I'd arrived, Colin had spent considerably less time with his wife. I would have disapproved, but to be fair, she didn't take that well to his presence. To make it easier on everyone, Colin mostly met with Mary on the good days.

"I'm sorry to hear that." Colin moved away, leaning against a nearby wall. I felt an ache of disappointment, my shoulder missing his touch.

"How is the podcast?" I asked. I didn't feel like going over the minutiae of disturbing things Mary had said.

"Good! The numbers keep climbing. We just signed a new exclusive deal with Spotify."

I supposed I should congratulate him, but sometimes I just couldn't be bothered with the empty, expected social conventions. "I listened for a bit, you know. Of your latest episode."

"Oh? And what did you think?"

"It felt somehow trite and navel-gazing, to spend endless hours contemplating how to manufacture oneself into a better version. Surely there has to come a point where all has been said about the topic? How long can you possibly go on about it?"

Colin laughed. I relaxed a bit. This was one of the reasons the two of us got along: Colin never seemed offended if I offered a harsh opinion. On the contrary, he delighted in being taken by surprise.

"Well, there's a lot to cover. And even if it may seem…pretentious to you, I do genuinely believe everyone has the capability, if not obligation, to become the best version of themselves. With a little help." Colin waved at himself. "And what's the point of even being here, if we aren't striving to be the best versions of ourselves? Do those who aren't trying even *deserve* to be here?"

I nodded. I loved seeing Colin light up with excitement. "I agree. Although some people would call that harsh."

Colin shrugged. "Well, some people aren't fans."

"Don't get me wrong, I respect what you've done with the podcast. It's earned you this life, your position, all your opportunities. I can respect that."

"You know I came from nothing, right? My parents were just some junkies in a trailer park. If I hadn't met the people who taught me everything I know…well, who knows where I'd be? I made it out, against the odds. So I know anyone can. Because I did."

I hadn't known that about Colin. The fact that he had struggled so hard to make something out of himself, and succeeded, made me admire him even more.

"I understand. I came from difficult circumstances too."

"Mary told me about that," Colin said. "You really are incredible. Dealing with all of this…and still working on the film? You are strong, Kara. You are the strongest person I know."

"Thank you." My voice sounded hoarser than I'd intended. Was I…crying?

I hadn't meant to be so emotional, but being strong, gritting my teeth was something I'd always prided myself on. It's how I rose up in this industry despite my parents being undocumented immigrants and eventually getting deported, leaving me to fend for myself.

Colin cupped my cheek with his hand and wiped my tear with the side of his thumb.

He stared at me. His eyes were so blue, two pools of clear water. His lips parted, as if he was coming to some new realization about me. My heart skipped a beat.

"Kara…" he whispered. His mouth was inches from mine. I could feel his breath against my lips. My face instinctively followed his.

"I wish we'd met…before," I said. "That Mary wasn't—"

"I know," Colin finished for me. He pressed a small kiss on the corner of my mouth and withdrew.

The corner of my mouth where Colin kissed me tingled.

Like a seal for a secret pact I hadn't realized I was making.

38

Oh, Mary. If only I'd known.

If I'd believed you. If I'd realized what Colin had done to you. How he'd tried to inspire you.

Maybe then I wouldn't have said the things I said.

Or maybe it would've still taken walking in your shoes to truly understand.

But my patience had worn thin when a film I'd worked on a couple years previously was having its premiere. I'd been preparing for the premiere for weeks: I'd worked with a stylist to design and source the perfect look. A pair of hair and makeup artists had finished working on me and were now hovering awkwardly at my back as I hammered on the door of the sound studio in which Mary had locked herself.

"Mary, this is ridiculous. Open the door. Mary!" I shouted pointlessly, my voice straining with frustration.

"Kara, you can go," Colin said, glancing at the me. "I can take care of this."

"My purse is in there, Colin. I can't leave without it." I hammered vainly at the door again. "Mary! Open this damn door!"

The door opened just a crack. I could see a sliver of Mary's face—her pale cheek, a wide, darting eye.

"No. I don't want you to go."

I froze for a second, unsure of how to respond. Was she really doing this on purpose?

"You're bitter you lost the role and are now trying to get back at me. Is that it?"

Mary shook her head. "I don't want to stay here…alone."

I wanted to scream. To shake her out of her delusions. She had sabotaged my premiere just to keep me here. And I was late now. *Very late.* The cab had already sat outside for a good half an hour, and I was sure my phone, which was in that room with Mary, would be littered with angry messages about being a diva, about being inconsiderate of other people's time. I could already imagine the headlines, slandering me. Every minute here was a minute I wasn't on the red carpet.

Unable to hold back, I shouted, "Goddammit, Mary! How many times do I have to tell you? No one is out to get you. Colin is not your enemy." I tried to angle myself through the gap in the door. "Now give me my purse!"

Mary lifted her hand; my purse was there in her lap. I made to grab it and pull it back through the door, but the strap was looped around her wrist, trapped like an anchored ship.

"I thought you said you'd help me," she said, voice trembling, as I yanked her arm fruitlessly.

For a split second, I hesitated. I had said that, hadn't I? I had promised her I'd help. But not like this—not when it meant giving up everything I'd worked so hard for. Not by feeding into her insane delusions.

While I hesitated, Mary yanked the strap. Her gesture was unexpected; it tripped me against the door, trapping my arm through the gap.

"Mary, stop!" I sucked in a sharp breath and tried to rip my arm back out, but now that she could hold onto me, Mary had latched onto my arm.

"Mary, let go of Kara," Colin tried, but Mary wasn't letting go of my arm any time soon. And I really needed this situation to be over an *hour* ago.

"Kara, I need you to stay," Mary was whining. "I need you to believe me."

I couldn't stop the words from spilling out. "It's all in your head, Mary! Everything! We've all had to bend over backward to take care of you, and it's not right. It's not right that we should have to bear this. You're *insane*!"

Mary's hand fell away as if I had slapped her, dropping my arm and the handbag, which I pulled out from the gap of the door. Her eyes, wide and hurt, met mine for a moment before she opened the door and stepped past me, walking slowly down the hallway.

I watched her go, my chest heaving, my arm throbbing from where she had grabbed me. The room felt too quiet, the stylists holding their breath, dreading to speak.

"It's okay," Colin said. "Let her go."

"Colin…" I whispered, unable to articulate exactly what I felt. Guilt, mostly. It was true that looking after Mary was taking its toll. But I had never meant to tell her that. Never meant to make her feel unwanted.

"I think you've done enough, Kara. I think she just needs a moment."

I watched Mary walk up the stairs, her silk nightgown reflecting lamplight. She moved like a ghost—and just like one, disappeared as she rounded the corner.

That was the last time I saw her alive.

39

MARY

I walked up the staircase, the stone cool against my bare feet. Somewhere behind me the distant drone of Colin and Kara's conversation continued, growing ever dimmer. Like it was occurring far below me, and I was floating away.

For a long time, I had felt like a ghost in my own house.

Some of it had to do with who I was. I'd never been able to trust my emotions. My brain chemistry had always been awry: in my early twenties, a doctor suspected I had bipolar disorder. But I never got it officially diagnosed or medicated. I thought it would ruin my chances of becoming an actress.

And then I'd met Colin. And he'd thought I was perfect just the way I was.

Well, he thought I *could* be perfect.

Colin believed anything was possible if one tried hard enough. He felt like he'd already perfected himself, so now he was looking outward.

He was a cultivator—he loved to push things, and I was his thing to push.

I entered my study and closed the door. My eyes immediately focused on the row of items neatly laid out on my desk. I walked up and laid my fingers over them, brushing them. Counting them...

Shortly after we began dating, Colin worked hard to get me roles and land meetings with the biggest agents in town. He staked out famous directors and had me run into them at opportune times. He read lines with me. He ran with me. He made sure to order food into the house, so I'd never be tempted to eat anything unsavory. He amped me up with pep talks and made five- and ten-year career plans for me, charting my trajectory to the top.

And all the while, he consulted his circle; the strange men that flitted in and out of the house, the ones he was always on the phone with.

My star started to rise. It worked.

Until it didn't.

Maybe he thought I could take it, but at some point, he broke me. Some days, I couldn't get out of bed. Some days, I couldn't find my voice. Some days, I couldn't stand for him to look at me because his gaze felt too intense, hot, like a concentrated beam of light. And on those days, when I failed him, he assured me he wasn't angry—no, he said he was never angry with me. Only disappointed.

But when he was disappointed, bad things happened to me.

Not because of him, of course. If anything was happening to me, it was my own doing. But I could never remember doing the bad things to myself.

I couldn't remember how I ended up with a deep cut along my arm from "accidentally" breaking the glass scale in the bathroom. I couldn't recall knocking over a pot of boiling water, scalding my foot so badly it blistered.

I could only ever remember *him*.

Micky would have tried to take me away from here, if I'd only told him. He was in love with me—I could tell. Poor, sweet Micky. It was too dangerous. If I told him, there was no knowing what Colin would do to him.

Four. Five. Six. Six EpiPens in two rows. Their plastic gleamed in the dim light. Colin had left them here for me. Likely filched from Flora. If Flora's carelessness could somehow be incorporated into my death, so much the better for him. Another little fish in his net.

I sat in the desk chair, strangely sanguine as I reached toward the first of the EpiPens.

I may have lost the ability to distinguish between what was real and what wasn't, but I knew a few things were true.

Colin had brought Kara here. At first, I thought it was to help me get better. To help me stay in line. A little carrot to go with the stick.

But Colin had not brought Kara here to help me. He had brought her here to replace me.

I wrapped my hand around the injector like a fist.

I placed the injector on my thigh, removed the safety cap, and pushed. A faint click. One. Two. Three.

My heart began an accelerated beat in my chest.

With shaking hands, I reached over for the second one.

If I could have made her believe me, maybe she could have saved me. But Kara did not believe me. And she never would. When Kara wanted something, she got it. She was too blinded by her focus to see anything else now. To see me.

I injected the second one. Then, in close succession, the third, the fourth, the fifth. *Click, click, click.*

My heart hammered madly in my chest. My face felt hot with blood. I hardly felt my hand grasping the sixth injector. With effort, I popped off the cap. Brought it against my thigh.

I'm sorry, Micky. I should have let you take me far away from here.

Good luck, Kara.

You've always got what you wanted. I hope it makes you happy.

Click.

40

KARA

When Colin and I got married, a little less than a year later, the ceremony was intimate and understated—a lot smaller than his extravagant wedding with Mary. Where they'd rented an entire Malibu villa, ours took place in a penthouse bar in a luxurious skyrise with a panoramic view of the sunset.

An elopement, the tabloids called it. Truly, it wasn't quite an elopement—just a small gathering of a few trusted people. I told people I preferred more upscale and exclusive events, but truthfully, I didn't have enough family or friends to justify a bigger celebration. My parents lived on a different continent; I hadn't seen them for years, but the last time I'd spoken with them, they'd had superstitious beliefs about remarriage and concerns about Hollywood's effect on my psyche. Most of my "friends" were industry colleagues who smiled to my face and gossiped behind my back.

As for Colin's side, it would have been inappropriate to invite his and Mary's shared social circle to a wedding so soon, especially since it hadn't even been a year since Mary's passing. His tight-knit circle of male friends made up most of the guestlist.

The fact that Colin was marrying less than a year after his wife's death had not sat well with the tabloid media, but for some reason *I* was the person everyone targeted. The tabloids, who took so much pleasure in writing scathing pieces about me were not-so-secretly desperate for any and all small tidbits about our upcoming wedding.

Well, so be it then. Let them bark. They had no idea what we'd gone through together. What we had *survived*. I glanced at the giant, radiant-cut diamond protruding from a thin platinum band, dangling from my finger to remind me of what I had.

I didn't want the memory of Mary surfacing on this day, but I supposed it was inevitable. I gulped it down with another cocktail and was just about to locate a waiter to wash it all down with another glass of champagne when I ran into Micky. The champagne sloshed over my arm, the leg of my ivory pantsuit, and his coat.

"Careful, Kara," Micky said, catching me. "Your outfit—"

"Oh, it's only archive Oscar de la Renta." I shrugged. "If insurance doesn't cover it, I'm sure the house will work as collateral."

Either Micky didn't catch the joke, or he didn't find it funny. Or maybe I was slurring again. Well, he could take his judgment and shove it up his ass. A girl was allowed to be a little or a lot drunk at her own wedding, wasn't she?

"Look, Kara, I came here for you."

"For me?" I didn't know Micky well—I only knew him from the times we'd run into each other in the house. He was *Colin's* friend. Why would he come here for me?

"Well...to be honest, I don't really care much for *you*. I came here for Mary."

I froze.

"It's *my* wedding," I said. Simple. Clear. Anyone but a complete idiot would have realized the implications: Keep my husband's ex-wife's name out of your mouth. I just wanted one day, one day where the ghost of Mary wasn't haunting either my dreams or my public image.

Micky shook his head. "Listen Kara, we may not be friends, but we both cared for Mary. And I just think there was maybe something else going on. Something we missed."

"Stop talking, Micky. I mean it."

"I can't. I just have to say this one thing."

"I'll kick you out. I swear to god."

"Nostromo."

Not what I was expecting. It bought him a few seconds of time.

"Nostromo, Enterprise, Millennium Falcon, take your pick. Just—if it's not what you thought it would be, let me know."

I had no idea why Colin was friends with this idiot. I didn't even dignify him with a thank you or a nod or an acknowledgment of any kind. He retreated awkwardly, turned around, and skulked away, aware he'd overstepped. Good.

I watched him walk away as I flagged down a waiter and snatched up another flute of champagne to replace the one I'd spilled. I glanced around: Guests were clumped up in their own little clusters. I could see Colin across the room, playing the host.

I was sure I was radiating rage because people kept to themselves, and no one approached me. I shouldn't have been surprised—of course people would give me a wide berth, even at my own wedding. My hands shook a little as I took another sip of the champagne, trying to expel Micky and what he had said from my mind.

God, what a presumptuous asshole.

41

Staring out of my bedroom window, I felt the glass cool and unyielding against my fingertips. My diamond ring still sat on my finger, though I didn't look at it as much as I used to. It had been almost a year since the wedding, and I didn't need the reminder anymore.

I took another sip from my glass, the liquid a pleasant burn down my throat.

Mary's painting hung on the wall, taunting me. Maybe I was a masochist for keeping it there.

I set the glass down and headed outside for a cigarette, walking idly around the lawn as the daylight faded. The dark iron gates loomed in the distance, casting long shadows on the lawn, but I knew better than to head out beyond them unannounced. Colin always had questions when I did. It was just easier not to.

I took another drag of the cigarette, blowing the smoke out into the pink sky.

Guilt gnawed at me. Guilt about Mary. I thought I'd be rid of the feeling by now, as if it were a simple illness that would eventually run its course. But guilt was a cancer. It developed new ways to thrive. It metastasized.

Simple things that reminded me of her triggered the guilt. A song we used to listen to. The smell of burnt toast. Someone laughing with the same nasally wheeze. Even a puddle of murky water, resembling the color of her sad eyes.

During the day, I could push these thoughts aside. But in the late hours, they overwhelmed me. That's how it worked, didn't it—the power of attrition. Wear someone down enough, and eventually they give up.

I didn't give up; I gave in. To alcohol, which numbed and blurred. To cigarettes, which gave my nervous fingers something to do. To my temper, which flared dangerously on set.

From behind the metal fence lining our estates, I saw our neighbor ambling about his lawn. I hadn't cared enough to learn his name, and I gave even less of a shit about him when I'd seen him exchange whispered words with the paparazzi once. You know when gossip magazines quote "a source close to" their target? Well, I guess it turned out they meant that literally.

I wasn't dressed to leave the house: just a silk slip dress, the strap drooping over my sharp shoulder, my dark hair a mess. I noticed he was looking. I gave him the finger, finished my cigarette, and headed back indoors.

I saw Flora in the kitchen, rearranging our stacks of mineral water. She was always ambling about in the house, working at completely menial tasks, bumping into things now that she was almost due to have her baby. Frankly, I could not understand why she was still here. Without this job, Flora would have a tougher time providing for her baby, but who cared? She could find work elsewhere. Somewhere where her patient hadn't killed herself.

Still, Colin had let Flora stay on as long as she was loyal to him. He claimed she could be useful. I suspected it had more to do with the fact that Colin enjoyed collecting people.

The noise of someone dragging luggage broke my introspection when Micky rounded the corner with a suitcase in tow. Another of Colin's strays. He'd stayed in the guest room for a few weeks or so while working on a project in the sound studio.

"Off then?" More of an observation than a question.

"Duty calls," Micky replied, pausing to fix his glasses and regard me with a look. Like he was trying to figure out what was going on with me. It should have endeared him to me, but instead it made me angry. Micky had one of those white-knight personalities, where he concerned himself too much with the issues of others. Colin was always careful to present a wholesome front in public, but Micky was annoyingly perceptive. He sensed I was having trouble coping.

Who knows, maybe the constant drinking was a bit of a giveaway.

It's my life, my problems. I'll deal with it.

"Good luck with that," I said. We'd both made it clear we weren't friends—I was just glad we could stop pretending.

Micky offered a half smile that didn't reach his eyes. Then he stopped, as if he'd remembered something. He rummaged through his bags a moment before retrieving a package and held it out for me.

I accepted the crumpled paper bag. "Exquisite," I said dryly.

"I found them while packing. I've had a few boxes in the sound studio for years now. Kept telling Colin I'd deal with them." He paused. "It's cassette tapes. Like the ones that reprogrammer guy made Mary record. Colin seemed really pissed he couldn't find them all. She must have hid some of them in there. Before she…"

Mary.

I weighed the bag in my palm. A rattle of cassette tapes. There couldn't have been more than four or five inside.

"And why," I asked, "are you giving them to me?"

"Well," Micky said, shifting from one foot to the other. "They have your name on them."

I felt a sudden tightness in my chest. I had half a mind to push the tapes back to Micky. To tell him to take them away and never speak of them again.

But this was Mary's voice from beyond the grave. And she'd left them for me.

What had she wanted to tell me?

42

The sun had set by the time I found myself on the threshold of Mary's study. The room had remained practically untouched since Mary had killed herself here—a place stuck in time. I'd changed the rest of the furniture, desperate to stake a claim to the house and my place in it. But in this room, the colors Mary had picked still reigned.

I lowered myself into Mary's chair, the leather creaking softly under my weight, and placed the paper bag Micky had given me onto the desk. There was a recorder in the drawer. With trembling hands, I pulled out the first tape and placed it into the recorder, snapped the slot shut.

I took a deep gulp from the bottle I'd brought, not bothering with a glass anymore. And then I pressed play.

The click of the button echoed too loudly in the quiet, a small gunshot.

Mary's voice filled the room.

I was on my fifth swig of vodka and second relisten of the tapes when Colin walked through the door.

"Kara? What are you doing holed up in here?" His tone was concerned.

I pressed the button of the recorder, cutting off Mary's confession.

"You lied," I said, turning to face him.

He sighed, the sound weary. "Kara, we've been over this. You have to let go of the past." He crossed the room in measured strides, coming to a stop by the desk. "You have to concentrate on your own life. *Your* future. Eyes *forward*, Kara."

The uncomfortable doubt that had haunted me had dissolved, leaving a stark, cold certainty in its place.

"She told me you were hurting her. She told me you punished her for not obeying you. I didn't believe her. You made me believe she was insane!"

"Well, she was, Kara," Colin said, taking a step toward me. "Or at least she believed she was. Whatever it was, she debilitated her own capabilities to succeed in this life. I really thought I could help her. Weed out her less constructive behavior…"

My jaw tightened. "Oh. I get it. *You* are the insane one. You really thought you could 'weed out' Mary's mental illness, one she had struggled with all her life? You thought you could just boost her career with a bit of tough love? Is tough love locking someone in a closet with a script and water, and only letting them out once they've perfected a monologue? Is it shredding a script and feeding it to them piece by piece because they've fumbled a line on set? Mary said once you engaged her in a brutal argument for an *hour* only to calmly retrieve a camera and play back the footage, all in order to make an argument in her upcoming film more authentic! That's insanity, Colin. No one would want that."

"Mary was paranoid, Kara. She was making up stories. You know this."

I waved my hands, splashing vodka over my sleeve. "She mentioned forced fasts. Grueling workout routines. She said you made her listen to countless motivational speeches and then locked her out of the house in the frigid cold because she'd 'failed to pay attention'—"

His blue eyes flickered. "I'm sorry to say this, Kara, but you are starting to sound like Mary. Imagining things. Imagining that the world is against you. Ask yourself: Have I treated *you* like this?"

I shook my head, trying to clear my thoughts. Colin did help me read lines. He did wake me up to go to the gym, and he did ensure there was clean food in the fridge. But anything as brutal as on the tapes? No.

But could Colin sometimes be harsh? Could some of his methods be considered extreme? Had I thought he was occasionally overstepping? Maybe. But I was *tougher* than Mary. I had more drive.

The haze of liquor had made everything more confusing. Mary had been so convincing in her tapes. Was it possible her paranoia could be so elaborate?

"You wanted this," Colin was saying. "You wanted me to help you."

"I did want this. I *do*. But—Mary said it started the same way. Innocuously. Then it ramped up—"

Colin laughed. "Mary said a lot of things. Mary said there was a group of us watching her, evaluating her, deciding things for us. Does that sound real to you?"

I hesitated. "Well, no…"

Colin spread his hands. "You, and thousands of other people, have faith in me. You were right to put your faith in me. Can't you see everything you've achieved with me already?"

"I'm an actress scorned by Hollywood," I spat. The strange night had made me abrasive, volatile. I tried to soften my tone. "My career is in shambles. No one in this town wants to work with me."

Colin leaned forward, covering me in his shadow. "That's on you, isn't it? Your temper, your inability to make friends, the drinking—" he gestured vaguely toward the bottle in my hand. "And then there's the obsession with Mary."

"Yes, maybe I am obsessed with Mary. Maybe I am torn up about the way she left us, and how I failed her. But isn't it strange that only one of us is? That you never talk about her? The only way you ever talk about her is her career—what she worked on, what you helped her achieve. But she was more than her career, more than her talent. She was a beautiful person. Did you even see that?"

Colin tilted his head and spoke calmly, not rising to the accusation. "I think you're being a little hard on yourself." His tone softened, almost concerned. "You know, Mary wasn't as perfect as you like to remember. And don't forget what you told me…that night."

His gaze flickered to my eyes. "That you wished she wasn't around. You wanted a chance…to be with me."

Heat flared in my cheeks. I got up from the desk and stumbled out of the room, Colin hot on my heels. His shoes clacked violently on the marble as he followed. I darted onto the balcony and pulled out a cigarette, lighting it with shaking fingers.

"Right before you kissed me. Or have you forgotten?"

"You kissed *me*," I whispered. As if it mattered.

"And you've been so proud of being better than her," Colin continued, pressing up closer against me. "Stronger. Going further. And you could go so much further. You just have to let me *help you*."

Hot ash fell on my hand as I tugged at my wedding band and my obnoxiously large diamond. "I don't want your help," I hissed. I yanked the rings off my finger and threw them over the balcony.

Colin watched them arc out over the air, expressionless. We both stood still. The heat of my cigarette approached my fingers. The only sound that broke the silence was the beat of my heart, thudding in my ears.

"You know," he said, after a long moment. "Mary had something you didn't. I didn't appreciate it at the time, but without it, you've grown difficult. Without it, the audience finds you…unlikable."

"And care to share what that is?" I asked from between gritted teeth.

"Humility," Colin said. He glanced over the railing.

"You should go get those rings," he added, almost as an afterthought.

And then he pushed me.

The whole world suddenly turned, and I was staring at it from an unnatural direction. Something was pulling me into its embrace: gravity.

You have time for a surprising amount of thought during freefall. My first was a clawing panic. A realization that I was falling, tumbling back-first toward the pavement below.

The second thought was that this was going to be really, really bad.

The third was that Colin had made a terrible mistake.

I heard an urban legend once about a drunk who fell six stories and didn't get hurt because he was so relaxed. He bounced off the ground like a cat.

That definitely didn't happen to me.

The ground under the balcony was paved with slabs of rock that rushed up at me like a black wave and punched all the air out of me.

I crumpled.

I would have screamed if I could, but all I managed was a bloody gurgle.

After what felt like an eternity, I heard the crunch of glass as Colin's shoes walked toward me and came to a standstill. He kneeled beside me and slipped my rings back on my finger.

43

The pain of the accident had been so violent I had thought nothing could ever compare. But the following months came close.

I wasn't sure which I preferred: the instant, overwhelming, and reality-defying pain of simultaneously breaking several bones at once or the agonizing and slow process of surgeons piecing them all back together again.

I lost count of how many screws I had in my body now. With a torn rotator cuff, I couldn't move or lift my arms. My neck, braced and fragile, was held together by what the doctors referred to as the C1 vertebra. Injuring it, one doctor had cautiously mentioned, could've led to full paralysis. They still didn't know the extent of the damage, but they said I was lucky to be alive.

I didn't feel very lucky.

My whole body incessantly screaming at me was enough to make me wish I wasn't alive. I had more sympathy for Mary, who I was embarrassed to have considered weak. It was one of Colin's mantras that I'd swallowed: that Mary was too weak to hack it, that her personal pressures and the pressures of the industry had been too much for her, and she'd taken the easy way out.

It was a neat little explanation for why she wasn't here. It absolved me of blame. But now I knew how natural it was to want to die…how the urge was a response to when our tolerance for pain was exceeded.

Mary deserved better. She deserved gentle, caring people, a proper diagnosis, and medication.

Intense pressure makes diamonds, as Colin would say. He just didn't seem to care that it breaks people.

The thought of Mary and how I had failed her was almost as painful as the constant ache radiating from my broken body. But luckily, at intervals, the doctors gave me morphine, and I gladly slipped into its warm, woozy sleep.

I woke up from one of those drug-fueled naps to find Colin sitting next to me. He was clean shaven, wearing a customary cotton shirt, and watching me with those bright blue eyes. He looked like he'd just stepped out of a perfume commercial. I blinked to diffuse the nightmare, but he wouldn't fade. He was real.

If I could have torn off my casts and drips and lunged at him, I would have. But I couldn't move.

"That's the spirit," Colin said, smiling. "I was hoping you'd make it. You are a fighter."

In the absence of anything else I could do, I silently fumed at him.

"I know you are angry, my dear," he began, his voice smooth and soothing. "You've been through a lot and deserve your rest, so I won't bother you for long. And seeing how recent your injuries are, I know you will struggle to admit this…you always were so stubborn. But I do think this will be for the best. I want you to know that I did this for you.

"Your career was dying, Kara. You may not have seen it, but it's true. No one makes it in Hollywood for very long if they are universally disliked. You were starting to piss a lot of people off. Directors. Producers. The general public. The drinking got out of hand. You were...unruly.

"Once you recover, Kara...it will be different. You'll be better. You'll be loved," Colin continued, his voice almost hypnotic. "Everyone loves a survivor, Kara. You come back, having survived alcoholism and a violent incident. With a newfound appreciation for life. With more humility and grace. You'll defer to me and follow my advice. And there will be no limit to how far you can rise, Kara. You'll be a legend."

Colin stroked my hair, gently pushing it away from my face. From my position there was nothing I could do about it. He sighed softly, as if reluctant to leave.

Then he got up and walked to the door. "I'll never give up on you, Kara."

My finger twitched, eager but unable to lash out at him. I watched him silently, my eyes narrowing ever so slightly. God, I wished I had my mobility so I could bash him on the back of that perfectly formed head with a metal tray.

But that's when I began to consider that perhaps recovery was not the smartest move.

If Colin was capable of pushing me off a balcony, he would most certainly kill me if I didn't obey his whims or if I threatened to try escape. Recovering from my accident, I'd be more vulnerable than ever.

But I had to find a way. I wasn't going to let him get away with this.

44

Masterminding a plan to murder your husband while incapacitated in a hospital bed, and then a wheelchair, wasn't easy. It wasn't easy to recuperate just enough to not be instantly institutionalized, but not enough to be seen as a threat.

Do you know how many times a doctor waved a lit pen in front of my face? How many nurses, physiotherapists, friends, lawyers, patronized me? Insulted me? How many hours I had to spend staring off into space?

I had people wipe drool off my chin. I had no privacy. I was helped to the toilet and wiped like a baby. I was dressed like a doll and carted around and talked down to, and I hated every second of it.

And the worst thing to endure was Colin. Colin's act of the despairing husband, the endless sympathy he was given. Poor, lovely, likable Colin stuck with an invalid wife. What a *hero*. And then the things he said to me! That I should be thankful. That I'd be stronger for it. That I'd learned my lesson. That I should trust him. That I'd get better, and I'd be more popular than ever before. That if only Mary and I would have just followed his instructions, he wouldn't have had to resort to such extreme measures. He wouldn't have had to keep us in line.

But he loved me, he said. And he believed in me. Believed in *us*.

Do you know how much self-control it took not to punch that smirk off his face?

When I felt the sensation return to my limbs, when I stretched out in the quiet hours of the night and eventually, tentatively took walks around the room, I wanted nothing more than to throw myself against the door and hurtle down the hall and out of this gilded cage, down the streets, to run far, far, far away from the man who had ruined my oldest friend's life and then mine.

But I chose to stay. I chose to sit day in and day out in that cursed chair. Because I knew there had to be a way I'd get back at him. That I'd take him down without taking the fall. I knew I'd find a way if I could just endure and out-perform the grieving-husband-Colin.

Inhuman self-control. That's what it took.

I'd never get my career back. I'd never win an Oscar.

But damn, did I know I had it in me.

The advantage of being perceived as essentially brain dead and incapable of discussion or movement was that I had a lot of time to think. And another advantage: people always underestimate someone in a wheelchair.

From my chair, I had a lot of time to think of the past.

After the accident, looking back, I'd put all the pieces together. Mary's illness. Mary's strange suicide. How I'd felt like Colin and I were fated to be. Colin's strange philosophies and then his violent outbursts, which he blamed on frustration and grief.

The signs were there, but I hadn't wanted to see them.

45

After a month in the hospital, I was discharged. I spent the first months at home pretending like I learned nothing in physiotherapy or recuperation. I tried my best to ignore attempts to engage me and reverted back to the simple code I'd used with the nurses—one tap yes, two taps no—to communicate base needs like using the bathroom.

Sometimes, I purposefully soiled myself to prevent the image of undue progress. It was undignified, and I hated myself for it, but I recognized that Colin would be suspicious if I showed perfect restraint in one area but progressed in no other. So I steeled myself for Flora's disgusted expression and the discomfort of what followed. I tried to remember my end goal: Get even with Colin.

I would have gone through a lot worse to achieve that.

Speaking of Flora, she rarely left my side. Even after my extended hospital stay and the birth of her baby, Colin had kept her on. I assumed Flora's purpose was twofold. First, Colin had someone around who had been able to testify to my drunkenness and irritable behavior. And now, he had someone loyal to him keeping eyes on me.

Now with a child to support, Flora was holding onto the job like an iron vise. Although Colin had told her to report any of my progress to him, I was sure she wouldn't. It wasn't in her interest for me to get any better. Still, even if she wasn't cataloging my every glance and gesture, Flora's devotion to Colin meant I had to watch my step.

With Flora always watching me, it was increasingly hard to prepare or realize my plans. In the beginning, Flora or Colin checked up on me throughout the night. But eventually, as the months passed and I continued to be bedbound, I was given a bracelet with a pager, something easy enough for me to press, and left to my own devices during the night.

That was when I had a chance to work on myself.

Before the accident, I'd been in good shape. Yes, there'd been the drinking. But I was on a regimented workout routine, and I had always been disciplined enough to eat exactly what a trainer prescribed to me. I'd always worked out for an hour a day minimum, in addition to doing laps in the pool. I could leg press my own bodyweight.

But bedrest is devastating to muscles and bones. I lost ten percent of my muscle mass in the first week in the hospital, and about five percent every day after. Rehabilitation had initially helped, but I couldn't be too cooperative. I couldn't be too eager. I couldn't seem capable.

Colin began sending me to an expensive physiotherapy practitioner in the city, where they fed me high-protein shakes and zapped my muscles with mild electric shocks to keep them from atrophying further. It was about as unpleasant as it sounds, but it was convenient because suddenly Colin had a reasonable explanation for why my muscles weren't shrinking further and were, in fact, returning.

Maybe it had something to do with the squats, jumping jacks, and burpees I was doing in my room at night. I knew that when my time came to confront Colin, I'd need all the edge I could get. Colin was bigger, faster, stronger. I had the element of surprise, but I'd only get one shot at it.

This was the plan.

I'd wait for Colin to grow bored of having me as his pet project. I could already sense his excitement waning. At first, I had been an exciting prospect, this invalid Kara. When he came to visit me, Colin never stopped yapping about how great my comeback would be, how it was all *mind over matter*. But there's only so long someone can try to amp-up another person who just…won't engage. I gave him nothing. I'd outlast him.

Next, I'd wait for Colin to run out of obvious ways to inspire me. He'd already tried talking, bribing, threatening…and even bought his own electric zapper. It stung like a bitch. "Tough love," right?

But I knew Colin. High up in his arsenal was psychological warfare. He'd resort to the same trick he tried with Mary: inspire me by finding and lavishing attention on someone else.

The idiot still thought I had a thing for him.

But I knew for this to work, I'd have to seem like I did. I'd have to seem like I was seething, and that his strategy was on the verge of working. That I was jealous as hell. But eventually, he'd grow bored of this. He'd pack me away or push me off another balcony, clear the slate for the next diamond in the rough.

I was not going to let that happen. I needed to strike before then, right as he was at his most distracted. When he didn't expect anything from me anymore.

And the someone else? The "new" Kara? Well, was there a more perfect scapegoat for Colin's death? If they had an affair, so much the better. I knew Colin was willing to cheat. And many a mistress had killed once she discovered her lover didn't intend to leave his wife. Or at least, I'm sure that's what the police would believe. It would be between that and believing an invalid woman could suddenly kill.

See, I didn't intend to be convicted for Colin's murder. That asshole had already stolen so much from me; I didn't want him stealing the rest of my life, too. Someone would have to take the fall, but the world needed to be rid of Colin, and that would be good deed enough for letting someone else take the blame.

I couldn't do it alone. I needed an accomplice.

So one day, when Flora was taking care of me, I threw up all over her.

"Oh my god," Flora exclaimed. She inhaled deep breaths in and out, her nostrils flaring, as if trying to control her temper, while staring down at the splattered, chunky damage. You'd think she'd be used to it, having a baby and all. "Oh my god."

I didn't really throw up on her. I just kept some of the gruel she'd fed me for breakfast in my mouth for an hour, waiting for her to come into proximity. Truly, it was a miracle I didn't throw up for real.

Flora removed my splattered shirt and, muttering some barely audible curses, retreated into the bathroom. I waited for her to close the door and then lunged at her phone.

I tapped in the passcode. I opened the browser window.

In the bathroom, Flora turned on the faucet.

I didn't know Micky's number, so I had to search him up online. His webpage took eons to load. Time I didn't have.

I heard the water turn off.

Finally, Micky's number. I copied it and closed the browser, then opened the messaging app. I tapped in the message. My fingers were shaking.

I heard Flora walk toward the door. I'd run out of time. I froze.

Flora walked out of the bathroom and turned right, toward my closet, without casting a glance at the bed on which I was frozen, sitting upright, clutching her phone. She must have been so used to me not moving she hadn't even thought to look. I stared back after her for a single second and then returned to my task.

Press send. Delete conversation.

I'd just set the phone back on the chair and settled myself in bed when Flora walked back into the room, carrying a fresh set of folded loungewear.

"All right, Mrs. Harrington," she said. "Let's get you into these fresh clothes."

I played limp while Flora rested me against her and maneuvered the shirt onto my head, guiding me like a child. For once, I didn't mind. I was too preoccupied thinking about my message, wondering if Micky still remembered the conversation we'd had more than a year ago. At my wedding.

"If it's not what you thought it would be…just let me know," Micky had said.

I'd sent him a single word.

Nostromo.

46

After I'd returned home from the hospital, I hadn't caught a glimpse of Mary's tapes anywhere. It was safe to assume Colin had destroyed them. After all, even if Mary was an unreliable narrator, they challenged the image of Colin as a wholesome and caring husband. And the account she provided of Colin's regimented push for her to be the optimal version of herself was so detailed that it was difficult to imagine it was fiction.

Of course, it had been easy for me to believe her voice on the tapes. I recognized what had happened to Mary because it had also been happening to me. If someone else heard the tapes, would they believe her?

It turned out there was someone who did.

One day, through the crack in my door, I heard conversation.

"It's been a while. I thought you'd forgotten me," Colin was saying.

"Never. It was just all a lot, you know? Kara's accident…I needed some time to process."

A familiar voice. *Micky.* Had he seen my message?

"You ignored my messages." A testy edge in Colin's voice. His tone was jovial, but there was an undercurrent of accusation. I knew Colin. Even if Micky had not been his focus, Colin liked having people who orbited him, deferred to him. Micky leaving to do his own thing and not seeking out Colin for advice must have irritated him.

Micky hesitated. "I was...embarrassed. You are so confident in your podcast, so honest...I don't know how you do it, man. We're not all as strong as you."

Smart boy. Play to his ego.

Colin's tone lightened when he replied. "Come on now, you're going to make me blush. It's good to have you back, Micky. Now—drinks?"

"Please!" Micky exclaimed.

I listened to the sound of chatting and laughter carry out from the poolside deck for hours, as Flora wheeled me out to the balcony for air and then back into my bedroom, where she preferred to keep me. She took me to the toilet, showered me, changed me into clean loungewear, and tucked me into bed. Flora had recently begun showering me twice daily in her desperate campaign to expel the smell of stale sweat that inevitably clung to me in the mornings after my secret midnight workouts.

I waited in bed, breathlessly, for hours. Eventually, I heard footsteps. I reclined backward just in case, but when the door cracked open, it was Micky. He slipped inside and closed the door.

"Kara?"

I sat up a little straighter. "Hi," I croaked.

"Kara," Micky repeated, eyes wide. He stepped up to the bed and kneeled beside it, clasping my hands in his. "It really was you. I didn't dare reply to the message…"

"I was counting on that."

"Everyone thinks you're essentially braindead. How long have you—"

"Been lucid? The whole time."

"All this time!" Micky exclaimed, then thought to lower his voice. "Jesus, Kara, it's been almost ten months…"

"Nine months, fifteen days," I croaked. I would have added some expletives if talking didn't hurt so much. "I'm aware."

"But…why?"

I had a feeling he already knew, but he needed confirmation.

"He pushed me, Micky," I said simply.

Micky closed his eyes and took a deep breath. When he opened them, they were brimming with tears.

"I think he destroyed the tapes…" I continued.

"Not all of them," Micky interrupted. "I kept some of them for myself."

"Why?"

"I wanted something to remind me of her. It was her voice."

"Did you listen to them?"

"I did, and the ones I gave you too. But I didn't know what to do about it. It would have been my conspiracy against Colin's word. I thought you were closer to the situation, and you'd decide what to do once you heard the truth. But then there was your accident…"

"Didn't it seem suspiciously timed?"

"Well, it seemed like a clear case. Flora and some neighbor both swore you'd been wandering around with a bottle of liquor. I… remembered that as well." Micky finished, ashamed. "And Colin just seemed so torn apart. Wrecked. Watching him take care of you made me think I'd been insane to imagine he'd ever hurt either of you."

"He's an excellent actor," I whispered. "He knew the whole tortured husband act would boost his image."

Micky was silent for a moment. "Do you think he killed Mary?"

"That, or as good as. Found some way to give her a little *push*."

Micky bristled. "God, I hate him," he whispered, and it was the first time I'd seen Micky look dark. He'd always been so geeky, so cheerful and jovial, that I confess I'd never taken him seriously. It was the first time I considered Micky might have an internal world of his own, one I knew nothing about.

"I've been roped into at least half a dozen dumb projects while waiting for him to get drunk and go to bed," Micky continued, grumbling. "He's like the devil, you have to sell your soul to get anywhere."

"Don't I know," I muttered hoarsely.

"So how do we get you out?"

I laughed. I really, genuinely laughed, even if the coughing sound that emanated from me sounded like someone strangling a cat. I don't think I'd laughed for more than a year, even long before my accident.

"I'm not *leaving*, Micky. I didn't fall off a balcony and sit in a wheelchair for nine months and have my body stapled together in order to just walk away. No, I'm taking him *down*."

"…down?" Micky asked, fishing for my exact meaning.

"*Down*," I replied with a tone that left little room for interpretation. "Now, will you help me?"

Micky considered for a moment.

"All right," he said, more forcefully than I expected, and gave my hand a little squeeze. He hadn't let go this entire time.

"All right," I said. "I've got a plan."

Micky did not like my plan. More specifically, he did not like the idea of framing someone else for Colin's death.

"Shouldn't you have more sympathy toward someone tricked by Colin?" he asked me one night. It was easy for him to come into the house under the guise of using the recording studio and crashing in a guest room due to working a late night.

"No," I said flatly. I was eating a burger Micky had brought me. Something *solid*. I'm pretty sure it was the best thing I'd ever had, and I'd eaten at Michelin star restaurants on four continents. "Look, Colin needs to be stopped. He's powerful, and he has influence. It's not going to be clean."

"It's just all so extreme…"

"Yeah, and so is killing one wife and maiming another." I swallowed a mouthful of burger. "Listen, Micky. Both of us know what Colin is capable of. We know he has millions of people lapping up every word he says. We don't know what kind of damage he could do down the line. He *has* to be stopped."

"Well, whoever Colin hires might decide he isn't such a good guy after all. They might discover what happened to Mary on their own. What will you do then?"

I stopped, fixing Micky with a serious look. "You can't tip them off, Micky. I forbid it."

"It's possible..." Micky murmured.

"Look, Micky. You wish Mary had told you what a monster Colin was at the time, don't you? Even if it put you at risk? Even if it meant you'd have to do something about Colin?"

"Yes," Micky said, without hesitation.

"Well, I'm telling you *now*. Colin is a monster. We are the only ones who know him and are close enough to him to do anything about it. Help me do what you were never able to with Mary. You can make it up to her."

Micky sighed wearily and adjusted his glasses. The fight had left him. "Okay, okay. I trust you, Kara. You say jump..."

I crumpled up the wrapper of the burger into a ball and thrust it at Micky. "Perfect. Now excuse me, I have to go scourge the scent of this burger off me."

I walked into the bathroom softly and began to violently brush my teeth. I stood in the dark with a cup of water Micky brought me; I couldn't risk someone seeing light coming from my room or hearing running water.

I was alarmed by Micky's morals rearing their head, but I had to trust him. I had to trust that he would not allow Colin to get away with all of this, now that after all this time he finally had the truth—and a chance to do something about it.

47

It would have been easy to frame Flora. But no matter how much I disliked her, Flora was a single mom struggling to get by and provide for her baby. She wasn't a legal citizen, and I knew what it was like to have your parents deported. She sucked up to Colin because she had no choice. Framing her would have been wrong. I couldn't take a mother away from an innocent child.

But someone else taking the fall? Some desperate Hollywood wannabe? That, I could live with.

I didn't have to wait long for Colin to start floating the idea of hiring someone to keep me company. He'd been growing really frustrated with me for a while now.

"You must be getting so bored pent up here in your room, Kara. I've come up with an idea. I'm thinking of hiring you a companion," he started. "Someone young and lively, to keep you company. To share their infectious joie de vivre."

I kept quiet. But I flicked my eyes up at him. I projected a feeling of annoyance.

Colin seemed taken aback by my sudden attention. But then, slowly, he began to smile.

"My friends agree. They've already begun looking. We'll find someone to inspire you. Perhaps another actress, hmm? Someone with a promising career. Someone for you to look up to."

His *friends*. Colin had always been well liked and well connected, but anytime he consulted his boys' club, I'd never liked the outcome. Sometimes I couldn't tell if Colin was just acting on whims, or if his decisions were being guided.

God, I wished I could have strangled him right in that moment. But I wasn't strong enough. Not yet.

I didn't respond to his goading.

A week later, Colin had a slew of candidates for the role of my companion.

Micky had been helping Colin vet the candidates for the position. It wasn't an easy search, I'm sure. Colin would want someone talented and beautiful, but also just fragile enough to control.

He'd hired and fired a handful of pretty, yet easily intimidated, young women before one candidate stood out from the rest.

"Kara, trust me, this one is perfect. I recognized her from a sound conference a while back. I'd spoken with her because no one else would. She's kinda desperate."

Micky showed me a social media image of a young woman with a round face, delicate features, and dirty blonde hair. For a second, my heart stopped until I recognized the small, unique details that distinguished the woman from Mary.

"Wow," I said.

"Right? She looks a lot like Mary, doesn't she?"

The resemblance couldn't hurt. It was what Colin had always wanted: someone not quite like Mary, and not quite like me, but somewhere in between.

"But that's not the best part. She's a total pariah in her community because she tried to sleep with a director for a role. A *married* director. Not long after her role got cut, he wound up in a coma. Word spread there was a connection, and now she's struggling to find work."

I perked up. "Interesting." I thought for a moment. Ultimately, Colin would be making the choice. But Micky and I could sway his decision, one way or another.

"You said she's desperate?" I asked. Whoever Colin hired would have to be. She'd need to withstand a hostile environment—not just from me, but from Flora as well. She'd need real motivation to stay.

"She will be if she thinks this job could help her get back into the voice acting world. I'll dangle a role in front of her—tell her she just needs to secure a sound studio, which this companion role so conveniently offers."

"And why would she need to find a sound studio? You could use Colin's anytime."

"Because this is an indie passion project of a cult favorite fantasy horror video game, and we have to save money where we can. We've got a built-in audience, and crowdfunding is sure to take off eventually, but until then, it's all coming out of my pocket. The other actress up for the role is offering a free sound studio. I can't pass that up. I really want to work with you, Anna, but you have to at least match that deal."

"Have you been rehearsing that?" I nearly laughed at Micky's pitch.

"Maybe."

"Hmm," I mused. "That might convince her. But how will Colin be swayed?"

"I've already begun planting the seed. She actually is quite talented. I was thinking of showing Colin some of her work. I'll convince him she's special—worthy of his attention. He'll want to see her in action in the studio. He'll be swayed, guaranteed."

I wasn't entirely sold. She'd have to be charismatic, attractive to Colin, and a whole host of other things for this to work out. I couldn't tell if she was all of that yet from second-hand accounts. I'd have to see her for myself.

48

I watched, standing, from my bedroom as Anna Albright descended the driveway toward the house for her interview. Flora had just headed off to fetch something from her bag, and I had a moment of blissful solitude.

Though, of course, this young woman was vying for a position tasked with interrupting all of that.

Anna glanced up at the house and froze as she saw my window. I froze in response. Had she seen me? But then I relaxed. You couldn't see anything from down there, I was sure. Or at least nothing that would blow my cover. If she saw something, it was only a fleeting shadow.

I dropped the curtain and sat back down in my wheelchair, painstakingly settling into the position in which Flora had left me. Every finger arranged just so. It had been risky, getting up, but I was curious about these new contenders for the position. Especially Anna, who Micky had told me so much about.

Another fifteen minutes or so, and she finally made an appearance.

I heard the door open behind me. "Kara, this is Anna," Colin said. "She's come to meet you and see if you might get along."

"Hi, Kara, it's lovely to meet you," Anna piped up. Though I kept my eyes half shut, I could see her in my periphery—young, delicate features, and eerily like Mary. No wonder she had caught Micky's attention.

"Perhaps you could read her something?" Colin suggested.

She had a pleasant voice. She was good, even. I glanced at Colin. His polite expression had slipped for a moment, replaced by a look of evaluation. I knew that look—he was already calculating her potential. Wondering what he could make of her.

And then he looked at me.

Showtime.

I turned my gaze to Anna, mustering a look of hate and contempt. I imagined I was looking at Colin. I imagined I was looking at myself, a few years in the past, ignoring Mary's legitimate pleas for help.

My expression must have been terrifying. Anna faltered, nearly dropping the book.

"I think that's enough for today," Colin said gently, kissing my forehead before leading her out. I suppressed a shiver.

Colin needed to believe Anna could get under my skin—that I was threatened enough to get better.

Two days later, Anna arrived with a beat-up car and a cheap duffel bag. I hadn't thought she'd done anything remarkable, but something had impressed Colin.

God, I thought. This might actually work.

Flora took an instant dislike to Anna, as she had taken to every companion before. After all, she wasn't an idiot—this insistence to find a new person to share her responsibilities and hours? Her position was threatened, and she knew it.

When Anna asked how much I understood, Flora curtly replied that I had *not been cooperative in neurological exams*. You could certainly say that. Following my accident, I'd been wheeled around to countless specialists who all attempted to provoke some kind of reaction from me with their lights, cards, and various other increasingly irritating stimuli. It took an incredible amount of self-control not to scream or get up and leave.

So, believe me when I say that Flora's condescension almost made me miss the specialists, that sometimes she *really* got under my skin.

"So," Flora continued, "do not expect riveting conversation."

It was fair to say I was feeling less and less guilty about disposing of Flora. I knew she was going to be a problem for Colin and Anna. I'd have to find a way to have her fired sooner, rather than later.

In the weeks that passed, Anna kept trying to make contact with me. It was almost enough to pity her, knowing what was going to happen, but I steeled myself against any sentimentality. I needed to go through with this plan. For Mary. For myself. For anyone Colin had ever—or *would* ever—hurt.

It's not like Anna was a person of integrity. If she suddenly and unexpectedly grew a moral backbone, she would know to leave. But I already knew she wouldn't. She was desperate.

From the first time she changed my clothes and took me to the toilet, I knew she had lied on her CV about taking care of a sickly person.

"I'll just lower your pants now," she said, voice shaking. "And then we can get you onto the toilet."

I sat in silence as she awkwardly rolled down my slacks. I had to concentrate on a point in the far distance to keep the humiliation off my face. I'd always hated this part of my act, but it was necessary. If I started going to the toilet autonomously, Colin would redouble his attention on me. I couldn't risk that.

In the bathroom, Anna hoisted me against her shoulder, trying to move me onto the toilet seat. Unattended, my wheelchair rolled away on the slick tiles.

"Shit," she said, unsure of what to do. Eventually, she managed to get me onto the seat. I instinctively gripped the railings, hard, to actually not topple over given how clumsily she sat me down. To sell my feeble act, I made sure my hands shook.

I really did have to go. Shit, indeed.

One part of my act that had always been hard to juggle was the limits of my mobility. How much could semi-paralyzed Kara really do? Well, I kept everyone guessing. In contrast to other areas of life, consistency was *not* key. One day, I'd open my mouth cooperatively for food, and another day, I wouldn't; some days, I'd focus my eyes, and others, I'd gaze endlessly into space.

This approach helped cover up any mistakes or odd behavior on my part. Flora and Colin chalked up anything strange to brain damage. With me being uncooperative in neurological examinations and doctor appointments, what was going on in my head was anyone's guess.

"How's that for an icebreaker?" Anna joked as she returned me to my bedroom. It required all my training in acting not to roll my eyes at her.

"I'll get better with practice. You'll see."

I steeled myself for the months to come, trying to imagine the culmination of my work and efforts. The day when I'd bound up from the chair. The look in Colin's eyes when he understood what I had done.

He'd never see it coming.

In the months that followed, I played up the act of a deranged, jealous wife every chance I got. I stared after Colin, I broke our wedding picture, I'd cast lingering looks at Anna whenever she conversed with my husband. Sometimes, I stared at her for twenty minutes straight just so I'd be staring when she finally looked at me.

And Flora? Well, it wasn't hard to fan the flames of the animosity between Anna and Flora. I had Micky rummage through Anna's things in her room. I saw her linger in my walk-in wardrobe with my expensive red carpet dresses and haute couture, so I left it a mess and listened to Flora give her an earful about it. When Anna drove me to the physiotherapist clinic, I slyly unbuckled my seatbelt. When Anna spotted my undone seatbelt in the rearview mirror, I swear she almost had a heart attack.

Colin was her only friend in the house. The animosity from Flora and the strange, unexplained, creepy things that kept happening would make her seek him out.

And then, once Flora and Anna were at odds, Colin would be forced to make a choice. If he chose Anna's side, he'd almost certainly get closer to her. Colin loves saving people, feeling like he owns them. Feeling like he has license to control their lives.

I'm not heartless. There were moments when I wanted to drop the act and scream at Anna to get out of here, to leave and go far, far away from Colin and never look back.

Especially when she reminded me so much of Mary.

These were the moments when she brushed my hair. When she picked out earrings or colorful clothes to give me a break from my drab wardrobe of unoffensive neutral tones. When she chattered on about her life or had a sudden freak out about my work.

"These are all the films you've been in!" Anna exclaimed excitedly as she discovered the books on my bedside table. "Wait, is this the novel for that space movie you did? The one where you played an astronaut?"

There was a knock on the door. As Colin walked in, Anna's cheeks instantly flushed. He smiled at her, and watching the two of them was like watching a conductor lead an orchestra. Anna's eyes followed his every move. Her body moved to accommodate him. I wondered if she realized how obvious she was.

She'd been here less than a month, and Colin already had her wrapped around his finger.

"Anyway, you should call it a day—I can take over from here," Colin was saying, picking up a book from the nightstand. I felt the hair on my arms stand up. I had no idea what Colin intended, but I was sure he didn't come here to read me a sci-fi adventure.

Colin continued reading for a minute or two before calmly setting the book down in his lap.

"She's nice, isn't she? Young. Pretty. *Pliable*."

I wanted to spit at Colin, but I had to control my expression. I settled on a scowl.

My reaction seemed to satisfy Colin. He leaned forward. "When you look at her, I want you to imagine all the things I could do for her. Personally *and* professionally. She would be such a nice project. I bet she would follow all of my advice. She would be…grateful."

I retained my expression, even when Colin withdrew something from his pocket. A device the size of a sunglasses case, with cords attached leading to square fabric pads. He twirled the cords around between his fingers.

"You remember this, don't you? It's the same thing you use in physiotherapy to stimulate your muscles."

He parted my shirt, peeled off the sticky sides of the pads, and attached them to the sides of my stomach.

"But this device is a little different. It's modified. A bit more…potent, if you will." Colin pressed a button on the device, and the patches began to buzz. I inadvertently jolted. I had to clench my fists not to cry out in surprise and alarm. Colin pressed the button again, and the shocks subsided.

"Doctors will usually only recommend the treatment for brief intervals, for a week at most and at less than half this intensity, so as not to overtax your muscles. But I think that's going a little easy, don't you?"

He pressed the button again. I gritted my teeth and counted the seconds. My fingers clenched the sheets until my knuckles went white.

"I've been lax with you. I've thought your natural ambition would be enough to get you to recover. But you've plateaued. Don't you want to get better?"

Colin pressed the button and leaned over again, close enough that I could feel his breath in my ear.

"I know it's all in your head, Kara. Mind over matter, Kara. *Mind over matter*. You are stronger than this. Prove to me that you have the will to recover, and I will send Anna away. You'll have a comeback the likes of which no one has seen."

He smiled. "You and me. A power couple. Like how we were before, right?"

I said nothing. It was impossible to imagine that I had once found him charming. Irresistible. Like we were meant to be.

Colin leaned back in his chair and picked up the book again from his lap, flipping a page as if what he had been doing was the most natural thing in the world.

"You have until the end of this chapter to say something, Kara," he said casually, device in one hand and the book in the other. "Or it's going to be a whole lot more of this. Just tell me to stop, and I will."

You are going to beg me *to stop by the time this is over.*

49

"She's been asking about Mary."

Micky was crouched next to me by my bedside, his dark silhouette barely visible in the dim room. The reflections on his glasses were the giveaway that I was talking to a person. We never risked turning on lights.

Micky always visited me at night. Courtesy of being Colin's old friend and having license to use the sound studio, he had a key: He came and went as he pleased. But since he didn't want Anna to know how well he knew the two of us, he'd taken to sneaking in and out of the house when we presumed she was asleep.

And my plan was working perfectly: Anna had been scared into Colin's arms. As time passed, more and more people could testify to their involvement. Then, when the house was empty, Colin would be killed, and Anna would be the only possible suspect.

But now she was asking questions about Mary. Something she really shouldn't have been concerned about.

"You wouldn't happen to have anything to do with that?" I asked.

Micky shook his head, but I continued peering at him. In the dark, it was impossible to read his expression. He had probably done something stupid. But Micky was a fool if he thought the mystery surrounding Mary's death would derail Anna. I'd seen her around Colin; she'd already fallen for him, hook, line, and sinker.

"Don't you think she deserves a chance? To figure out what is going on?"

"We've been through this, Micky. We've gone too far to scare her off now."

"But isn't that what you're doing? Scaring her?"

"Scaring her *just enough* so she runs to Colin. And it's working."

"She might figure it out," Micky muttered. "She's not stupid."

"Love makes *everyone* stupid," I said bluntly.

"We'll see," Micky muttered.

He wasn't going to drop it. It dawned on me that Micky might be attracted to Anna. That could throw a wrench in the plans. He could be compelled to save her.

Micky was sweet, and he wasn't bad looking. But he was no match for Colin in Anna's eyes. He would see that soon enough.

Micky was invaluable, even if he occasionally questioned the morality of the plan. I had him sneak around the grounds and pretend to be a paparazzo, snapping pictures of Anna. She ran right to Colin after that.

"She's completely under his spell," Micky whispered when we reconvened in my bedroom a few days later.

"Yes, as expected."

Micky hesitated for a moment. "I tried to scare her off. I ransacked her bedroom."

I had to fight to resist the urge to raise my voice. "What?! Micky, that's too much. You could have ruined *everything*."

"Relax. It worked in your favor. Just one more thing to run to Colin with," Micky said. His tone was dejected, and he seemed to be slurring slightly. Had he been drinking?

"Micky, I understand the urge to numb yourself with liquor better than anybody. But now is not the time. We have to focus."

"Yeah, yeah." Micky got up. "I'll do what you say. Doesn't mean I have to like it."

I steeled my voice. "Look, I can't have you going rogue again. No more stunts. Okay?"

"Okay." Micky walked to the door. "Just remember, I'm not doing this for you. I'm doing this for Mary."

A few times, everything almost fell apart. A few months into Anna's stay, I could sense there was tension between Anna and Colin, and not the good kind.

I had to act fast. I had to do something drastic.

The perfect opportunity arrived when Anna took me out for lunch. Not having been out of the house to a restaurant for more than a year, I allowed myself a moment of relaxation as Anna read a tabloid magazine to me and gossiped about the celebrities within.

I'd always prided myself about being independent, about needing nothing and no one. But perhaps that wasn't entirely true. Those first few years after I'd met Mary, it had felt like a hole inside me had been filled, a hole I hadn't even realized was there. For the first time in my life, I'd had a best friend. Until we'd drifted apart, projects and life and competition putting distance between us.

Sitting here with Anna reminded me of better times.

Anna's phone rang, and she glanced at the screen. I could see panic light up her face as she picked up. Flora's sharp tone carried, even with Anna's phone pressed against her ear. After a brief negotiation with Flora and a trip to the restroom, Anna pushed me out of the establishment, and we waited outside on the curb, in the heat.

Before long, Flora arrived in a cab. Without exchanging a word, she strode over and made to grab the handle of my wheelchair.

I was gazing absently ahead but following the exchange between Anna and Flora with the rapt attention of someone following a tennis match. I was confident Colin preferred Anna to Flora, but how viciously would Flora fight to retain her position?

I eyed traffic. Flora had to go; she was turning out to be a bigger obstacle for Anna than I'd anticipated. But for Colin to fire Flora, she would have to mess up. Big time.

Like letting me slip into traffic.

I contemplated my options. The sidewalk was at a slope—all I needed was to yank the wheels, enough for Flora to release her grip, and I'd be rolling onto the street. If I timed it right, the cars would be far enough to have time to stop. I hoped.

I'm sure anyone would say it was crazy. I'm sure they'd say that about everything I'd done so far.

Sure, then. Maybe I was a little crazy.

"You are not a qualified nurse," Flora was saying. "You are a fraud and a liar, sneaking into this household, and—"

I yanked the wheels.

Flora let out a shriek as my wheelchair slid down the sloped pavement, picking up speed. Horns blared, and I realized I miscalculated. A car was coming straight at me, and it wasn't slowing down fast enough.

I braced for impact.

Suddenly, I felt a decisive yank on the wheelchair, interrupting my fatal trajectory. Anna must have lunged in after me. I heard her frantic breathing.

"Oh my god," she muttered. "Oh my god."

I was lucky there was so much happening around us. It gave me time to compose myself before she kneeled beside me a moment later. "Are you okay?"

I stared off into the distance, although my heart was hammering in my chest. But not just because of the near-accident.

Anna had saved my life.

Could I really ruin hers?

But right as I began having doubts, Anna once again refused to save herself. She once again elected to choose Colin.

The following night, I was working out when I heard someone creeping around the house again. I paused my jumping jacks, trying to calm my ragged breathing. It had to be Anna. What was she doing sneaking around?

Then I heard the steps escalate. Shit. She'd be here in just a few seconds.

I suddenly had a flash of clarity. *I could use this.*

Lightning fast, I sprinted toward my bed and dug around for the shard I'd concealed in the mattress.

Earlier that evening, Colin had forced me to watch our wedding video. Maybe he thought it would push me, make me yearn for the life we had together.

I pretended to sleep through the whole thing.

Colin was, unsurprisingly, angry about that. He'd put on a charming face when Anna walked in on us. But after she left, he stormed over and took the disc out of the DVD player. I opened my eyes to see him snap it in half, then drop it into the waste basket beside my nightstand.

I'd retrieved one of the pieces, hoping for an opportune moment like this one.

I didn't even have time to wipe the sweat from my brow before the door swung open, and I saw Anna there, framed by the dim automatic lights of the hallway.

And she was wearing my ink-blue archive Armani ballgown. I was *not* expecting that.

"Kara?"

I gritted my teeth against the pain and dug my palm into the sharp edge of the disc. It sunk into my skin, sending rivulets of blood running down the length of my arm.

"Kara, please calm down."

She reached out for me, and I flinched, slashing her arm. I hadn't meant to attack her, but the shard was at an angle, and it was sharp.

"Kara! Just calm down!"

Anna pried my fingers off the shard, which fell to the floor with a clatter. Just then, someone called out from the hall.

"Anna?" Colin's voice hollered. "Is everything all right?"

Anna froze and glance down at her—*my*—dress, now splashed with blood, and then she made a decision. Quick as a flash, Anna tore off the dress and stuffed it under my bed. Now she stood in my room in her skimpy underwear. A moment later, Colin entered, also just down to his boxer shorts.

I'd thought Anna would run off to Colin after discovering me with the shard, but this was even better than I had hoped. I had the two of them in the same room, practically naked, adrenaline flowing.

Not too long after, Flora arrived. I saw her exchange a glance between Anna and Colin in their states of undress. She couldn't be blind to the attraction between them. If she let this go on long enough, Colin would undoubtably choose Anna. I saw her make a calculation and turn to Colin.

"I have to be honest, just like I have for previous candidates. I don't think Anna is suited for this position."

"Oh?"

"And let's not forget…yesterday she put Mrs. Harrington's life in danger."

"That's not how it happened," Anna objected. "It was *Flora* who let the wheelchair slip—"

"Oh *I* let it slip now? Come on, Anna."

They went back and forth like that for a while until Colin turned to me. "Kara, darling. Please. Is there someone here who makes you feel unsafe?"

There was an awkward pause. I glanced at Colin, and then at Anna, wondering what he was after, and then I understood.

I could have pointed at Anna. I'm sure that's what he wanted. He wanted me to prove to him that I was getting rid of competition, that I was going to work hard to reclaim what I had. My marriage. My career. I could have sent her home then and there.

But I'd come too far to stop now.

I lifted my finger and pointed at Flora.

And I could see it on his face.

That's when he gave up on me completely.

It wouldn't be long now.

Anna had enough evidence against her; she'd been sighted in multiple places with Colin, and the bitter Flora could attest to their presumed affair. Even Micky could testify, if he could get the better of his remorse. He'd briefly popped into my room after an incident with Anna to inform me that Colin threw him out. It wouldn't be safe for him to appear around the house anymore.

I was on my own.

But I had it. All the evidence necessary.

All I needed was an opportunity.

50

THE PRESENT

ANNA

I woke up to the sound of the studio door opening with a gentle whoosh, like a vacuum seal being broken open. There were purposeful footsteps, then a pause. The pause of someone contemplating.

Contemplating me.

Have to get up.

I tried to push myself up, but my body felt weak and unresponsive. My mouth was dry, and something coarse pressed up against my cheek. Carpet.

Looking around, I saw that I was sprawled across the floor next to the console. My limbs, twisted in awkward angles, made my back ache. I reeked of liquor.

Without having to reach over and feel it, I knew there was a bump on my head. I must have slammed it against the table on my way down.

It would explain the headache pounding against my skull, doing its best to split it in two. I felt more tired than I had in my entire life.

Still, that was the least of my concerns. The thought of Colin returning filled me with dread. With a twinge of horror, I realized he must have completed what he left to do: He must have killed Kara.

And now he was here to frame me for her murder.

I thought fleetingly back to my desperate attempt to upload Colin's lines from when we'd practiced Micky's script together onto the internet. By this point, I'd listened to them enough to know them by heart.

I had no choice but to kill my first love, and I'll do the same to you if you won't obey me.

I watched the light die from her eyes. I'll happily watch it die in yours.

Try anything...and I'll grind you to pulp. There will be nothing left of you.

And then, a blood-curdling scream. Courtesy of me. It had taken nearly everything in me to produce.

I knew Colin's passcode. He'd shown me how he uploaded episodes to his podcast channel. But everything had been swimming together...

Had I managed the upload? Had Colin's incriminating words been uploaded online for everyone to hear? Maybe it didn't matter. Even if I had succeeded, Colin would have deleted it as soon as he found out about it.

My feeble attempt at retaliation had been just that—weak.

I waited for his voice, for threats or orders, but nothing came. Maybe he wasn't in a position to hurt me directly anymore. Perhaps there were police officers standing beside him, craning their necks, eager to get a good look at the crazy woman who had tried to claw her way to the top by infiltrating this Hollywood family.

I wanted to say something in my defense. Or perhaps it was better to stay silent? What was it police said in these situations: Everything you say can and will be used against you?

I braced myself for the cold metal of handcuffs against my wrists.

Instead, I felt soft steps approaching me and a gentle hand resting on my shoulder.

"Anna? Are you all right?"

I craned my neck just enough to catch a glimpse of her, my eyes watering against the bright light in the room.

Her sharp cheekbones were flushed, and she was wearing her customary beige loungewear. Her dark hair was a tousled mess, framed by a halo of fluorescent light.

There she was, impossibly. Kara.

Her chest was rising and sinking rapidly, near breathless, as if she had rushed downstairs—to me. Her eyes were not unfocused, the way I was used to seeing her, but keenly fixed on mine, sharp like an eagle's.

How long had it been? Was I dreaming? And was that *blood* on her cashmere sweater?

So many questions raced through my mind. I tried to speak, but fatigue, alcohol, and whatever else Colin had spiked my drink with made my tongue thick.

All I managed to say was the most pressing question. It came out in a husky croak.

"What is *happening*?"

Kara leaned over and looped an arm under mine, helping me stand up. It was strange: It felt like tumbling through a mirror into a world where everything was backward and nothing made sense. Anchoring myself against her, I allowed her to help me to my feet. Although nothing should have surprised me anymore, I was shocked to see how strong she was. Wiry. But strong.

"We need to move fast, Anna," she said, her voice urgent, focused. "There isn't much time."

Kara led me out of the sound studio and through the basement toward the stairs. I clutched my side, wincing in pain. She waited a few beats for me to catch my breath, then pushed on. She seemed impatient at my sluggishness. I would have laughed at our strange reversal of roles, if it wasn't entirely inappropriate, if I weren't half scared to death, if it wouldn't have hurt so much to do so.

So strange. Kara impatient at *me* for moving so slowly.

"Hold onto me."

I did as I was told, wrapping my arm around Kara's shoulder and clutching her arm with the other, and hobbled beside her, up the steps from the basement. My legs ached and tingled with every step, pins and needles.

"Don't touch anything," she instructed. Then, more gently, she added, "Just in case."

Just in case of what? I was too tired to argue. Besides, I was clinging desperately to Kara with both arms: I didn't have an extra hand to do whatever it was Kara didn't want me to do.

"Where are we going?" I whispered hoarsely.

"Up," she replied simply, and continued to hoist me up the steps.

"Why?"

She waited until we were at the top to answer.

"To help me decide what to do."

I opened my mouth to reply, then closed it. I was too weak to argue. And perhaps it was easier to be led. That was what had happened all this time, wasn't it? I'd thought I'd been making my own decisions, but Colin had been manipulating me all along for his own twisted ends. Trying to make me replace Kara. To get rid of her.

I glanced again at Kara.

"Colin wanted to hurt you."

Kara nodded, guiding me past the gleaming steel kitchen and around the corner. To my dawning horror, we were faced with a second set of stairs. She paused at the foot of them and gave me a look.

"And I wanted to hurt him."

I gaped at her. "How long have you—"

Kara laughed, a short, bitter sound, then sobered. "A while," she said simply, leading me up the stairs.

Talking and climbing hurt too much, so I concentrated on the latter. At the top, I froze.

"Micky?"

He was busy dismantling something, his hands moving with a practiced ease. He glanced at Kara and me but didn't seem surprised to see us.

"I'm almost done with the cameras," he told Kara.

I turned to her, still in shock. "But Micky…he—"

"Don't worry, Anna. He's on our side."

"I wiped the floors and your bedroom," Micky continued, addressing Kara. "Anywhere else?"

"That should be it." Kara reached over to a bucket with cleaning supplies and extracted a few pairs of silicone gloves. She paused to give him a meaningful look. "You should leave, Micky."

Micky nodded to Kara. A flicker of worry breached his purposeful manner. "You're pretty beat up."

She really was. Now that I could see her clearly, dark bruises blossomed across her neck and under her ears. Her forearms were mottled with inky fingerprints, bruises that made me shudder.

"I'll deal with that later," she said, pulling on the gloves and urging me forward down the hallway.

"What is he doing?" I asked as we left Micky behind.

"Dismantling the cameras. We don't need them anymore, and they might raise suspicion."

My head spun. "Cameras?"

"There was one in the sound studio, you know. That's how Micky knew to rush over. He saw Colin lock you in there."

I was struggling to piece things together. "But why?"

"To capture incriminating footage," Kara said, as if it was obvious.

All this time, Kara had known Colin was dangerous. All this time, she'd been working against him.

"Of Colin?"

Kara hesitated before answering. "Of you."

I thought of everything that had happened in that sound studio. My flirtatious reading of lines with Colin. Us being…intimate.

"I don't understand…"

Kara stopped and faced me. "I'm going to confess something, Anna. I underestimated you. I thought you'd fall for Colin—become his new little pet."

A pang of shame and guilt tightened my throat. "I did."

"But you stood up to him. You fought back. Not to mention, you saved my life. And I've had to…re-evaluate my stance on you."

She sighed and shook her head. Did I sense a note of shame? Of regret?

"You hurt him."

My heart skipped a beat. "The upload…"

Kara nodded. "Colin was too busy cornering me to notice. But it's spreading as we speak. Soon it will be everywhere. The lawn will be teeming with press."

I swallowed. I wasn't ready to think about how my life would change yet, but at least I was still here. Alive, and not being convicted for a crime I didn't commit.

"Where is Colin?" I asked carefully.

"He's here," Kara said. "And now I need your help. Again."

"With what?"

"With deciding what to do with him."

I almost didn't want to ask. "What were you *planning* on doing with him?"

"What he was planning on doing with me," she replied. She considered for a moment, then continued. "I won't force your hand, Anna. But I think you'll want to be here for this."

With a jolt, I realized we had stopped right in front of a familiar door. It was the same room Kara had collapsed in front of, the dusty one I'd investigated once before. With furniture that didn't match the rest of the house. Mary's old office.

Kara pushed the door open, and I saw him. Back facing us and tied to a chair.

My boss. My lover. My enemy.

Colin.

51

"Put these on," Kara instructed, handing me a pair of silicone gloves. I did as I was told, tugging the plastic over my clammy skin. Kara watched silently. Then, she urged me through the door and closed it behind us.

The air inside was thick, the curtains drawn just enough to let a sliver of orange light through. In a few hours, it would be bright; the sun was already teetering on the horizon. A single lamp on the desk cast a halo of yellowed light over its immediate surroundings. Aside from the lamp, the only thing on the desk was an unmarked leather case.

In the center of the room, beside the desk, sat Colin, slouched in a leather chair. He was loosely belted to it, though I had a sense it was mostly to keep him upright.

Kara circled around to face him. Colin slowly lifted his head. He scoffed at his surroundings.

"Mary's office? How nostalgic, Kara," he sneered.

"It was that or the balcony you threw me off."

"You were drunk," Colin growled. "You fell."

Kara leaned over, her dark eyes gleaming in the half light.

"Easy to fall when someone pushes you, wouldn't you say?" She turned to me. "I brought a guest."

My heart hammered in my chest. Even though Colin appeared to be helpless, I didn't know if I was ready to face him. But right now, I didn't have a choice.

Shakily, I stepped forward, my footsteps muffled by the room's giant rug. I stood beside Kara and looked down at him, trying to keep my chin propped up high.

The dim desk lamp cast an eerie glow over his haggard face.

He had a black eye and a split lip, but it wasn't his disheveled appearance that made him look like a completely different man. It was the expression in his eyes: The warm, kind look had been replaced by a predatory gaze. His brows furrowed over his blue eyes, casting them into shadow and making them look much darker than they had any right to be.

Then, unexpectedly, he broke into a small smile, and he turned to look at Kara.

"So it worked, didn't it?"

I glanced at Kara, whose eyes had narrowed. "What is he talking about?"

Colin let out a little strangled laugh, a twisted version of the chuckle I once loved. I thought about how just yesterday I'd been head over heels for this man. How excited I'd been for our future, and how scared I'd been that something could snatch it away from me.

What a difference a night can make.

"I know you find my methods extreme, but admit it. It worked. You had lost all motivation to recover, but when Anna arrived..."

"You idiot," Kara hissed, flashing her teeth. "Do you actually think I gave a shit about your little fling with Anna? Please. I've been well and able for over a year."

"So all the dressing, the showering..." I whispered, recounting all the time I'd spent with Kara. "It was all for show?"

Kara glanced at me, unapologetic. "I'd never have gotten the upper hand, otherwise."

Colin scowled. "Why didn't you let me know? We've wasted all this time. We could have worked together on your comeback. Your career..."

Kara's tone was cold but vicious. "Aren't you listening? I don't care about my career. I don't care about anything you could offer me."

"Then what *do* you want?"

"I want Mary back from the dead, you piece of shit."

That wiped the smile off his face. But he recovered quickly.

"Oh, this is about Mary, is it?" he said, face serious now, his smile transformed into a sneer. "You still haven't gotten rid of that strange obsession of yours. Don't pretend you were best friends, Kara. You didn't care that much about her when you were competing for the same roles. When you let it slip to casting agents that she was bipolar, that hiring her might be risky. Don't think I don't know, Kara. I have my sources."

Kara seethed beside me. It was about the most terrifying I'd seen her, and I'd been scared by Kara on multiple occasions.

I shifted my eyes from Kara to Colin, who was staring at us from under his dark brows. Still confident, despite his circumstances. Calculating.

"We should call the police," I finally said. It was the right thing to do, wasn't it? But even as I said it, I felt unsure. Colin had money, and he was powerful. He had the means to hire the best lawyers on hand. And what evidence did we have?

"The police don't always get the guy, Anna," Kara replied evenly, her eyes fixed on my expression. "And even if they did," she paused, considering me, "would it be enough for you?"

We exchanged a long look, and I glanced at Colin. Was it what I wanted?

"Good try, Kara," Colin chuckled. "If Anna really had it in her, you'd be dead already."

A surge of anger welled up in my chest. I turned to face Colin.

"You underestimated me, Colin. Both of you have."

I took a step closer to him, my voice gaining strength.

"But there's one thing I really hate: being betrayed. And you know I'm not afraid to take justice into my own hands."

52

I'd trusted Colin. He'd promised me the world, and I'd been stupid enough to believe him.

But he'd been an idiot to disappoint me.

A few years ago, when I was desperately trying to book gigs, I met a director. His name was Marcus Berg. He said I was perfect for a role but made it clear he expected *something* in return. It was entirely inappropriate: I was in a relationship—engaged, actually—and he was old and married. But I weighed my options and decided I didn't need to be so particular about those kinds of things.

I guess it's fair to say I really wanted that role.

I may have skimmed over some of the particulars when I told Colin the story, but a lot of the general parts are the same. I let Berg parade me around as his newest arm candy, and I laughed at his lecherous jokes. My fiancé didn't like the idea of my sleazy boss forcing me to attend all these social events, but I told him it was part of the job. That he was a product of his time. That my fiancé had nothing to worry about: I found my boss gross.

And I did, most of the time. But then there were the moments he complimented me. When he told me how talented I was, how I'd be a big star. How this role would *make* me a big star. In those moments, he was the most beautiful man in the world to me.

If I could have afforded therapy, some therapist would probably have pointed out it was part of the draw: having a paternal figure admire and compliment me. Something I'd never experienced growing up. Maybe that's why I've never been. No one wants to hear they're a cliché, right?

Here's another cliché: I should have known it was too good to be true.

The role I'd been promised, Elsie Wyatt, shrank, was relegated to a supporting role. Then it disappeared entirely. I waited for Berg to offer me another role in the production, but it never materialized. He stopped calling.

Just as quickly as I'd been picked up, I was unceremoniously disposed. And what's worse, he'd started going around blabbing that I'd *tried* to sleep with him for the role, but he'd had to decline. It wouldn't have been *ethical*.

Should I have just sat by and let that happen? Hell no. There was a familiar little voice in my head, egging me to do the opportune thing. The voice sounded a lot like my father's. *Seize the moment. Utilize your environment. Attack an opportunity.*

And I'd done that. I'd utilized Berg's coke habit as the opportunity it had afforded to spike his stash. To silence him. To protect myself.

Sure, it didn't work out the way I intended. He didn't die. But he did end up in a prolonged coma. For over a year, I'd been visiting him as Elsie Wyatt after selling a few of the nurses a story about being his illegitimate daughter. Did I visit him out of guilt or because I was scared he'd wake up and tell everyone what I'd done? I wasn't sure myself. Maybe I'd never know for certain.

The rumors got some of it right. The part about me spiking his coke with fentanyl to get him to shut up about me sleeping my way to the role. It was the truth, but not the whole truth.

I also wanted him to pay. Not because it was necessarily the right thing to do.

But because letting him get away would have felt wrong.

53

Colin's body tightened in response to my claim. I saw an unfamiliar uncertainty in his expression.

"Excellent!" Kara said, like she was chairing a board meeting. "Now that that's settled, I have a few ideas."

She walked up to the desk and unclasped the locks of the case upon it. The lid opened with a sharp click, revealing a row of plastic-wrapped EpiPens. I recognized them from Flora's medical kit. The one she'd been adamant I didn't touch.

"Is that Flora's…"

"She was always paranoid about anyone touching her stuff. Probably because things kept going missing," Kara said matter-of-factly, withdrawing one of the EpiPens. "You had something to do with that, didn't you, Colin?"

Colin glowered at her and said nothing.

"So the first punishment I'd suggest is what I'm going to refer to as the *Mary Choice*. Inject yourself with half a dozen EpiPens, and you get to walk away a free man. What do you think, Anna?"

"It *was* Mary's *choice* to inject herself with those," Colin interrupted with a growl. "She could have stayed."

"You abused her, isolated her, made her believe she was worthless, and then left her in a room alone with a viable way to kill herself. I've heard the tape, Colin." Kara twirled the EpiPen between her fingers.

"Besides, you'll be afforded the same luxury of choice, Colin. You can choose to inject, or there's another option. I call it the *Kara Way*. You can hurl yourself off the same balcony you pushed me off. It's a long way down. And I can tell you from experience that it hurts. A lot. But what was that thing you always said, Colin? Mind over matter?"

For the first time, a current of fear flashed through his eyes.

"What do think, Anna? Does that sound fair?"

"Anna," Colin implored me. "This is insane. You are not going through with this, are you?"

I made myself look him directly in the eye.

"Earlier, you told me I hadn't been bold enough. Is this bold enough, Colin?" I slapped him across the face, hard. My hand stung from the impact.

"Maybe I was wrong about you, Anna. Maybe you've proven your point. We were good together, weren't we? I can still give you everything..."

I didn't reply but turned to Kara. The sun was rising rapidly, casting a dull, orange glow into the room. Whatever we were going to do, we had to do it now.

"Tick tock, Colin," Kara said as if she'd read my mind, tapping her foot. "We don't have all day."

"And if I don't choose?"

Kara's lips curled slightly. "We'll choose for you," she said, her voice cool and casual. "And I know which one I'd pick." She leaned over and pinched his cheek. "It's not so bad," she cooed. "The pain is only more than you can ever imagine."

Colin's gaze locked onto the sliver of window peeking through the curtains. He seemed unable to pull his eyes away from it, fear creeping into every line of his face.

"Do you remember the doctors telling me I was lucky to have survived?" She continued. "How lucky do *you* feel, Colin?"

"Mary, Mary. The EpiPens," Colin said quickly.

"You know, I had a sneaking suspicion you preferred her." There was a note of amusement in her voice, but she didn't smile. She pushed Colin's chair toward the desk and pushed the case toward him. "Fair enough. There's six EpiPens here, Colin. That was enough to kill Mary, but will it be enough to kill you?"

Colin eyed the pens. "And if I do this, that's it? Right?"

Kara looked over to me. I gave her a short nod.

She turned back to Colin. "An eye for an eye."

54

Epinephrine is a medication that reduces the body's allergic response. It relaxes muscles and makes breathing easier. For people with life-threatening allergies, it can be lifesaving, which is why Flora had always kept them close when caring for Mary.

Side effects can include dizziness, headache, heart palpitations, muscle weakness, nausea, sweating, tremors, and vomiting. And those are just the ones that do not require medical attention. More serious side effects include dangerously high blood pressure. Stroke.

Death.

But a single shot, or even multiple shots, is unlikely to be fatal to a healthy adult—unless that person has underlying heart issues. Unless someone repeatedly injected themselves with no reason to do so.

And what happens then?

By the third shot, the color had drained completely from Colin's face, his hands were trembling, and his breaths came in rattling wheezes, as if he couldn't get enough air.

"Look," he rasped, his voice breathy and strained. "I was just trying to help. You wanted—you enjoyed my help. Both of you."

"You still believe your Machiavellian games were some kind of favor?" Kara shook her head. "Keep going, Colin. If I were you, I'd just get it over with."

With trembling fingers, Colin reached out for another EpiPen.

Colin had lied to me. He'd let me down. I should have just let him keep injecting himself in silence. And yet something bothered me.

"I don't understand, Colin. You said you cared for me. You said we'd be together. And then suddenly everything changed, and you wanted me gone..."

Colin glanced up at me. His eyes seemed unfocused. "I didn't have a choice," he coughed.

Colin wasn't making any sense. "What does that even *mean*?"

"It means he's trying to deflect. Dodge responsibility," Kara spat. "Eyes forward, Colin."

Colin glared at Kara, and with a strained click, administered the fourth EpiPen. Hand shaking, he let the administrator drop onto the carpet.

"You just weren't good enough for us, Anna," Colin continued softly.

I wondered if Colin had already lost it. "Who is *us*?"

Colin looked like he was going to throw up.

"It's that creepy group of his," Kara said, her voice low and dark. "These strange men. The one who visited Mary. The ones who are always in and out of the house."

Had this strange group collectively decided that it was time for Mary to go? Time for Kara to fall? Time for me to replace Kara? Time for me to be disposed of too?

"Who *are* they?" I repeated, insistently.

"A pathetic boys' club with a power complex and a bad hobby," Kara spat.

"We're more influential than you would even believe," Colin said, slumped against his chair. "And closer than you'd think."

"Well, they're not here to help you now," Kara said. "So I suggest you keep going."

Shakily, Colin reached out for the fifth EpiPen. His hands shook so much it was a surprise he was able to steady the pen against his thigh. He administered the epinephrine with another sharp *click*.

"Good boy," Kara remarked dryly. "One to go."

Colin gagged.

"I'll call the police when you're done. They'll bring an ambulance along. That should take you to the hospital. Or the morgue. Whichever it is."

"You're going to regret this, Kara," Colin muttered, his lips almost blue. He was breathing quickly. Too quickly. "We're going to make you pay."

Kara quirked a brow but said nothing.

"Anna," Colin implored, his voice cracking. His once confident demeanor unraveled. "You know if you side with Kara, you're through. No one will ever work with you again. But it's not too late. You can still prove yourself—to me, to *us*."

Kara looked at me. She didn't say anything, but her expression did all the talking for her. Had she been wrong about me? Was I still the foolish girl she had pegged me for when this had all started?

Colin floundered for the final EpiPen, his hands shaking, his face pale and slick with sweat.

"What do you want, Anna? Name your price."

Name my price? After everything he'd done to me? After he'd spent months gaslighting me, wrapping me up in some twisted test in the guise of love?

"Money," I said, my voice cold and detached. "An obscene amount of money."

"Done," Colin gasped, nodding frantically.

"I want you to sing my praises to all of your director friends. I want a career."

"Okay. Anything you want. We'll fix it. We'll make you the star you deserve to be. I'll explain everything to them…"

Kara looked between us, unsure of what was happening. Colin smiled at her, triumphant.

"Anna was always better than you. And I can offer her everything she ever wanted. You choose me, don't you, Anna?" His victorious expression faltered as he saw the look on my face.

"Anna?"

I stepped toward him, my fingers wrapping around the EpiPen in his trembling grasp. His eyes widened.

"I'm sorry, Colin," I whispered, my voice soft. Lethal. "I don't. You're too much of a disappointment."

And then I pressed the EpiPen straight into his chest, leaning on it with the weight of my whole body, feeling the resistance of flesh beneath the needle that had shot out of it. His breath hitched, his body jerked, as the epinephrine shot through his veins. As it spread from his heart.

His hand weakly reached for the EpiPen still lodged in his chest, his mouth working silently.

Even though I'd been prepared for it, I instinctively winced, brought my hand up to cover my mouth from the strangled scream that threatened to escape. Or maybe the vomit.

The room was eerily silent except for the faint sound of his ragged breath slowing down. Until finally, it stopped. Colin's body went slack. His eyes were glazed and unfocused, fixed on something beyond me.

Beside me, Kara had her eyes closed, like she had averted them, or maybe she was savoring the moment—I couldn't tell which. When she opened her eyes, she looked from me to Colin and then back again.

"God," she said casually, crossing her arms. "I'd *kill* for a cigarette."

55

The police officer's name was Carver. I didn't remember him introducing himself the way they do in movies or on TV, but his surname was stitched onto his uniform. It was easy enough to make out, especially when he leaned over me as if to punctuate his questions, which he kept repeating over and over.

"So, you say you were locked in the recording booth since last night?"

"Yes," I said for what felt like the hundredth time, trying not to squirm on the uncomfortable chair they'd seated me in. I was exhausted, frazzled, and I desperately needed a shower. I was still wearing the dress from last night. It was wrinkled and sticky with stale sweat, adhered to my skin.

After a long back-and-forth about where to conduct the interview, they had driven me to the station. I suspected it was partly to make it easier to search the house. I'd been shepherded into the back of a patrol car just as more officers arrived—crime scene investigators, uniformed cops putting up yellow tape. I caught a glimpse of the neighbor standing on his lawn, decked out in designer sweats and pristine white sneakers, craning his neck to see what was going on.

The press had started to show up too, but they were too slow to catch me being whisked away.

Though the fan on Officer Carver's desk was anything but high tech, and I could still feel the relative LA heat on my skin, I shivered. I'd shivered enough over the last two hours for the younger officer, who stood in the corner, to drape a hoodie over my shoulders.

It wasn't my first time being questioned by the police—after the Berg incident, I'd spent hours in a station like this. Back then, the officers had seemed more suspicious and less sympathetic. That said, it definitely felt like all the officers then and now were questioning my life choices.

"And Mr. Harrington locked you in there?" Officer Carver continued, shifting to another line of questioning.

The police had smashed open the door to the sound studio when they found me. I was frazzled, hungover, and half hysterical.

"Like I told you, I have no idea why. We'd just had dinner..." I thought about adding a dramatic sniff but decided that would be overkill. "He didn't even leave me any water. There was no way to get to the bathroom."

Kara had told me to go on the carpet before she left. *It'll add authenticity to the scene*, she'd said, her tone all businesslike, before locking me inside. She would know about creating authentic moments—I'd helped her to the bathroom enough times to know she was used to people seeing her at her most vulnerable.

"Hmm. The private chef Mr. Harrington hired said you were...experiencing some withdrawal symptoms from alcohol. Do you think that has affected your recollection of last night?"

"I've had trouble with drinking," I admitted, leaning into the narrative Colin had crafted for me. If there was one thing Kara had drilled into me, it was that appearing weak made you seem less of a threat. "Colin—I mean, Mr. Harrington—he said he'd help me sober up. But I slipped. Maybe that's why he left me in there, to dry out or something. But I can't believe he'd just...forget about me."

"And before Mr. Harrington left...he uploaded something to his channels?"

I nodded. My head was starting to ache from the repetition.

"Hmm. The audio is very incriminating. Admitting to killing his first wife...You didn't find it suspicious? That he would upload something like that?"

"I don't know. I wasn't exactly coherent at the time. But Colin had strange moods. And he'd been talking a lot about Mary lately."

"Hmm."

Officer Carver exchanged a glance with the younger officer in the corner.

"This isn't the first time you've had an entanglement with a married man, Miss Albright. And both men have ended up hurt. Wouldn't you say that's a suspicious pattern?"

I tried to look shocked by the implication. "I mean...I hadn't thought about it like that. I must just have terrible luck with men."

I heard the officer in the corner snort. Officer Carver cast him a sharp glare.

"And Mrs. Harrington?"

"Kara? What about her?"

"You were hired as her personal companion, but last night, you were dining with her husband instead. No one was on duty to watch Mrs. Harrington. What do you think of that oversight?"

I dropped my gaze, letting the guilt show. "I'm not proud of it. But Colin said he had it under control. I didn't think—" I faltered, trying to play the helpless woman. "I didn't think he would try to hurt her. I thought he was going to…I thought he cared for her."

"Here's what we know, Miss Albright. Mr. Harrington locks you in the sound booth. He roughs up his incapacitated wife. Then he uses EpiPens to end his life. But why?"

"Like I said. I…I think it had something to do with Mary. He never really got over her death. It haunted him."

The other officer shrugged. "Maybe he felt guilty after all."

Carver sighed, skepticism wavering. "I'm really sorry to keep going over this again and again, Miss Albright. You must be exhausted after the ordeals of last night."

I sniffed. "I wish it never happened."

I wished they would have offered me breakfast.

Carver turned to the younger officer. "And this Micky person?"

"Picked up last night by CCTV entering a club in Santa Barbara."

"What time?"

"Ten thirty. He left a few hours later."

Carver nodded.

"There's something else," the younger officer added, handing over a sheet of paper. "The contacts on Mr. Harrington's phone."

Carver swiped the paper and scanned through the list of names, absorbing it with a furrowed brow. For a moment, his bulldog expression softened, replaced by something else. Weariness, maybe.

"You may go, Miss Albright. I'm sorry to have troubled you. We'll call you if we need anything further."

I stood, glancing around for something to gather, but I had nothing but a paper coffee cup, long since cold. I turned to leave.

"Miss Albright," Carver called out, just as I reached the door.

"Yes?"

"Mr. Harrington was well connected to some…interesting individuals. I'd be careful if I were you."

A coldness gripped me. *You just weren't good enough for us, Anna.*

Who was *us*?

"Don't worry," I said. "I will be."

As I walked down the station hallway toward the double doors leading outside, I heard the officers exchange a few words before the door snapped shut behind me.

"What a mess."

"Well. You know, famous people are all messed up in one way or another."

56

Over the next week, Colin was all over the news. His face stared up at me from every glossy tabloid, bright blue eyes wide, tousled hair falling over his forehead, features distorted by the bent paper, crinkled by some curious onlooker who had already skimmed the pages for the juiciest gossip.

The headlines screamed out the scandal: *The Real Monster Behind the Voice: Colin Harrington's Shocking Downfall.*

It was a stupid question, but I wondered where they had found so many haunted images of him. I'd only ever seen Colin look truly shocked once: the moment I'd pushed the EpiPen into his chest.

And it wasn't just Colin. Kara was everywhere too. Gaunt Kara. Haughty Kara. Even a blurry, shadowy silhouette of her in a wheelchair, captured by some audacious paparazzo from beyond the fence. Ever since Colin's confession had been broadcast, the tabloid press had been struggling to decide what role Kara should play. A tragic victim? A resilient survivor? I even saw badges proclaiming *Save Kara Harrington!*

Kara would have hated it.

Worst of all, there were pictures of me. Caught in a silk slip through the estate window, creeping around at night. Arguing with Flora by the roadside. Going to a restaurant with Colin.

I had become a reluctant tabloid sensation: *Anna Albright: The Girl Who Survived Colin Harrington.*

Who IS Anna Albright?

The Spell of Colin Harrington and the Dark Side of the Hollywood Dream!

The covers of the magazines felt like tiny windows into the last months—time I tried to actively push from my mind whenever it threatened to encroach. Which was constantly. Every time I closed my eyes, I would see Colin. Colin smiling at me, laughing with me. Colin leaning in for a kiss. Colin hovering over me, menacing, dark. Colin tumbling away from me. The sound of Colin impacting the pavement. The bloody mess he'd left behind, like a wet patch of paint on one of Kara's paintings where the artist had used too much medium.

To make things worse, this whole mess had dug up the Marcus Berg scandal all over again: *Anna Albright's Dark Past: A Trail of Manipulation?* Even if the story didn't cast me as a villain, it didn't make the suffocating attention any easier to bear.

Besides, there was no way I could slip into the care home to check on him now—not when my face was plastered all over the newsstands. My career, which had seemed dead and was surprisingly revived thanks to Colin's intervention, was now irrevocably buried. I was damaged goods. Every promising connection I'd cultivated by getting close to Colin had turned to scorched earth after his death. I didn't even try calling anyone—I didn't know who of these connections could be among Colin's creepy circle.

And then there was Officer Carver's warning. *Mr. Harrington was well connected to some interesting individuals.*

He hadn't named names, but I remembered the way his brow furrowed when he'd skimmed through Colin's list of contacts from his phone. The resigned look on his face. I needed to get out of the city.

I avoided the Harrington estate, which had become overrun with reporters swarming the gates. The media had probably captured enough footage of the exterior to last them a century, but they didn't seem to realize that yet. I wondered how long they were planning to stay. Maybe they were camped out there, waiting for Colin's ghost to burst out and give them a full report of what had happened.

Eventually, they'd move on to the next story, but Colin had been popular—a voice millions listened to—and his gruesome death only fueled people's morbid curiosity. Everyone wanted more details, but there was no one left to interview. My phone, which the police had returned to me in a plastic bag, had been going off nonstop since I recharged it. I'd abandoned social media and ignored all the calls.

Even the ones from my father.

I knew the call was inevitable—judgmental, somehow twisting this situation to be my fault. Or maybe he'd criticize me for not leveraging it to my advantage.

I didn't want to admit that it stung. I wanted to be emotionally distant, immune to the need to please him. But there it was, creeping up on me—relentless, insidious. I didn't know if I would ever be rid of it.

In the end, though, he surprised me. When I finally opened my messages, scrolling through endless interview requests and spam, I found one from him. It was short, just two words:

Come home.

Micky picked me up from my hotel. I had no way of contacting Kara, and it wasn't safe to try—she'd still be deep in her cover. But I needed a way to get my things and my car.

As I clambered into his black Volvo and buckled the seatbelt, Micky watched the rearview mirror like a hawk, eyes darting for any sign of paparazzi. His knit cap was pulled low across his forehead. He adjusted his glasses, the same wire-rimmed pair he always wore. Given the level of subterfuge he was attempting, sunglasses might've suited him better.

"I thought you were staying at the Regency?" he asked, voice casual but curious.

I'd been snapped there last week, despite my best attempts to blend in with an unassuming hoodie and shades. It wasn't an extravagantly expensive hotel, but I'd chosen it for the high-end promise of privacy. That hadn't worked out as planned.

"I've been moving around a lot," I replied.

"Smart," Micky said, nodding as he guided the car onto the street. The weather was overcast, the gray sky hanging low over the city like a lid, promising rain. The streets were slick from an earlier drizzle, and the occasional gust of wind rattled the branches of the trees lining the road.

We drove for a while in silence, the muted hum of traffic filling the air as the city pulsed around us.

"Tinted windows," I remarked, tapping the glass with my knuckle.

"Yeah."

"Smart," I said.

Micky gave me a small smile. "We are going to have to talk, aren't we?"

That was putting it mildly. Micky had been keeping secrets from me the whole time I'd worked for him. If I hadn't wanted answers so much, I might have screamed at him.

"I was waiting for you to start."

Micky sighed, his fingers tightening on the wheel. "As you probably guessed, I've been around the Harringtons for a long time. I knew Colin first, from way back before he got mixed up with all…this. Before the fame."

"Why lie?" I asked, watching him adjust his glasses again, his eyes flicking nervously between me and the road.

"Would you have applied for the job if you didn't need a sound studio?" he asked, keeping his voice level.

I shook my head. "Probably not. But I hate that you sold me out like that, like a lamb to the slaughter. I hate that you all trapped me."

"I knew it was wrong," Micky said softly. "That's why I hid Mary's tapes for you to find. I was hoping you'd piece it all together."

"Kind of a pathetic way to make amends," I muttered. Micky hung his head, ashamed, and didn't say anything. As much as I wanted to yell at him, there was something nagging at me.

"Some of those tapes made Kara look pretty bad," I said after a pause.

"I just wanted you to hear Mary's whole story."

"I didn't. I never found Mary's last tapes. At least, I never heard the one Kara was referring to."

"Colin found some and destroyed them, but he knew there were more missing. I think he started to suspect me. That's why he expelled me from the house."

I thought back to Colin discovering Micky and me arguing. How he'd told Micky to leave, to not show his face around the house anymore. I thought Colin had been chivalrous, but it hadn't had anything to do with me after all.

"Oh," I said.

We drove in silence for a while. The traffic had slowed to a crawl as we approached a busy intersection. I glanced out the window at the line of brake lights ahead, the muffled honks of impatient drivers creating a steady, agitated rhythm. I had a feeling this was going to be a long, painful ride.

"You said you were Colin's friend. How long were you working for Kara?"

A pained expression crossed Micky's face. "Ever since I realized what happened to Mary was not an accident."

I put two and two together. "You loved her."

He nodded. "For the longest time. I didn't know what was hurting her, but I told her we could leave together. That I'd take her anywhere. But she didn't want to leave." He thought for a moment, before correcting himself. "Didn't think she *could* leave."

"Reminds me of someone I know," I muttered.

"What do you mean?"

"Why didn't Kara just *go*? Why did she stick around all this time?"

"Well, that's one of the reasons I guess I agreed to all of this. Kara was never going to let Colin get away with it. She had to see it through, even if it killed her."

"*I* could have *died*, Micky," I exclaimed.

Micky winced. "I never wanted you to get hurt. I only wanted Colin to be exposed. But we never should have used you. I'm sorry."

I couldn't say I forgave him, because I didn't. But maybe in time I'd understand.

Slowly and gradually, the traffic lurched to life, and we were moving again.

57

Micky drove the car right up to the gates, where perhaps half a dozen bored-looking journalists and cameramen suddenly sprang into action. He did his best to ignore their waves and knocks on the window as the driveway gate slid aside, and then he drove down the shallow ramp.

"Do you think they saw me?" I asked, glancing at the receding crowd in the side-view mirror.

"Maybe. They'll be more insistent on the way back if they realize you're here," Micky remarked as we entered the cover of the garage, where the door slid smoothly shut. Micky parked and pulled up the handbrake with finality, like a punctuation mark to his sentence. I got out of the car and paused, taking in the whole collection of luxury cars.

"What will happen to all of this?" I asked, trailing behind Micky as he made his way to the elevator.

"It's Kara's now. Though I doubt she'll keep it forever," Micky said, pressing a button to take us to the upper floors. The doors slid shut, and only the very slight shift beneath my feet told me we were ascending.

I'd been so preoccupied with the spiral my own life had taken that I hadn't spent much time pondering Kara's next move. "What's she going to do now?"

"Why don't you ask her yourself?" Micky replied, just as the doors opened, revealing the hallway that led to Kara's bedroom. It was exactly as I remembered it: the same furniture, the same lighting, the same grim contemporary art Kara had once been so fond of lining the walls. Though now, all of it felt somehow foreign, alien. Like a staged set for a production I hadn't realized I'd been a part of.

Micky lingered behind while I walked up to Kara's bedroom door, the way I had a hundred times before. Strangely nervous, I knocked, then pushed it open, unsure of what to expect.

"Kara?"

"Hi, Anna."

There she was, resting in bed with a thin blanket over her knees, positioned the way I'd seen her countless times before—except this time, her eyes were sharp and focused. When she saw it was me, she relaxed perceptibly and sat up straighter in bed.

"Were you expecting someone else?" I asked.

"You can never be too careful." Kara raised her long arms above her head in a languorous stretch. "I didn't spend more than a year in a wheelchair just to be exposed by some wayward maid at the wrong moment."

"It's quite an achievement," I remarked.

"I did get caught by one of our maids once. I told her if she ever breathed a word to anyone, I'd ruin her life and have her whole family deported. Not my proudest moment, but I did what I had to do."

I thought back to the young maid I'd run into during my first weeks in the house. She had barely wanted to look at me, much less speak. I'd assumed she was snooping through my things, but it turns out she'd just been terrified of Kara, like the rest of us.

That explains it.

"How long do you plan on keeping it up?" I asked.

"For a while. Especially now that Colin is dead and the police are still investigating. It would be awfully suspicious if I regained mobility now. But my lawyers have conveniently found documents outlining my will and suggestions for conservatorship in the case of Colin's death. My lawyers will handle the estate, while Micky will be responsible for situating me in a comfortable care home. I'll spend six months or so there, then gradually make a miraculous recovery."

She laughed at my expression. "Nothing too extravagant. Not the flamboyant comeback Colin was planning for me—that would attract attention. Not just from the authorities, but from whoever Colin was working with. No, the fact that I'm fully mobile will be a secret entrusted to few. Whenever I'm in public, it will always be in a wheelchair."

I thought of Kara's life before: the endless galas, award ceremonies, press tours. Being photographed by paparazzi while lounging on the deck of some yacht in the Riviera sun. She had sacrificed all of that to get away with revenge. She'd forever be playing a role.

"That's…quite the price to pay," I said.

"It was worth it," she replied decisively.

"At least you have Micky."

"Yes. I think I'll take him on as a new companion. It'll be a relief, not having to pretend all the time." She paused, then added, "He had a soft spot for you, you know. He's a good guy."

"I know. But I don't think I can ever forgive him for the deception. Either of you. You wanted me to go down for *murder*…"

Funny, they wanted to frame me for a murder I didn't commit, but in the end, I actually did it. I was guilty. Even if I didn't feel like it.

Kara nodded slowly. "I understand." She studied me for a moment, then her gaze wandered, almost involuntarily, to the painting of a skyline on the wall—the one Mary had given her. "You know, I tried to hate you, Anna. It made everything easier. But there were moments when I genuinely enjoyed your company."

"Me too," I said quietly.

In different circumstances, we might have been friends.

She rolled her shoulders, as if trying to shrug off the vulnerability.

"So what are you going to do now?" she asked.

"Me? I'll go home."

"And what about Marcus Berg? The director you drugged?" She raised an eyebrow at my surprised expression. "Please. I knew about that well before you ever entered this house. I also know you've been visiting him under an alias. Why?"

"I wanted to keep an eye on him," I admitted. "To have the upper hand, if he ever woke up. To be prepared."

"He deserved it," she said immediately, her voice uncharacteristically sincere. "He and Colin both had it coming. You shouldn't feel bad about them for a second."

I didn't know what to say. Berg had been a liar and a manipulator with a reputation for using young actresses. Colin had been an abuser. They'd both deserved justice, but I couldn't erase the discomfort I felt when remembering their final moments. Colin wheezing in his chair before I plunged an EpiPen into his heart. Berg's face when he snorted the fentanyl-laced coke, clutching his chest as he fell to the ground.

Which was scarier? Bearing the weight of causing someone pain or admitting that part of it—the part where I'd wanted to punish them for hurting me—felt good?

Finally, I settled on "I don't know if I agree with you. But thanks, Kara."

"Micky will give you some cash, off the books. Be smart with it. The authorities will keep an eye on you for a while."

"Okay." I walked toward the door. "Good luck with acting…I'm sure you must be tired of it by now."

"You have no idea," she said with a tired smile, sweeping her dark hair off her shoulders. "But it has its uses," she added with a twinkle in her eye.

Micky walked me out of the room and down to the basement, where my things—all my new expensive cashmere clothes, lingerie, and accessories—were stuffed into the same beat-up cardboard boxes I had first carried into my room at the Harringtons'. We picked them up and headed to the garage. I tried not to look up at the bar as we passed. If I had stared long enough, I am sure I would have been able to conjure up an image of Colin behind it, beaming, shaking me a cocktail.

Now he was on a slab somewhere, tucked into a freezer.

In the garage, we loaded everything back into my beat-up car. After I slammed the trunk shut and wiped my hands on my jeans, I turned to face Micky. This was goodbye.

"I take it the project is canned," I finally said. The whole time I'd packed, we hadn't exchanged a single word.

"You'd be right. I'm afraid it's not a loyal interpretation of the video game source material," Micky said, scratching his neck awkwardly. "I took a lot of inspiration from my own life, the people around me. The fans would be very confused."

At this point, I'd figured as much. "It was based on Mary, wasn't it? The Countess was Mary, and the Count was Colin?"

Micky nodded. "That's right. But more than that, it might attract the wrong kind of attention, having your name attached to it. We still don't know exactly who Colin was connected to—although I have some ideas—and whether they suspect any…foul play."

It wasn't anything I hadn't expected, but it still stung. Now I truly had nothing tethering me to the voice acting world anymore, to what had for so long been my dream. "I understand."

"For what it's worth, I thought you made a great Countess. And here…" Micky reached into his pocket and pulled out an envelope. It looked thick, secured with a rubber band—like one of those clandestine hand-offs you see in movies. "For all the work you've done so far."

I stared down at the envelope. The Harringtons had paid me well for my time with Kara, and this stack of money looked like more than I had ever had. It was probably at least thirty thousand dollars. But even with all that, my dream for my career was all but scrapped. I'd ended up even worse than when I had started.

"Thanks."

"And…you know, if you need work down the line, I'm sure I can set you up with one of my connections. Maybe start fresh, under a new name. Small projects. A clean slate."

I shook my head. "You know, I think I might be done with acting. With this world. It brings out the worst in me. I'm going home."

Micky nodded slowly. "I understand. I think I do." He hesitated for a moment, then dug into his pocket again. This time, he pulled out something bulkier and held it out to me.

"What's this?" I asked, accepting it and turning it around in my fingers. I knew what it was, of course. But I didn't know why Micky was giving it to me.

"A tape player. And one of Mary's tapes. I've gone over them for years, but I'm no closer to figuring things out. Apart from Kara, you're the only other person who's heard any of Mary's tapes. Maybe you'll catch something we didn't."

"I'm not sure I want to listen to any more of Mary's tapes," I said, though I still tucked it into my pocket.

"Just let me know if you do," Micky said. "And Anna…I'm sorry. For everything."

I looked at Micky—his tired eyes, the lines etched deeper into his face, his posture slumped with the weight of everything that had happened. I should have been angry with him, furious for his role in all of this. But if he hadn't slipped me those tapes, I might never have given Kara the chance to trust me. In his own way, Micky had at least tried to help.

"Thanks, Micky. See you around," I said. It was one of those things you say to someone you're almost certain you'll never see again.

"Take care of yourself, Anna," Micky said softly.

I climbed into the driver's seat and forced the ignition to life. I pressed my foot down on the pedal and steered away, leaving Micky behind in the garage, alone with the ghost of Mary.

As I drove onto the driveway, the lingering press snapped to attention like a pack of hungry wolves, cameras flashing wildly. But I drove past them, left them in my wake.

I didn't look back.

58

KARA

The Green Village care home was a fine enough establishment, but there was a note of disbelief in the director's tone when Micky called to let them know he was hoping to situate me there.

Disbelief, and maybe a tiny hint of hesitation. After all, following Colin's death a few weeks ago, a new miasma of notoriety had descended on me in addition to all the rumors that had circulated before, and the bad press still hadn't died down. But eventually, he'd conceded.

It was a sunny autumn afternoon when we arrived. I was wearing a dark blue suit and a blue scarf and sunglasses to hide my face. I'd instructed Micky to dispose of anything Colin had bought me in the house. I'd never wear anything beige again in my life.

Micky rolled me through the parking lot, dodging the half dozen or so paparazzi who had materialized out of thin air. Someone must have been tailing our car and tipped them off. I continued to stare straight ahead as Micky pushed my wheelchair forward, yelling at the paparazzi to back off. Their sounds faded as we went through the doors of the care home, where they blended with the sound of a gently dripping water feature.

The director of the home, David Colburn, was waiting for us along with a pair of nurses. He welcomed us, glancing at the door and the dim sounds of paparazzi from beyond as he did so. I wondered if he regretted his decision. But then he smiled. After all, a celebrity client is a celebrity client, and all publicity is good publicity. Or so someone once told me.

What a laughable idea.

After all, bad publicity was what had ruined Anna's career. It had stopped what could have been a promising ascent and made her desperate, willing to clutch at any opportunity that came her way. Made her easy prey for Colin. And—I admit—to me, before I thought better of it.

One of the nurses took command of my wheelchair and pushed me onward into the building as Micky and David trailed behind, talking.

"Recreational time on the terrace…"

"Bright, airy interiors…an integrated ambient sound system, based on the latest, cutting-edge research…"

"Homemade meals from fresh, organic ingredients…we are on a first-name basis with all of our suppliers…"

But I wasn't here to listen to ambient rainforest noises through sophisticated speakers while someone fed me saltine crackers and organic carrot puree soup. I was here because I owed someone something.

Because I owed Anna.

The nurse rolled me through a sandstone corridor lit with natural light and stopped in a common room to point out the residents. All of them were older than I was, probably by many decades. She leaned over and removed my sunglasses as she did. I wished she hadn't; it had been easier to study their faces discreetly with shades on. To see if I recognized any of them. I didn't.

"Most of the people here have had long and illustrious careers in show business," the nurse said brightly. "You'll have a lot in common. I'm sure you'll make many friends."

I doubted it. Making friends wasn't really my forte. For a long time, I hadn't had a single person I would have referred to with that title. Mary had been my first and probably only real friend, even if the world had forced us apart. When she died, I'd lost myself.

I would never forgive Colin for what he had done to her or to me: Twenty years from now, I'd probably still visit his grave just to vandalize it. But I admit, finding out what he did to Mary gave me a purpose. Avenging her had been the greatest and proudest achievement of my life.

But now I had a new friend to protect. Anna.

Even if she didn't see me that way.

The nurse continued pushing me down the hallway until we passed a few closed doors and came to a stop by an open door to a nice, spacious room, not unlike some hotel rooms I'd stayed at in an upscale villa in Mexico.

"Obviously, many of our clients are high-profile, so naturally, the public is curious. But not to fret—we have a freshly installed state-of-the-art security system to guarantee our clients' privacy," Colburn was saying.

Something about his forceful insistence told me that when Colin's death scandal broke, Colburn learned about Anna's unwarranted visits. He must have had the shock of his life when he realized a potential murder suspect had been sneaking into his exclusive clinic under a pseudonym.

"That's a relief," Micky said. He nodded at the doors beside my new room. "The place is fully occupied, then?"

"We are a very desirable establishment," Colburn said. The urge to roll my eyes was great, even with my years of practice in restraint. Please. There'd been no wait to speak of, or maybe he really had tripped over his feet to get me to stay here.

"Just to your right, you have Elvira Anne. Multiple Oscars for screenwriting in the '70s, if you'll recall. And to the left, Marcus Berg, a renowned director…"

Colburn faltered, probably recalling that Anna had worked for me and wondering how much or how well connected I was with her circumstances.

"What a coincidence!" Micky exclaimed, dissipating the tension. "I'm a big fan of his work."

What an incredible coincidence, indeed.

"We'll give you a few minutes to settle in, and then someone will be with you to take you through the rest of the paperwork."

"Excellent," Micky said.

Micky waited for the staff to leave before kneeling beside me.

"It's not too late to change your mind."

"I have to recover somewhere. Might as well be here, where I can do something useful."

Micky sighed. "Aren't you tired of pretending to be sick? You could have stayed at home. With me. And not have to pretend."

"I've built this ruse up for so long. Might as well have it be useful one last time."

"I still don't see how this is necessary."

I didn't respond. Micky was not reassured by my silence. A scowl formed on his forehead, above the rims of his glasses.

"No rash actions, okay?"

Poor Micky. He would always want to restrain my darker impulses.

But I wasn't here just to observe.

It was time to repay the favor.

59

ANNA

The TV in my father's living room was blaring news, with capitalized headlines and anchors sporting their bleached smiles, while the rain outside pounded against the stone exterior. The warm glow from inside extended twenty feet through the steel-framed windows, casting an orange hue over the traditional, columned front porch and pooling onto the shadowed lawn, where it was eventually swallowed by darkness. It was a different sky than the one I had gotten used to in LA, but I welcomed the change. It felt good to be anywhere but there.

My father and his new wife Dina lived in a contemporary cottage—an urban retreat with minimalist interiors in white, black, and gray, complemented by oak flooring. It was stylish, though they hadn't done much to make it particularly personable.

"You'd make a fine teacher. It's important for a teacher to have a pleasant voice," my father was saying.

We had just finished dinner and had retired to the dark leather sofas with our coffees. The meal had been another exceptional if slightly clinical one. I'd seen Dina measuring cuts of lamb with a ruler. She hadn't spoken to me much since I arrived. I wondered if, after years of politely cool interactions, I was now intruding in their lives, silently judging her compulsive behavior with meat. But at least she'd made me coffee.

I was curled up on the sofa, cradling my cup, with thick socks on my feet. The wood crackled in the fireplace, which my father lit when he detected the first autumn chill. It was hard to believe that just a few weeks had passed since I was in sunny California. It felt even stranger to be this relaxed around my father. I had expected him to reprimand me, to set me straight, but the welcome had been gentler than I'd anticipated. It was as if he understood that I had at least *tried* my best, and that was worth something.

He was determined to steer me toward another career path. For the past few weeks, he'd come up with various plans and schemes, suggestions for my future. For the first time, I wasn't objecting. In a way, it felt nice, having him care for once. For so many years, I'd felt like I hadn't even been worth his consideration.

"...as we continue to learn new developments about the death of director Marcus Berg in a Los Angeles care home..."

I almost dropped my coffee.

"Careful. The carpet is new," my father noted, though his gaze was fixed on the TV. We continued watching in transfixed silence. My fingers tightened around the porcelain handle.

For so long, I'd worried Berg would wake up and come for me. That I'd end up in jail. That he'd use his connections to do something far worse to me. I'd snuck into the care home out of desperation, convinced I'd figure something out if he showed signs of waking up. Negotiate with him. Figure out a way to keep him under...

But now I didn't have to make that choice. I was free.

"...a name you may recognize from projects like *Scott! A Free Dog!* and animated films like *Robot Redux*. Authorities are still trying to piece together the circumstances and determine whether there is cause to suspect willful neglect or malpractice..."

"It's a strange world, Hollywood," my father remarked. "You have to be uniquely devious to make it there."

I set my cup down on the coffee table, willing my fingers to stop shaking. "Well, I've left that world behind now."

"A wise choice. You don't have to excel at something glamorous to succeed. You just have to excel at something. Look at Dina's occupations—cooking, cleaning, exercising at the gym. Frivolous pursuits in the grand scheme of things, but mastery in anything is a worthwhile act."

His wife looked like she might cry. "Dinner was lovely, Dina," I said to her retreating back. I watched her leave the room and glanced at my father.

"She knows who she married," my father said coolly.

"You're taking another trip then?" I asked, hoping to shift the topic away from self-improvement and his peculiar relationship with his wife. I had almost preferred it when my father treated me as a lost cause—it meant he wasn't so involved in my life.

Though, I had to admit, being welcomed into his home and receiving a warmer, more interested attitude felt good. It was as if something I'd been chasing my whole life was finally falling into place.

"New York," he said, lifting his coffee cup to his lips and taking a long sip. "Just for a few weeks. I have a client there who has some harmful thoughts that need reprogramming."

My heart skipped a beat. "What did you say?"

"New York. Why, what was it you wanted to clarify?"

"It's nothing," I said, rising from the sofa. "I think I'll go relax in my room for a moment."

"It will be good for you to find a pursuit. An idle mind is the devil's playground."

I forced a smile. "I'll think of something tomorrow."

A staircase with blackened steel banisters led to the guest bedroom. I'd never had a bedroom in this house, even though we'd moved here after my mother's death, and even though I hadn't been old enough to leave home yet. I had spent most of my time at my aunt's house, feeling like an unwanted guest or intruder whenever I visited what was officially considered my home.

I closed the door of the bedroom and sifted through my things, looking for what Micky had given me: a recorder with one of Mary's tapes.

Maybe you'll catch something we didn't.

I hadn't wanted to listen to it. I didn't want to give Kara and Micky the satisfaction of being any more involved in their world than they had already made me. I didn't want to think for a moment longer about anything related to Colin Harrington, the man I had helped kill. The man who had been planning to frame me for murder. The man I had loved.

You just weren't good enough for us, Anna...

But the same curiosity that had driven me to desperately search the Harringtons' house for more of Mary's tapes had prevented me from disposing of it. So there it had sat, untouched, at the bottom of my luggage through the long drive from Los Angeles to Minnesota and these few weeks I'd spent at my father's house. Such an innocuous thing, nestled among the high-end periwinkle blue sweater I'd invested in when I was trying to fit into the Harringtons' world.

I picked up the recorder and turned it around in my hands. Listening to Mary's tapes had felt different when I thought Kara might be guilty. When I was desperate to prove that I wasn't mad for imagining she was up to something. Before I had known Colin was responsible.

But from Colin's words, I had pieced together that he wasn't the sole person responsible. There was some sort of larger organization behind Colin, people who were helping him make and enforce his decisions.

But who else? Who were they?

Dreading what I'd find but desperate to expel the uneasy knot in my stomach, I drew a breath and pressed play on the recorder.

With a click and a whir, the recording sprang to life.

The first voice, that of the interviewer, was clearer on this tape. But it was still obscured, as if he were leaning back in a chair, speaking out of range of the recorder.

I could make out some words: session, growth, progress.

I caught the end of his sentence: "—lost sight of who that is, haven't you?"

Mary's voice was tense. "The real me? I'm not sure you even know what that means, Doctor. I don't."

"—why I'm here—piece yourself back together. Not—you've become confused. Lost—who you are—condition—"

Mary paused, her voice softer. "Colin says I'm paranoid. Sometimes I can see why. Sometimes I think it's all part of some great plot. That everyone is lying to me, even you."

The other voice huffed, amused. "There's that paranoia—creeping in—peer-reviewed techniques—your benefit."

"You are saying I need to trust the process. But sometimes what Colin does, what you are telling me is for my benefit, feels more like a test…what happens if I fail?"

The interviewer's voice was too distant to piece together the words of his reply. But Mary repeated some of his words right back to him, laughing incredulously.

"Unlock the version of you that you've forgotten? Sounds like something in a sci-fi script." But then her voice broke slightly, vulnerability bleeding in. "I just…don't know who I am anymore. Maybe you're right. Maybe I am lost. And I do need someone to tell me who I am… But I can't shake it. I can't shake this feeling that none of this is real."

"—why we are doing this—in the end you'll thank me—see that I was always—by your side."

Mary's final words were whispered, almost to herself. "Something bad is going to happen to me, isn't it?"

The interviewer seemingly leaned forward, the microphone picking up his voice clearly as he replied:

"No, Mary. You are going to be reborn. Now, are you ready to begin?"

The recorder tumbled from my fingers and bounced on the soft bed, whirring and spluttering for a moment before the tape ran out.

That voice. The reprogrammer on the tape. I knew that voice.

As I stared into space, the same voice rang out again, except this time from down the stairs.

"Anna? Could you come downstairs?"

A voice I knew as well as my own.

My father's.

60

I stood, rooted to the spot by shock, my fingers still extended and spread from where they had relinquished their grip on the recorder. The recorder that had just unveiled a final and terrible secret.

What I knew: Colin had struggled growing up, lost touch with his childhood friends and family, but eventually found a group of like-minded individuals whose philosophies resonated with him. He'd built his empire—a podcast empire—around these ideologies, delighting in spreading them to the masses.

This group was a constant, shadowy presence in his life. Members came and went freely in his house, using each other to manipulate their partners and friends in what they called "reprogramming" sessions. They vetted each other's staff members, friends, and partners. They claimed to pursue self-improvement and self-help, but their methods were violent, brutal, manipulative, and abusive. This was Kara's theory, something she'd pieced together from her time in the house and from listening to Mary's tapes.

I hadn't been entirely convinced. I'd seen some of Colin's friends and acquaintances come and go, but I hadn't had any solid proof of another member of this group.

But what I'd now learned: One of them was my father.

It wasn't a coincidence that they knew one another. And I hadn't been suggested the job at random. I'd been *nominated*.

My father had sent me straight to the lion's den.

"Anna?" My father called out again.

"Just a minute!" I shouted back, shoving the recorder under a stack of clothes. My heart pounded furiously in my chest. There was a door and a staircase between us. It was impossible he had heard anything, right?

I cracked open the bedroom door and started descending the stairs, gripping the handrail to stop my fingers from trembling. Halfway down, I saw my father waiting at the bottom, his silhouette framed by the dim light from the hallway.

It wasn't just my life he had jeopardized. I'd spent years wondering why my mother killed herself, why she had left me. I'd thought my mom's relatives, insistent that my father had somehow failed her, were sad and bitter, directing their grief at an unlikable and flawed man, who nonetheless was no villain.

But now I knew different. I had experienced firsthand how someone like my father could draw a woman in. How their sole focus was to work her into something pleasant, something with purpose, something valuable. Regardless of the cost.

"Sorry," I said, forcing a casual tone. "It's hard to hear over the rain."

He studied me intently before glancing at the rain-soaked window. The storm outside was furious, the rain lashing down and rattling the giant panes of glass.

"Yes, it is. The storm's really picking up. The gutters are clogged. Water's seeping into the attic again, and if we don't fix it tonight, we'll be dealing with major leaks by morning."

I stared at him, trying to make sense of his words. *The storm's really picking up. Peer-reviewed techniques for your benefit. The gutters are clogged. Unlock the version of yourself that you've forgotten. Reprogram. Leaks by morning.* Everything was blurring together into a chaotic fog.

My father was *they*. My father was *us*. I didn't know how many there were in this group Colin and Kara had referred to, but I knew one was standing here right in front of me.

The rain was coming down in sheets, and thunder growled in the distance.

"Just come and hold the ladder for me, Anna. I'll need someone steady." His voice was calm, but it carried an edge—impatient like he was done pretending to ask. Like I should have known better than to make him wait.

He limped down the hallway, grabbed a jacket from the hook near the door, and slipped it on with practiced ease. I pulled on the thin windbreaker I'd bought in California and followed him silently to the door, my heart pounding. Was this really about the gutters? Or did he know something? Had he heard something? Was he testing me?

We stepped outside into the storm, the cold rain immediately soaking through my clothes, clinging to my skin like an additional, unwelcome layer. The wind howled, making the house creak and groan as though it were trapped in a giant tunnel. My father moved with determined strides toward the side of the house, grabbing the ladder that leaned against the wall.

"I'm going up. You hold the base."

The rain turned the metal ladder treacherous, slippery. It glistened in the rain like an oil slick. I could barely see through the blur of water streaming down my face. My father grabbed the first rung and began to climb, and I instinctively gripped the ladder's sides, trying to steady it.

The rain pounded relentlessly on the roof, turning the ground beneath me into a muddy stew. He was halfway up now, his body swaying precariously on the slick metal rungs.

The rain intensified, slashing through the night, and lightning flashed across the sky, briefly illuminating my father's face, twisted with concentration. He reached the top of the ladder, his hands stretching toward the clogged gutter.

My father had an upcoming trip to New York. Another client who has *harmful thoughts that need reprogramming.* How many people had he worked with? How many of those were trapped, like Dina was or Kara had been, and how many had been pressured to take their own lives, like Mary or my mother?

Another blinding flash of lightning lit up the sky, followed by a deep, rumbling thunder that shook the earth beneath my feet. In that stark light, I saw my father's hands gripping the gutter, preparing to clear the blockage.

There was one thing he had taught me that I could agree with.

Sometimes all a person needs is a little push.

END OF THE COMPANION

Do you love gripping psychological thrillers? Discover an exclusive extract from Jo's *The Photographer.*

ABOUT JO

Jo Crow crafts chilling psychological thrillers that delve into the shadows of everyday life, where dark secrets and twisted motives lurk just beneath the surface. Her stories capture the eerie tension of family life, where the familiar can suddenly become dangerous.

When she's not writing, Jo is a mom of two, often drawing inspiration from the unpredictability of parenthood. She enjoys curling up with a good thriller, taking her golden retriever on misty evening walks, and imagining the hidden fears that keep us awake at night.

Connect with Jo on Facebook, visit her website, or sign up for her mailing list for exclusive sneak peeks and updates.

You can contact Jo on:

- facebook.com/authorjocrow
- goodreads.com/authorjocrow
- bookbub.com/authors/jo-crow
- amazon.com/Jo-Crow/e/B0781194Q5

MAILING LIST

If you enjoyed my book and would like to read more of my work please sign up to my mailing list at:
www.JoCrow.com/MailingList

Not only can I notify you of my next release, but there will be special giveaways and I may even be on the hunt for some pre-release readers to get feedback before I publish my next book!

BLURB

I was crying. I couldn't help it.
"It's Ben. He's missing."

My husband is gone. No note, no explanation—**just vanished**. And he left our four-year-old daughter, Fay, alone in the house.

He also left behind a mountain of bills I have absolutely **no way of paying off**.

So when my old sorority sister and Instagram celebrity Marissa Jones turns up offering me a job as her personal photographer, **I can hardly refuse**. I have to provide for my little girl.

Even if it means going back to Milwaukee—the place I swore years ago that I would never to go back to. The city that still **haunts my nightmares**.

At least Marissa's brother, Teddy, is there. Back in college, he was always **my protector, my safe space**. And maybe, just maybe, he can be a whole lot more than that.

Before long, Fay and I start feeling **right at home** in Marissa's gorgeous home. But something isn't right.

I feel eyes on me—**watching, judging…waiting**.

And even worse than thinking I'm in danger, I fear my **daughter's life** might also be at risk.

Get your copy of *The Photographer*
eBook
Paperback
www.JoCrow.com

EXCERPT

Chapter One

After what felt like forever, I finally made it to the car and slid in behind the steering wheel, heart jittering, hands clammy, skin prickling with the sensation of being watched. Beside me, on the passenger seat, I set down my purse, my camera, and my keys.

The darkness outside was pressing up against the windows of the car, bringing with it a chill that made me shiver. The community college parking lot was badly lit and although in the distance I could see the muted light of the classrooms, the space in between was filled with nothing but darkness. With the tip of my elbow, I pushed the interior lock until it clunked loudly and sealed me in.

Safe. I was safe.

Taking some long, slow breaths—in through the nose, out through the mouth—I reached into the inside zip pocket of my purse and took out a small unlabeled plastic bottle. From it, I shook a quarter-sized dollop of hand sanitizer into my palm. Slowly, I rubbed it into my fingers and then carefully wiped the steering wheel. It was the good stuff; the kind used in hospitals and commercial kitchens. It was fragrance-free and left my hands papery, raw, and looking older than they should have. But it did the job.

After I'd cleaned the steering wheel, I started on my camera, carefully wiping the body and the controls then dusting the lens six times counterclockwise with the brush Ben bought me for my birthday. Midway through the seventh swipe, a vicious tap-tap-tap on the window shook my concentration. My breath caught in my throat. But then Jenna's face was pressed up against the glass and she was smiling at me, laughing, gesturing for me to open the door.

I didn't. But I did wind down the window.

"Jenna? Did I leave something behind in class?"

"No, silly. We wondered if you wanted to join us for a drink. Every week you say, 'Maybe next time.' But next week's the last class, so…" she trailed off and shrugged, glancing back at the others who were watching us expectantly.

My fingers tightened around the body of the camera in my lap. "I'm so sorry. I can't. Next week, though, I promise."

"Sure," Jenna replied, clearly not buying it. "See you."

Sitting back and trying to steady my breathing, I watched Jenna's silhouette disappear. The interruption meant I had to start my ritual all over again. Hands. Steering wheel. Camera.

I hated saying no to her. Jenna was so nice, and she hadn't given up on asking me yet. Me, the thirty-something mom in night class with no social life.

But when I'd pictured myself in a crowded bar with bodies I didn't know jostling up against me, and too much noise, and floors sticky with who-knows-what, every time I'd said the same thing.

I'm so sorry.

I can't.

The same thing happened when I thought about walking to class and back. It was only a few blocks from home, but now that the evenings were closing in and there were ominous shadows and dark corners to contend with, I couldn't make myself do it. Plus, it was the one night of the week I had sole use of the car, and I wasn't going to give that up.

More often than not, the class, or the car, or both, caused a fight between Ben and I, and tonight had been no exception. Ben said he needed to 'take care of something' at Frosted, our bakery, and wanted the Honda. Before I knew it, I was waving my arms and raising my voice, even though our daughter, Fay, was right there staring at me with her big watery eyes.

"Ben, you work late every night of the week. This photography class is the only thing I have that's for *me*. You *know* how important it is."

"I'm not telling you to stay home. My mom will—"

"I don't want her around here all the time."

"It's not all the time, Laurie. It's one night."

"I *need* the car."

"Can't you walk?"

"No, Ben. I can't. You don't understand." And with that, I'd grabbed the car keys from the hook, slung my camera over my shoulder, and strode out decisively. I refused to feel guilty for leaving Ben to care for Fay on the one night I had for myself.

Now, though, my bravado had faded, and I was starting to wish I didn't have to return home. Maybe I should have said 'yes' to the drink? At least it would have drawn the evening out a bit, made Ben wonder where I was, given him time to miss me. But I didn't. As usual, I simply couldn't let myself be free. So, I had no choice. I had to go back.

Heading away from the college, I noticed Jenna and the others up ahead. They were laughing. Maybe they were laughing at me. I didn't look at them as I drove past, just stared straight ahead and pretended they weren't there. And soon enough, I was pulling into our neat little street with its neat little houses—the white picket fences, and the porch swings, and the gabled roofs that had made me fall in love with Arlington all those years ago—and I knew I was going to have to apologize to Ben.

I'd overreacted.

Why had I yelled? Ben never yells.

Me, on the other hand... I had trouble finding the words to explain why I wanted something done a certain way, or to articulate how I felt. And the more frustrated I'd get, with Ben or myself, the louder my voice would raise. Afterward, I always felt irrational.

Walking up the four stone steps that led to our front door, I inhaled deeply through my nose and let the air expand in my chest. I held it there for a moment, counting slowly from ten all the way down to one, then reached into my purse for the house keys. My fingers snaked through its insides—wallet, compact, phone—but couldn't locate the keys, so I turned back to the street and angled myself toward the light coming from next door's porch. Our own porch light went out weeks ago. Ben said it looked like kids had broken it because he'd found shattered glass and a couple of small round stones not far from our welcome mat. But neither of us had gotten around to fixing it.

As I finally found the keys, a car pulled into the street. It had a loud engine, dimmed headlights, and it slowed as it approached me. Something about it made me wrap my arms around myself. I narrowed my eyes, but the driver was just a blurry silhouette, obscured by tinted windows.

The car stopped, lingering in the middle of the road. Then, as I turned back toward the house, I felt it start to move again. I glanced over my shoulder. This time it parked right in front of our Honda. Almost directly in front of our house. The headlights went out. The engine stopped. But the door didn't open. And then, just as I was about to run inside to fetch Ben and tell him something weird was going on, it jumped back to life and sped off.

Clutching my purse and camera close, I stared out after the car anxiously. If I mentioned it to Ben, he'd tell me it was nothing. I was always suspicious of new cars on the street, and nine times out of ten they were simply lost and looking at the house numbers. It was the dark that was making me nervous. I always felt on edge when I was out at night, but starting to rant about strange cars watching the house would only cause another argument.

Pull yourself together, Laurie, I whispered, reaching out and unlocking the front door.

Inside, the house was still and dark—quieter than normal. Ben would usually be slumped on the couch with the TV blaring, half-asleep with his laptop open and paperwork all over the floor, but the lounge was empty.

I set my camera down on the kitchen worktop and flicked on the coffee machine. Perhaps Ben was in bed. Sometimes, he crashed out in the basement—his 'creative lair,' where he came up with new ideas for the bakery and pored over business plans and cash-flow forecasts. But when he did, there was always a telltale sliver of light bleeding out from the gaps around the doorframe.

With the absence of any such light, I sighed, and pulled my hair back. I hated it when Ben was in bed before me because it meant I had to simply wash, change, and crawl into bed, rather than giving the bathroom a quick once-over with the steam mop and some bleach. Still, at least it would delay any confrontation until morning. Maybe by then I'd have figured out how to say what I wanted to say: *I miss you. I'm lonely. You work too much, and you don't share things with me anymore.*

The green light on the coffee machine started blinking, releasing a piping hot stream of extra-strong espresso into a short white cup and nudging me out of my tangle of thoughts. I always did it this way—a short sharp hit of caffeine that would keep me awake long enough to tackle the shots I'd taken—because if I didn't edit them straight away after class, life would get in the way and they'd be resigned to a permanent 'to do' list. Coffee in hand, I took my camera to the nook under the stairs that had become my workspace and plugged it into the computer. Scrolling through the photographs I'd taken in class, I pinged a few Instagram-worthy shots over to my phone and—not for the first time—wished I'd drummed up enough freelance photography work to pay for one of the models that linked seamlessly with your social media profiles and editing software.

Maybe I'd ask Ben about it. If he was working all these hours, things at the bakery must be going well.

Right?

I stayed in my nook for a little over an hour, playing with the post-production lighting effects we'd been learning about and, as always happened when I was engrossed in my photography, I managed to forget everything else and just... be.

Eventually, I glanced at the clock in the corner of the screen. It was getting late and the espresso was wearing off, so I tidied my desk, washed up my coffee cup, tucked my shoes neatly onto the rack in the hall, and padded up the stairs toward mine and Ben's bedroom.

Fay's room was on the left, opposite the family bathroom. She was a light sleeper, so I almost didn't dare nudge the door open to check on her, but something told me I needed to.

The door creaked as I pushed it back far enough for me to stick the upper half of my body into the room. My eyes slowly adjusted to the darkness. I scanned Fay's bed for the familiar bundle of legs and arms cocooned beneath the covers. She had a habit of sliding right down into the middle of the mattress, burying herself so it was almost impossible to tell which bumps were her and which were bundled up blankets. But there was always a foot or an elbow that gave her away.

I blinked. The covers were flatter than normal, smoother. There was no lump in the middle. No leg protruding to the side or crop of messy hair peeking out of the top. I flailed for the light switch. A dim orange glow illuminated the room.

Fay was not there. Her bed was empty.

**Get your copy of *The Photographer*
eBook
Paperback
www.JoCrow.com**